D1737890

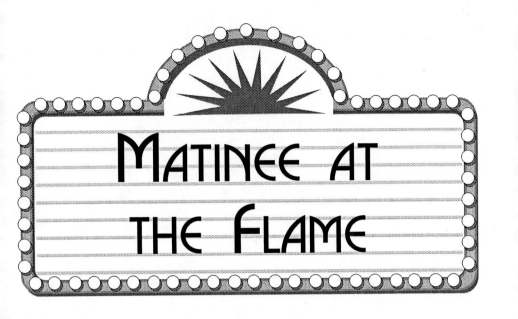

# MATINEE AT THE FLAME

# CHRISTOPHER FAHY

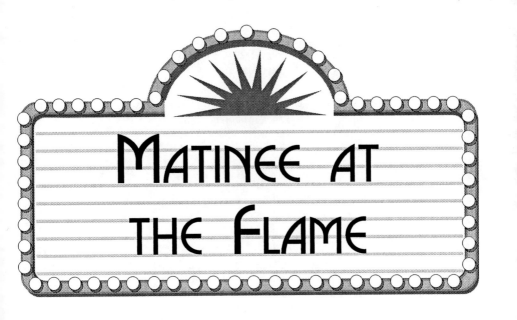

# MATINEE AT THE FLAME

# CHRISTOPHER FAHY

OVERLOOK CONNECTION PRESS
2006

Published by
Overlook Connection Press
PO Box 1934, Hiram, Georgia 30141
www.overlookconnection.com
overlookcn@aol.com

A signed limited hard cover of 500 copies
is available from OCP and Specialty Bookstores.
You can view complete details at:
www.overlookconnection.com/ocpmain.htm

Also available as a trade paperback
ISBN: 1892950731

Book Design & Typesetting:
David G. Barnett/Fat Cat Design

These stories have previously appeared in the following publications:

"Matinee at the Flame": *The Twilight Zone Magazine,* Volume 1, Number 6.
"The Last Temptation of Tony the C.": *Cat Crimes,* edited by Martin Greenberg & Ed Gorman (Donald I. Fine).
"Transformations": *Isaac Asimov's Magical Worlds of Fantasy 11, Curses,* edited by Isaac Asimov, Martin Greenberg & Charles Waugh (Signet).
"The Pharoah's Crown": *Predators,* edited by Ed Gorman & Martin Greenberg (Roc).
 "Hunger": *Cat Crimes II,* edited by Martin Greenberg & Ed Gorman (Donald I. Fine).
"The Man in Black": *Frankenstein, the Monster Wakes,* edited by Martin Greenberg (DAW).
"Want": *The King is Dead: Tales of Elvis Postmortem,* edited by Paul Sammon (Delta).
"Carnival": *Gallery* magazine, Volume 8, Number 8.
"The Real Thing": *Santa Clues,* edited by Martin Greenberg & Carol-Lynn Rossel Waugh (Signet).
"Trolls": *Night Screams,* edited by Ed Gorman & Martin Greenberg (Roc).

# MATINEE AT THE FLAME

Elmer Hutchins sat in his truck and stared through the mist at the brown brick wall.

Four fifty-one Blake, that's what the guy had said, rear entrance, Elmer was sure he'd heard him right. He looked at the scrap of paper again, then back at the battered green metal door on the other side of the alley. FOUR FIFTY-ONE REAR, it said. He looked at the rusted fire escape, the cinderblocked windows, the line of pigeons along the roof, the water dripping grayly onto mossy dark cobblestones. Four fifty-one Blake Street—the old Flame Burlesk.

Elmer opened the door of his truck; it slipped a notch, then groaned. He stepped out into the drizzle-slick alley, sad-faced, bent and tired, a crushed fedora hat with its brim turned up perched crookedly over his ears. He hitched up his baggy trousers and limped across the cobblestones, his bad hip aching in the damp; looked back at the rust-eaten faded blue truck with *Hutchins Light Hauling* along its side in greasy, dirty yellow. *Left the door open. Damn. My memory's goin', there ain't no doubt.* But he still had ears, and the guy said four fifty-one Blake Street, he *knew* he did.

The Flame: he'd started going there at seventeen, when he worked at the market across from Schlosberg's department store. Now Schlosberg's was gone, knocked down for a mall, and the Flame had been dead for what, twenty years? At *least* twenty years.

On the wall by the door was a faded poster: THE MARINES ARE

LOOKING FOR A FEW GOOD MEN. It made Elmer think of the last time he'd gone to the Flame, back during the war, spring of '43. And afterwards he went to a bar, got drunk and made the decision, signed up. Fort Dix and Europe. Battle of the Bulge. He shook his head and whistled "Jesus" between brown stumps of teeth. Raw rain dripped in puddles at his feet.

He stared at the dark, imposing wall, the stained and moldy bricks. Why hadn't they cleaned out the place before now? And why had they chosen *him?* The building was huge, he'd have to make a hundred freakin' trips. He shrugged. Well, he was only here for an estimate, nobody said he had to take the job.

Beside the massive door frame, peeling paint said, NO ADMIT- TANCE RING BELL. He pushed the button, heard nothing. Water dripped on his hat; the pigeons gurgled high above his head. He pushed the button again. He waited. Nothing.

Suckered. Jesus Christ, some son of a bitch had suckered him. But why? Who the hell would want to pull—? He was turning away when the door scraped open a crack.

A burly guy with a bouncer look, thick cauliflower ears. He raised his eyebrows, "Yeah?"

"Elmer Hutchins, Hutchins Haulin'. You called me, right?"

"Oh, yeah. Come in."

Elmer stepped inside. A dim red bulb poked out of the brown brick wall. In the background muffled music, upbeat jazz.

"So where the hell were you?" the rough-looking guy said. "You couldn't find the place?"

"It's a long drive from where I am," Elmer said. His nose felt suddenly stuffy; the smell was sour, damp. "Lotta traffic today." A muted trumpet, cymbals—and whistles and shouts. He frowned. "They still…? I thought this place—"

A woman's angry voice, a flash, a rustle of heavy velvet, and then she was there: a redhead bathed in dim red light, stark naked except for a glittering G-string and high-heeled shoes. Her ample breasts were covered with goose bumps.

"Jesus, Murphy, I froze my ass off, give us some heat for Chrissakes! I ain't gonna do no second show unless I'm *warm!*"

The rough-looking man said, "Keep it down, Lily, they'll hear you out there!"

The woman glared. "I'm tellin' you—"

"I turned the heater up an hour ago, it takesa lotta time— "

"Aah, time my frozen ass. Now Trixie's coolin' hers—" again Elmer heard in the background the bump-and-grind music, more whistles "—and when she's done she'll land on yer head too, you ape."

Elmer tried not to stare at the redhead's astounding flesh. Nobody told him the Flame was back, it musta just started again. They probably needed to haul off the crap that was sitting around all those years. But why did they have him come here now, when a show was on? Somebody musta screwed up.

The background music loud, climactic: sharp trumpets, brisk cymbals, a drum roll, *thump!* Then shouts, applause.

"Murphy, I don't feel no heat! I swear to God, I ain't goin' out there unless—"

The thick velvet curtain parted again and the redhead was joined by a blonde with long breasts and sharp hips. "Christ, you can't even work up a sweat!" she said. "This place is as cold as a morgue, what's the big idea?"

Beyond the curtains a man's voice said, "And next on the Billy Pagan Revue…" and Elmer thought: Billy Pagan! Is *he* still around? Christ, I saw him when I was a *kid.*

"…That king of comedy, that clown of clowns…"

"Well, ape?" Trixie said. Murphy held up his hands. "Hey, girls, hey, gimme a break. Like I just got done sayin', I turned it up. Rollie set it at forty last night and it's gonna take —"

Once again the thick curtain parted. The face of another man appeared, a thin, pale, bony face. "Hey Murphy," it rasped through ratlike teeth, "let's go!"

"Good Christ!" Murphy said with startled eyes, "now look what you girls done! Get out there, Hutchins, yer on! You goddamn girls…."

"What?" Elmer said. "I can't… the show—"

Murphy grabbed him and pushed him forward. "Come on, get out there, they're waitin'!"

"*What?*" Elmer said, and Murphy kept pushing, pushed him through the heavy curtain, and there he was in the wings, he could see bright light, and the thin-faced man looked mad. "Hurry up, hurry up," he whispered hoarsely, a frantic edge to his voice. And he grabbed Elmer's other arm, pulled, then shoved—and Elmer was out on the stage.

The spotlights stunned his eyes. He was vaguely aware of the balcony, black shapes of shoulders, heads, then saw the spread of bodies below in the dark. Directly down in front was the band. The bandleader—bald and paunchy, with a thin moustache—was staring. All was quiet. In spite of the chill, Elmer started to sweat.

Somebody snickered. A few people laughed. Elmer's throat closed up. He looked to the wings. Murphy was there on one side of the stage and the thin man was there on the other side, glaring hard. Elmer shrugged. The thin man scowled and Murphy made a fist.

Sweat poured down Elmer's face. Frozen, staring straight ahead, his tongue a leather flap, he stammered, "Ladies and gentlemen…"

His voice rattled starkly around the walls. He stood there, paralyzed. He had never been on a stage before in his life, not even in grammar school. His face felt numb; he thought he might faint. He forced his lips to move. "Uh, ladies and gentlemen," he said again, though he saw no ladies, only the bald and gray and shaggy heads of men. His voice made echoes, dissolved.

He glanced at the wings, where Murphy threatened; licked his gums, stared back across the lights. "Hey, listen, there's some kinda mix-up," he said in a shaky voice. "I come down to haul some junk, and the next thing I know…I'm out *here.*"

Dead silence. Slick with sweat, he hitched up his baggy pants. A suspender came loose with a sudden snap, flew up, and cracked his eye. He held his face, pain rocketing into his ear—and the audience howled.

He stood there, hand on his eye, as the throbbing died. Slowly, squinting, he lowered his arm. "Hey no," he said, "you got it all wrong, that was just a *mistake.* He whistled the "s" in "mistake" through his shrunken gums, and the audience laughed again. He clutched at his falling trousers, clipped his unruly suspender back in place. "Hold on a second, wait," he said in a louder voice. "I mean it. I don't belong out here, I ain't no comedian. I'm a junk man, nobody, a *failure.*" More laughter, some shouts, and somebody yelled, "Yeah, tell it!"

"A junk man, that's all," Elmer said. "A total flop. I ain't never succeeded at nothin' in my whole life!" He stepped forward to dodge the needlelike glare of the lights, and tripped. "Good Christ!" he shouted, catching himself. A quick drum roll.

The audience roared. An odd thrill raced through Elmer's chest; his heart sped up. He looked at the band. The drummer—tall and pale, with a huge mop-top of carrot-colored hair—was grinning crazily.

"I'm tellin' ya, I don't know any jokes, my life's a bore. It's *always* been a bore, a goddamn mess."

"Tell it!" cried the voice again. And other voices yelled, "Let's hear it!" "Come on!"

"Hear what?" Elmer frowned. "How my mother died when I was ten? How my old man drove a cab—and raised five kids on a cabbie's pay? Tell *that?*"

Another drum roll. Shouts of, "Yeah, that's it, go on!"

"I worked in the market across from Schlosberg's—a couple of blocks from here—when I was twelve. Had to, old man wrecked the cab, got laid up for a year, we didn't have no dough—except what me and my sister brought in. No disability checks in them days, just me and my sister Jean."

Sporadic clapping, some listless cheers. Elmer held up his hand. "That's right. Twelve hours a day I worked till my old man was back on his feet. By then I was fourteen, feelin' my oats. I was used to work—so no more school for me. I was a hotshot, had plenty of dough, you shoulda seen my clothes." He grinned. "And baby, look at me now." He hitched up his tattered pants again. The audience chuckled, guffawed.

Elmer's grin widened. He tried to see the faces down below, but all was black. "I even came here to the Flame," he said. "Philly was wide open back in them days, this joint was jumpin', you shoulda seen them dolls!" He pointed to the balcony and said, "I useta sit up there."

"Come on," someone shouted, "an old sack of bones like you?"

"I'm talkin' over fifty years ago," Elmer said. "That's where I sat, a steady customer." He flashed his gums, his stubs of teeth. "Oh yeah, I liked the women then, you bet I did!"

The drummer laughed, the bandleader laughed, and then the audience laughed.

"Oh, I was a hotshot, knew all about the birds and bees, met this cutie named Molly and fell in love. My first girlfriend—and damned if I didn't knock her up!"

At this, the spectators snapped to life: crisp laughter and sharp applause.

When the noise died down Elmer said, "We got married, of course, that's what you did, there wasn't no legal abortions back then. And Christ, what a match! Them first few years we fought like wild animals! But I was faithful, no foolin' around." A rush of laughter then, long and loud.

Elmer looked to the wings. Both Murphy and the thin-faced man wore grins. The dolls were standing there in robes, arms crossed, enjoying it. He faced the audience again, excited, flushed, and said: "That first kid was a boy, and then we had another one, don't ask me why." He shrugged his skinny shoulders. "You know how it is." A snicker down front: the trombonist.

"The thing of it is, I liked them guys. Sweet kids, I used to play games with 'em after work. I was workin' for Kelly scrap metals, out in the yard, makin' pretty good money, I couldn't complain, me and Molly was startin' to hit it off—then World War Two comes along."

He paused a second, swallowing. The dark was quiet. He said, "Now here's where I make a mistake. A mistake, Christ, it's a disaster! I got this bad hip, see, arthritis, I'm born with it. Two kids and a lousy hip, I coulda got outta the service easy. But I got this thing about duty, see, I'm *patriotic*. I don't even wait for the draft, I sign up. Don't tell 'em about the hip, and they take me in.

"And I'm over there two years. France, Belgium—the worst. The Battle of the Bulge! Christ, you never seen such a shootin' match! And I was there!"

"Hey!" a voice in the blackness yelled, "he's a *hero!*"

Against the fall of laughter Elmer grinned and said, "Okay, okay, but remember, I coulda stayed out. Two years in them trenches, the cold and the rain, and my hip was screwed up for good. My God, did it hurt! When I come back I have to take shots just to get some sleep!"

The crowd found this terribly funny. The saxophonist played a quick trill.

Elmer tugged at his pants again and licked his gums. He said, "Now while I was away, things wasn't exactly standin' still stateside. I go back to see Kelly—and the sucker's a millionaire! Scrap metal during the war? You'd have to be a total fool not to make a mint, and Kelly wasn't no fool. So I ask him for my old job back and—he turns me down!"

The audience cracked up. The drummer was laughing and shaking his mop-top head. "That's right, he turns me down! I'm over there gettin' my ass shot off so that he can get rich, and he won't even gimme a job!"

The place was pandemonium now. The dark walls rang.

"That's right!" Elmer said. "So I tell him to shove it and start my own business. Scrap metal, paper, all kindsa junk, I'll show that Kelly creep. And guess what? I done it for over forty years—and just about survived!"

When the laughter died down again he said, "Hey, that ain't all. Let me tell you about my boys. Great kids when I go away, and when I come back they don't even *know* me. And I don't know *them.* What a couple of brats!"

As the audience screamed, Elmer held up his hands. "Wait, you ain't heard the best part yet. My wife, cutie Molly, who I was faithful to? Even over in France, believe it or not? Well, she's got a little surprise for me. While I'm fightin' the Krauts, she's foolin' around—and another blessed event is on the way!"

This was just too much, and the crowd went wild. Whoops and shouts and cackles and cries. The band was doubled up.

Elmer waited a full three minutes before things calmed down. He was smiling a foolish, sunken grin. "And what a kid!" he said. "A little girl in a great big hurry, couldn't wait nine months, come out in seven. Three pounds, two ounces, scrawny little red-faced water rat, you never seen nothin' so ugly in all your life."

The goofy redheaded drummer was caught in a spasm. Laying his sticks on his drum, he clutched his gut.

"But get this," Elmer said. "This little girl, my little Alice—who her old man was I'll never know—turns out to be a prize. She's a beauty, a peach. And my boys? Lemme tell you where they are now: one of 'em's out in L. A., a hotshot ad man, brings in more dough in a year than I seen my damn whole life. The other one's in Kansas City—insurance company executive. They ain't had nothin' to do with me in years. You know why? Because I never took 'em to baseball games! I'm bustin' my hump twelve hours a day to make ends meet, and all they remember is—the baseball games I never took 'em to!"

He looked across the field of darkness, over the glare of the lights. The rustle and murmur were electric—he could actually *feel* them now. "And another mistake," he said. "Wait'll you hear *this*. I take all the money I save and stick it in a hotshot scheme to pay for my boys' education. My wife's crazy brother tells me the deal's a sure thing—and I lose my shirt! So the boys hafta work their way through college, and hate me for it. But little Alice—who ain't even *mine*—she thinks I'm great!"

Even Murphy was laughing now. The dolls were grinning and chewing their gum, the thin-faced man was beaming.

Elmer rode on the energy of the crowd. Then all at once it was gone. A weariness hit him; he sighed. "Ah, Alice," he said. "Used to curl right up on my lap. My little pusscat, I called her."

"Oh, how *cute*," a voice in the front row said.

"She'd bring me my coffee, I'd read her the funnies…"

"Who could ask for anything more?" said another voice.

Elmer stared through the lights. He was frowning now; beads of sweat rode the grooves of his forehead. "But you see, she was never strong," he said. "So scrawny at birth, always sick with one thing or another. She was eight and a half when she caught the disease. She turned real pale and didn't have no energy, lost weight, her eyes got dark, there was nothin' nobody could do. We went to five different doctors, nobody could help. Ten months of that torture and she finally died."

A chuckle up front. From the back of the theater, a laugh.

Shaking his sweaty head Elmer said, "No, you don't understand! I'm not kidding, it really happened, she really *died!*"

More laughter, and somebody said, "Oh please, oh stop, I can't *take* it!"

Elmer looked at the floor, sudden pain in his eyes. "To see that kid suffer like that, I swear to God, I wish she'da never been born." He looked at the blackness, mouth quivering now, and said, "It almost killed *me*. My wife fell apart—stayed in bed all the time, stuffed herself fulla candy and cake, watched TV. Got as fat as a goddamn elephant." As the laughter rang on the walls, he said, "Even now, after all these years, there are nights I can't sleep. I keep seein' her. Alice, my little Alice…"

He stood there, brushing away the tears, till the audience quieted down. Then he said: "Well, what can you do? Pick a different mother who ain't gonna die? Stay in school when your old man's laid up? Stay outta the service when Adolf Hitler is tearin' the world apart? Yeah, I coulda did that, I *shoulda* did that, I had that bad hip and two kids. But I *wanted* to fight, I wanted to help the good old U.S.A."

"So," somebody yelled, "yer a martyr, right?" The voice was brutal, raw. Elmer looked at the band, and the drummer's smile was gone.

The sweat was coming in rivers now. Mopping it up with his dirty bandana, Elmer said, "I thought I was doin' right—goin' into the army, puttin' in all that time at work. What was I supposed to do, forget about the work and go to baseball games?"

The bandleader chewed on his cud with a sour face. "Yeah, yeah, come off it, pops."

Elmer's eyes had a desperate look. "My brother-in-law said we couldn't miss. Wire recorders, a great investment, I took all my money…" He paused and stared into the silence. "Well, you woulda made the same mistake, I bet."

"Don't count on it, chucklehead," somebody shouted. A couple of people booed.

Elmer pressed his lips together; his jaw was tight. "My little Alice was turnin' out swell," he said. "Don't I get some credit for that?"

"Not from *me* you don't," someone sneered. Sarcastic laughter. The band looked bored.

"I done what I could to build her up, I give her vitamins. I didn't have the dough to take her down the shore or move to the country. Anyway, who says it woulda helped?"

"Hey," somebody shouted, "he gave her vitamins—and she died!" More laughs.

"You think that's funny?" Elmer said. "A little girl dying like that, and you think it's *funny?*"

"If that ain't funny, what is?" someone yelled. "G'wan, can it, ya bum!"

"I just want to forget!" Elmer said. His mouth quivered; he bit his lip. "I don't want to think about it no more, I just want to forget!"

"Hey, he wants to *forget*," somebody cried. "We *all* want to forget, Bozo!" And now, through the thick dark silence, movement: people getting up to leave. The bandleader's face was angry, hard. "Hey, wait," Elmer said, "don't go, you gotta let—"

"We don't gotta let you do nothin'!" a harsh voice roared. Then another voice yelled, "Take it off!"

Elmer stared through the lights in confusion: dark bulky shapes, the milling crowd. "Take it off?" he said.

"Take it off!" came another shout. Then the chant began, "Take it off, take it off, take it off!"

"I won't!" Elmer cried, the sweat pouring over his cheeks. "I won't take it off, goddamn it, I've had enough!"

Horrendous jeers, a deafening, angry roar. And Murphy was out on the stage and had Elmer's arm in a viselike grip and hustled him into the wings. In a flash the band flared up, the blonde pranced on, the claps and whistles began.

"What the hell's the idea?" said the thin-faced man, his cheeks flaring up in the blood-red backstage light. Murphy squeezed Elmer's arm.

"I was doin' good," Elmer said. "I was doin' *damn* good."

"You didn't take nothin' off," the thin man said.

"No," Elmer said with a head shake. "No, I ain't goin' to, neither."

The thin-faced man sucked his teeth in disgust. "You coulda went all the way, you fool!" He nodded to Murphy and said, "Let him go."

When Elmer was free he said, "What did you want? I come here for trash, you send me out there, make it all come back—" His voice was wavering, cracked.

"No excuses!" the thin man hissed through his ratty teeth. "Understand?" His eyes glittered, burned.

"There's such a thing as the breaks," Elmer said.

"We *know* about breaks, pops. We don't wanta *hear* about breaks— good or bad. Now get goin'."

"Get goin'," Elmer said. "I don't even get paid? For all I did? For all I said?"

"You'll get paid outside. Now scram."

"Outside?" Elmer said. "What kind of an operation—?"

"Yer outta here, pops," Murphy said. And he grabbed Elmer's arm, dragged him up to the door, jerked it open and pushed him out.

The rain had stopped. The sun split a cloud, hit Elmer's eyes as he thought: *Get paid outside, there's nobody here! Those crooks!* Then the thought made no sense.

He stood there, dazzled, the memory of brassy music fading in his ears. And the memory of faces fading, a thin man, a tough-looking man, two sharp young broads, a redheaded man with a drum; and superimposed on them all, the face of a child—a blond-haired little girl, nobody he knew.

He squinted against the light. There was his car, his navy blue Chevy, parked across the way. As he looked at the license plate—*Pennsylvania, The Keystone State, 1943*—he thought: Why did I pull in here? What the hell am I doing *here?* I'm in back of the *Flame!*

On the wall near the shining green door was a poster, a boat going under the sea. LOOSE LIPS SINK SHIPS, it said. Had he really been thinking…? Good God, a wife, two kids, a bad hip…and he'd thought of *enlisting?*

He laughed to himself and walked to his car. The clouds were whipping away in the sun, the street was drying fast. He slid behind the wheel and checked his watch. Twelve thirty-five.

He looked in the rearview mirror, adjusted his tie. Twelve thirty-five on a sunny Saturday in May and he felt terrific. He turned the key; the engine purred.

A great day for baseball, he thought as he pulled away. It was Connie Mack's A's and the St. Louis Browns this afternoon at Shibe Park. The kids would love to see that game. Even Molly might want to go.

# THE LAST TEMPTATION OF TONY THE C.

He couldn't believe she liked this halfassed town any better than he did—she simply refused to admit it, the stubborn bitch. Why the hell had he stuck with her all this time? Why hadn't he ditched her ages ago, before they left Paris?

Because she'd had money and even a shot at a job back then, that's why. And he had been lonely, she'd wanted some company on her travels—so here they were.

The job was supposed to be at the Peggy Guggenheim, but when they got down to Venice they learned it was gone. The bastards had hired some other artist, another American, right off the street instead. They figured that Tara had changed her mind, they said. Just because she was two weeks late. The bastards. The news didn't faze her, though: she had money. And jobs opened up at the Peggy G. all the time, she said, and if they could hang around for a little while, she'd score for sure.

So they hung around for a month, and nothing came up, and prices were high—not as high as they'd been in Paris, but high—and drugs weren't easy to get, so they split for Florence. They stayed in a little hotel in the center of town, saw Dante's tomb, Giotto's tower, the paintings at the Uffizi and lots more stuff—and he'd actually had a desire to pick up a brush. Nothing strong, not as strong as the urge for some good cocaine, but a definite twinge. They found some grass and some decent speed, one balanced the other out pretty good, and they ate good and slept good too.

## THE LAST TEMPTATION OF TONY THE C.

In Vienna it wasn't so good, it rained a lot, and Tara had stomach cramps—from something she'd eaten in Florence, no doubt. She was crabby and wouldn't sleep with him, and stayed at the pensione while he roamed the museums and walked the gray Danube's banks in the dreary rain.

In Berlin they had one whale of a fight. She had talked about going back to New York, as she missed her cat (her mother who lived in Queens was keeping it), and he'd told her she liked her goddamn cat better than him. "Well, Tony, I've known Sugar longer than you," she said in her lazy, sleepy way, with that curl of her upper lip he had grown to hate. "And she's nicer than you, and she doesn't blow all my money on drugs the way you do."

Her money. Sure. Like her CEO daddy had nothing to do with it, right? And she'd known from the very beginning he wasn't a saint. Well that was the last straw, that wiseass remark, and he'd stormed out into the street and hit the bars. Got away from li'l ol' Tara girl for a while. Tara, Jesus, what kind of a name was that? The name of that mansion in *Gone With the Wind?* Her real name was probably Debbie or Sue. That Southern accent, give me a break. When she'd grown up in Queens?

In one of the bars, quite late in the day, he'd found a dude who sold him something, and after a night that was lost forever he'd woken up in a tattered room with a headache the size of a house. He'd found Tara (Linda? Jane?) back at the hotel, drinking hot chocolate and reading the *Trib,* just as cool as could be. And the look in her eyes said quite clearly: You goddamn fool.

Then Amsterdam. Warm sunny days, bike rides, cheap tasty Indonesian food, cheap drugs—who could ask for anything more? Except maybe the turn, the change he had come to Europe for, the change that would break through the blockage that numbed his desire to paint. Every so often he got just a flicker, like back there in Florence, but nothing that said: This is it! Like it used to in Omaha and his first days on Riverton Street. That change hadn't come.

And it sure wasn't going to come in Amsterdam's opposite, *this* friggin' place, zero city, he thought as he rounded another bleak corner. The weight of these buildings, their dark brown baroque facades, crushed the juices right out of his soul. How could anyone ever paint in a burg like this? The Avenue Louise was sleepytime, the Grand Place medieval glitz, the cops wouldn't even let you stick your sore feet in the public pond. Eveything was *verboten* here. Bunch of tight-assed bourgeoisie. Whatever happened to Bruegel's peasants, dancing around with their dicks sticking up, swilling beer, eating platters of pig? They were rednecks, yeah, but at least they had *life*. *These* schmucks… And as for drugs—a billionaire couldn't buy a joint in this goddamn hole.

Why had he ever left Amsterdam? Now *there* was a city, a place where folks knew how to *live*. The kids smoked cigar-sized joints in the public parks while they waded around in the ponds, and nobody said boo. Cocaine, acid, smack, you could get it all. And the town even gave you clean needles! To go from that freedom to this was too much, too much. But when Tara had "done" the Van Gogh Museum, the Rijksmuseum and cruised the canals, it was time to move on, she said. To this. Verbotenville.

And now it was starting to drizzle again. Same thing as Berlin and Vienna. His hair was already wet, Jesus, where *was* this place?

When he looked up again, he saw it: *Musee Royaux Des Beaux-Arts*. Not bad looking. Huh.

He stopped for a moment and reached in his pocket and took out a foil square. Looked around—no cops—then opened the foil and popped the two pills in his mouth.

He'd gotten the pills in Amsterdam, and this was the end, sad to say. He'd done one yesterday and it wasn't bad: brought a bright clean edge and a mellow cool. A little too mellow, actually, and that's why he'd taken a double this time. Try to sharpen things up a bit.

As he walked through the entrance door, his depression deepened. Ahead he saw ornate gold frames and stern portraits of soldiers and kings.

Am I really ready for this? he asked himself. Then shrugged, bought a ticket and went inside.

A portrait by Jan van Eyck, 1434. Lotta water under the bridge since those days, man. Porcelain people: they looked like they'd shatter to bits if you knocked them down. Hands and fingers so white, so thin. Big nose on the dude, and the cuffs on the chick's robe two feet long. Good technician, van Eyck. The grain in the wood floors, amazing.

Stuff by Aertsen and van der Goes, and some others that left Tony cold. Good old Rembrandt, of course. Soldiers. Yeah, it was good—but *soldiers?*

On to a Bruegel—a famous one—*Landscape with the Fall of Icarus*. Old Ick is head down in the water, drowning, and who gives a damn? Life goes on. Hey, you fly too close to the sun, you fry your tailfeathers, right? And here was one of those peasant paintings, the dancing, the drinking—and what was that stuff going on in the corner? Somebody getting roughed up, getting robbed. Even back then, man, the world was royally screwed.

Then Reubens. He'd had a good deal: sketch out the compositions and paint the heads, get your lackeys to do the rest. Rake in the dough and keep most for yourself. Tony scowled at the canvas. Were all broads big mamas back then? Or was that all that guys liked to see in the buff?

Another room. Franz Hals. His smiling peasants had never made Tony joyous, not in the least. There was something about their teeth. He squinted. Ugly teeth, mean ratlike teeth. He thought: the pills are kicking in.

After Hals he had just about had enough. He was crossing another gloom-packed room when a triptych on a table caught his eye. He stopped.

A Bosch? No kidding? He hadn't expected that. Even though Bosch was Belgian, the Prado had most of his stuff, though God knew why. Tony had seen it his first trip to Spain.

He looked at the brass plate attached to the painting's frame. "Attributed to Hieronymous (Jeroen) Bosch, c. 1508."

Attributed to. Well it looked like the real thing, all right. Good old Hieronymous, Jerry the B., as they used to call him in art school. Now *there* was a painter, there was a guy who *knew*.

The triptych was smaller than most—each panel was only about two feet high and a foot across—and was darker than other Bosches that Tony had seen. Or was that the effect of the drugs? Couldn't tell. He squinted, leaned close.

The first of the panels, the one on the left, was brighter than the other two, with a lovely lush garden and naked slim people (no Reubens heavy-weights here). Way off in the distance, however, some bad shit was coming down: an ugly knot of insectile limbs was rolling across the green hill.

In the next scene—again, pure Bosch—things were radically falling apart. Some poor naked dude pulled a huge wooden wagon that over-flowed with green corpses; an arrow was buried between his shoulder blades. Another nude guy slumped against a stone wall while a huge fish with legs stuck long pins through his neck. There was one of those giant pathetic tree-men, fishing boats stuck to his severed limbs, and his broken-egg body was chock full of fat priests and nuns doing something obscene. Fish-like birds with thin murderous bills and the legs of humans sailed through the dark blue sky, as crowds of milk-pale people below were nibbled by monster rabbits. Above it all, Jesus sat on a cloud, shrug-ging and raising his arms as if saying: Hey man, I mean what can you do with these fools?

The third panel depicted all hell breaking loose—quite literally. The sky was a flaming red cauldron of sparks, and people were being devoured by cow-sized rats. A fat yellow pig had one sad skinny dude by

24

his ankles, and dipped him head-first into lava. Another doomed sucker puked bilious green bubbles, out of which black roachlike insects came crawling to feast upon babies' eyes. Not a fun time at all.

Tony wished he had waited till later to do those pills, whatever the hell they were. He wasn't feeling the same way he'd felt when he'd done them before; and now that he thought of it, these had been different, a different color, red, not blue, like yesterday's. Old Bosch was plenty without added zip, these golden haloes, these buzzing sounds, these shimmering wavy lights, and he thought: Maybe Jerry the B. used to take something too, like mushrooms or something, whatever they had in those days. Whatever, he'd gone all the way. You bet. It was almost as if he had actually *been* there, had actually visited hell and come back with the news. Or maybe to him the everyday world looked like this, like the underworld. Maybe that was it.

Despair sank its talons in Tony's heart. That vision, that singular way of seeing—what did it take to achieve it? He was starting to think—no, he'd thought for a while now—that he'd never be able to break through like that, make it over the edge.

He stared at the painting, that hellish third panel, and thought: Fantastic! I'd give *anything* to be able to see like that, take *anything*…

Shaking his head in awe, he turned away—and suddenly realized something.

He was all alone in this room. There was nobody else in sight, not even a guard.

He looked back at the painting, then up at the sign on the wall. *Defense de toucher aux pientures.* Well that was the same everywhere, no museums would let you touch paintings, that went without saying. But how delicious to touch one right here in Forbidden City!

He looked around quickly—left, then right—then caught his breath and did it: reached out and touched the right panel, the blazing inferno— specifically, a snarling cat—with the tip of his right index finger.

Ow! Gasping, he jerked his hand back.

An electric shock! The bastards had wired the paintings! Real sweethearts in charge of this place, oh yeah, the least they could do was tell you the damn things were juiced! He looked at his stinging, tingling hand, and his fingers were yellow and green.

He'd done some stuff in Santa Fe that had made his hand look like that, some peyote—or maybe mescaline. Made him puke like a dog all night and half the next day. Not *that* again, he said to himself. Man—

A guard was in the doorway now. He'd come out of nowhere, poof, like a friggin' ghost, and stood there scowling. Had he seen? Had the painting set off an alarm? Couldn't be—or the guy would be on him for sure.

He was one weird dude, that guard, one *mean* lookin' dude. His hair stuck up in silver spikes and his yellow-green teeth looked like fangs. His hands were black, with blue-black nails, like a friggin' gorilla's hands. I am *outta* this place, Tony said to himself.

As he started to walk, the floor seemed to ripple. The paintings, especially their golden frames, seemed to shine with an inner light. Not bad, he thought. Looks like I'll get something out of this stuff after all.

On the street, though, the light hurt his eyes, and his pupils contracted with sudden sharp pain. The rain had stopped, but the sky was still brooding and gray. Good thing the sun's *not* out, Tony thought, I'd be damn near blind.

The street was deserted—except for a guy at the end of the block, on the corner, waiting for the light to change. The light was huge, a blood-red sun, even this far away. Tony squinted against its glare.

It shifted to splintery emerald green and the guy crossed the street. He was hunched down, bent, was wearing gray, and looked for all the world like a giant bird. His nose was as sharp as a sandpiper's beak, and his arms in his floppy gray cape looked like wings. And—what? Did he actually lift off the ground and fly a few feet?

This stuff was *bad,* even worse than that Santa Fe crap or that junk he had done in Chicago with…yeah, Drusilla. A chick with a name like that, he shoulda known better. Drusilla, Tara—how come he always got stuck with these weirdo women?

When he reached the corner, his feet felt soft on the curb, soft and light. His whole body felt light, like he might float away if he didn't watch out, or like if he jumped…

He tried it—jumped. And got *up*—into slam-dunk range. Impossible, he thought. There isn't a drug in the world that could—

Someone was staring. She (*was* it a she?) stood in one of those dark baroque doorways, her thick eyebrows furrowed, skin doughy and pale, her huge eyes like lumps of black coal. Okay, so I jumped, Tony thought. So what is it, a crime? Is jumping forbidden too? As he finished this thought, those black eyes blinked, and a serpent's red tongue darted out from the woman's blue lips, sprouting spirals of flame.

Whoa!

He walked in the other direction. Bad stuff, and how long was it going to last? The Santa Fe garbage had taken three days to metabolize—and this shit seemed stronger than that.

It dawned on him then that he wasn't walking—not walking, but *capering* down the street. I don't want to do this! an inner voice said, I am making a fool of myself! But he couldn't stop.

They stared. The whole lot of them stared. They were naked or wrapped in rags, their eyes burning, beaks clacking, their vicious horns slicing the air. He snarled at them as he capered by and they shrank back or slashed with their claws.

Whoa!

Shaking their fists, they spat as he passed. "I don't speak your friggin' language!" he tried to say, but it came out all garbled, a jumble of noise.

His shoes were suddenly killing him. He tore them off quickly and dropped to all fours. That felt better, much better, yes.

Which way was home? Down here, this street? Yeah, down—

When he turned the corner, the world was fire. Flames poured from the roofs and windows of towering flat wooden buildings. The heat was unbearable. Christ! Where the hell were the fire trucks?

In the flickering darkness between two tenements, crowds of naked people screamed as coals rained down on their flesh. Lizard men with slick skin and long snouts lashed another nude throng with black whips. Further along the cobblestone street giant weasels chewed people's thighs. Much worse than Santa Fe, Tony thought. *Much* worse.

Then it hit him: It wasn't the pills.

He had touched the painting—had touched the forbidden painting and caused all this. The painting had been the gate, and he, Anthony Catalano, a sinner—

No! Tony said in his mind, his skin flooded with sweat, it's just the pills!

And a bird rushed at him, huge and blue. It brandished a thick black stick in its claws and the funnel-like hat on its head spouted purple-green smoke. Its beak went wide, snapped shut again, went wide, and the clamor that issued forth from that scarlet gash made Tony's blood run cold. He tried to scream, Stop! but the sound that came out was a hiss. The bird was on him, stretched its neck—

And Tony charged it, biting its leg. It screeched, flapped its sandpaper feathers at Tony's hot head. He ran—and ran, past grinning goats and toads with red coats and black tongues.

His stomach suddenly cramped with a horrid pain. He moaned and squatted, pushed—and out of his heat came steaming eggs which cracked and spewed forth monster crabs that clicked their claws and pursued. He ran. Had to get back to Tara, the room, lock the door, call a doctor—

He craned his head and the street was full of them, after him, all of them, lizards and fish-men, men with diaphanous wings and bright scissors where fingers should be. Foxes with beaks and long ears that hung down to the ground, giant snakes with the faces of men. The sky was roiling with sulfurous clouds and his breathing was filled with brimstone, he couldn't go on—

And suddenly here it was! This was it, this was it, his building! He yanked on the heavy entrance door, ran inside, slammed it shut.

And if *she* was a demon too? he thought as he crouched in the shadows, fighting for breath. If this hell was the way things really were—and touching that painting had merely allowed him to see it? No! he told himself, that can't be it, she'll help, she will, she *has* to help.

He raced up the high dark stairs, turned right, and there was the door to the room. He pounded on it. Tara! Tara! he tried to shout, but the noise he made, it sounded like—

«« — »»

"Did you have to shoot him?" she asked, looking down at the hallway floor. "Did you have to *kill* him?"

"Ah yes," the policeman said in his heavy accent. "He was dangerous. Quite dangerous, he bit one of us in the leg. He was wild, wild."

"It seems such a shame," Tara said.

The policeman shrugged. "He maybe had some kind of sickness? We'll have him examined."

"What kind of a cat is he, anyway?" Tara asked.

"I don't know," the policeman said. "I don't know cats."

"Such an ugly thing. Those teeth, those claws…"

With a look of disgust the policeman said, "I don't want to touch him, I'll send a man out right away." He nodded. "Sorry for all the trouble, madame. Goodbye."

"Goodbye," Tara said.

Brushing her stringy hair away from her eyes, she went back inside. The thought of that cat made her naked toes curl. So ugly looking, so mean. They had plenty of weird things back in Queens, but they didn't have cats like that.

She went to the window and looked at the street. Still gray, still raining. Depressing.

Yeah, Tony was right, this city could get you, could bring you down bad. It was time to move on again.

She'd tell him that as soon as he came home.

# THE BLUMBERG VARIATIONS

The stamps were *dreck*. "Gigantic collection of U.S. postage stamps," the ad for the auction had said, and it wasn't a lie, it was just that the stamps were crap, all common cancelled stuff that someone had cut off their mail and thrown into liquor boxes. Five liquor boxes of crap going back at least twenty years. Blumberg stared at them with dismay. He'd fervently hoped that today he would make the big find he so desperately needed. No. Another strikeout.

Blumberg sighed, thinking, Might as well just head home. But he'd driven a hundred and twenty-eight miles to get to this stupid auction hall and he wasn't ready for more dull hours behind the wheel, passing the now-familiar landmarks not in anticipation but in defeat, so he signed in and took a card. He figured he'd stay to see the stamps auctioned off, to see what someone would pay for boxes of junk. And maybe he'd be in luck and something of interest would make an appearance before the stamps came up, some inexpensive *tchotchke* to partly justify his trip.

His number was 42. For some unknown reason, it seemed like a lucky one. Taking a seat near the exit in case he decided to bolt, he thought: If the stamps *had* been something, would they actually have been *something?* Could the key to his problems lie in a bunch of *stamps?*

He'd started collecting again last spring after thirty-five years away from the hobby, hoping that now at the age of forty-eight he'd recover the old excitement he'd felt as a kid. Stamps had taught him about geography, history, nature—he'd loved them back then.

But now? He'd purchased a fairly decent lot at a bargain price last May, but after sorting through it for most of a rainy Sunday afternoon all he'd felt was a sense of viewing his preadolescence across vast fields of time. Even finding a pretty nice Zep in a packet of German postally used didn't give him the kick he'd thought it would.

Stamps seemed fraudulent now. So many were puff for special interest groups like service clubs or chicken farmers. Either that or they fostered myths like Washington kneeling in prayer at Valley Forge. As a kid, he'd been ignorant of the politics and had just *collected*. Impossible today. He told himself maybe the more time he spent, the more his interest would grow, but so far it hadn't happened. Collecting seemed merely acquisitive to him, compulsive and mercenary. Nevertheless, he attended more auctions and bought two more lots. They sat in his study untouched.

So why was he sitting here now when he had no interest at all in these boxes? He just didn't feel like driving back home right away and having Marilyn ask why he wasted his time on this stuff. She hated auctions. Shopping she loved, but not auctions. "Pawing through dead people's stuff," she said. "You know what an auction's like? A horse race in a cemetery, that's what it's like."

Blumberg could see her point, but didn't share her feeling. He watched as a skinny-armed, pimple-faced kid held a rocking chair up, and the auctioneer's patter began. "Original robin's egg blue, who'll start at a hundred? At fifty. Original paint, folks, so who'll give me twenty to set it in?" He pointed at someone who wiggled a card. "I have twenty, now thirty now thirty-five. Thirty-five and now forty. Now forty-five…"

The chair went for sixty. The kid took it off and a woman replaced him, brandishing candlesticks.

The stamps didn't surface for nearly an hour. Twice Blumberg came close to leaving, but what, he had something better to do? He stayed in his seat. He made no bids. Nothing was interesting to him. The stamps went for eighty-five bucks to a fat balding guy about Blumberg's age. *Dreck*. Eighty-five dollars for *dreck*. A novice collector? A grandfather buying a stash for a kid? Go figure.

So that was that, the big whoop-de-do for the day, and Blumberg was ready to turn in his card when the auctioneer said, "Where this next item came from I don't really know and don't really *care* to know. It's the real thing, though, a genuine piece of Americana, I guess about fifty years old."

What he raised in the air was a Klan uniform, the robe in his left hand, the hood in his right. "This isn't my politics, folks, I certainly don't condone their beliefs, but here we have it, and who'll give me fifteen dollars to set it in? Fifteen dollars now twenty, now…"

32

Horrified, Blumberg was thinking, *This shouldn't be auctioned off, it should be destroyed!* "I have twenty-five dollars, who'll give me thirty?" and now Blumberg found himself tilting his card and the auctioneer nodded. "Thirty now thirty-five..."

Blumberg got it for fifty. The acne-pocked runner presented it to him, folded, and Blumberg flushed as others watched. Tucking it under his arm he rose quickly and went to the counter and paid, then slipped out the door.

*I'll burn it,* he thought as he started the car. It was there on the passenger seat, one sinister eye of its hood staring up. Yes, he'd burn it—or if he should happen to pass a dumpster, maybe he'd shove it as deep as he could into garbage.

He drove and drove, but no dumpster appeared. He stopped for a bite to eat—no dumpster out back of the diner—then drove again, and soon enough he was home. He parked inside the garage and left the vile thing on the seat as he went in the house.

Marilyn was in the living room, on the phone. "Well, Sheila, I'm going to get off, Hy's home. So I'll see you in half an hour. Okay. Bye now."

Marilyn was forty-six, dark-haired with olive skin and a decent though *zaftig* figure. She'd always been *zaftig.* She wore too much makeup, especially around the eyes, but this didn't bother Blumberg. "So," she asked, "any luck?"

"The stamps were junk."

"And you didn't find anything else?"

A huge disappointment in her tone. She'd been cheated: no display. An expert at shopping, she never came home empty-handed, and loved the display, loved it almost as much as the shopping itself. "Just look at this dress!" she would say as she shook it in front of his eyes. "Marked a hundred and forty, and what do you think I got it for?"

God forbid he should guess too low. With a lift of his bushy black eyebrows he'd say: "Eighty? Ninety?"

Then, beaming, she'd crow, "Twenty-five! Twenty-five for a hundred and forty dollar dress, that's a hundred and fifteen dollars saved!" and Blumberg would act astounded, praising her prowess. He'd sit through the showing of all her great buys as she glowed with triumph. Month after month, year after year of their twenty-four years together, he'd acquiesced to this ritual. It was one of the threads that held their marriage together.

For him to arrive home with nothing at all was more than a disappointment, more than mere failure, it smacked of betrayal. "Nothing?"

**33**

she said with chagrin in her voice. "No, nothing," he said. Her reply was, "I see." This was code, and it meant: You're a fool. With Marilyn it was hard to win, hard to avoid that "I see," and Blumberg sometimes felt like slapping her silly. A purchase of stamps would have helped, but not satisfied; hoarding small scraps of old paper seemed only a whisker shy of *meshugge* to her, but at least he'd have *bought*.

"What a waste of a morning," she said, but he countered, "I had a good time. It was entertaining."

"Pawing through dead people's stuff," she said.

He thought of the Klan outfit there on the seat of his car. If she ever found out he'd spent money on that, *oy vey*.

"So listen, I'm going out with Sheila, Macy's is having a sale."

"Good luck," Blumberg said. This meant: What more do you *need?*

His first name was Hymen. Yes, with an "e," like the Greek god of marriage. He tried to avoid it, called himself Hy, but of course when it came to signing things, it had to be Hymen. Why, for the love of God, had his parents named him that? Nobody named their kids "Vulva" or "Testicle." Hadn't they known the word's meaning? Hadn't they known how to spell? They'd wanted to punish him right from the start? He'd never dared ask how they'd come by their execrable choice, and now they were dead.

They'd primed him for failure with that name. Those little smirks at Motor Vehicles and other official bureaus, the inevitable, "Hi, Hy." Okay, maybe failure was too strong a word, he wasn't a failure, he had a good library job, a nice home. Lack of outstanding achievement, then, they'd set him up for that. The only famous Hyman he could think of was that bigmouth admiral, Hyman Rickover. Spelled with an "a"— and not even a Jew? He didn't know. As for famous librarians—zip. Library work was an occupation devoid of fame, like plumbing, accounting, insurance. Nobody in those lines of work ended up on a postage stamp. Politicians, musicians, scientists, athletes—actors and cowboys, even—but not librarians. Not auctioneers. Certain fields lacked greatness in the public mind. Of *course* there were great librarians, he himself was a pretty damn good one, but no recognition would come to him for it. So what? If you liked what you did, who cared about fame? Did he like what he did? Yeah, he liked it okay, but maybe he'd like something better. Such as? No clue.

Marilyn worked in a bank, surrounded by money. Not that she got a lot of it, she was a teller. She constantly had her hands in it though, and wanted to keep what she touched. This was a major source of frustration.

And now she was going to spend some more of the tiny amount she got and said, "I ought to be home by five."

*Ought to be,* Blumberg thought, and said, "Have fun," which meant: Get a life.

When she left in her car, the Subaru, he went to his car, the Buick, and took out the costume. Costume? That probably wasn't the word to use, the Klan would probably not like that word.

He looked at the uniform (better word) there in his hands. He would burn it right now—in the fireplace? He wasn't even sure if the fireplace worked anymore, it hadn't been used for so long. If he started it up while Marilyn shopped, when she came home she'd smell it and start to ask questions. Fires in July? Any excuse would sound hollow, no, he'd hide the thing till he figured out another way to dispose of it. He'd put it in one of his drawers for now, she never looked in his bureau, he did his own laundry. He went to the bedroom.

He opened the bottom bureau drawer, the one with pajamas and bathing suits, preparing to stash the outfit there, when he changed his mind and set it down on the bed.

The bed was kingsize, and it was unmade. They almost never made their bed these days. Certain standards had slipped with the passage of time, along with other things. Slippage, marital and otherwise, was now a fact of life.

On Tuesday, he'd gone to the dentist to hear from a strapping blond *shiksa* a lecture on gum disease. He was falling apart at the level of bone, it seemed. Not only his jaws but the aches in his knees and lower back confirmed this. He brushed and flossed, took walks and tried not to eat too much fat, but it wasn't enough, the slippage kept gaining on him.

He looked at the outfit. It gave off a musty, cellary smell. Its fabric was off-white—yellowish, really. From age? It was rough, like one of those bags potatoes or apples came in. Muslin? Sackcloth? Marilyn would likely know, but of course she would never see it. God forbid! That "KKK" on the hood would stop her heart, her cousin had lived through the Holocaust!

What did those other patches mean? That drop of blood on the shoulder, a cross in a circle, a pine tree. The pine tree symbolized Maine? Blumberg wondered how old the thing was, who its owner had been. Some plumber, accountant, insurance agent? Some *shlepper* who'd never done anything, really, except attend meetings and maybe help burn a small cross on somebody's lawn? Had Klansmen burned crosses in Maine? They hadn't been active for years in the state, and this outfit had probably lain in a trunk for decades. And now it would lie in his bureau drawer? Good grief, he had paid fifty dollars for it!

Now he unfolded it, smoothed it out over the sheets, and saw that its owner had not been tall. Blumberg had always fantasized Klansmen as big guys, giants, almost. Not this one.

The robe didn't open in front. You slipped it on over your head like a night shirt, then fastened the sash and put on the hood...

And now he was holding the hood up and putting it down, and holding the robe up and putting it down, and now he was taking his clothes off except for his underwear. Now picking the robe up and pulling it over his head. It settled across his shoulders and covered the belly and breasts that he'd failed to subdue through diet and exercise. Slippage.

He wondered: Did Klansmen wear undershorts? How could he ever find out without talking to one? Some did and some didn't? All robes were as coarse as this? Maybe those in the South were smoother and lighter because of the heat down there. He tied the sash, which was blue with white bands at the edges, then put on the hood. The musty smell was strong.

The costume fit almost perfectly; its hemline fell to mid-calf. Whoever had owned it had been just about his size, five-eight.

He peered through the eyeholes at bureau and dresser. Felt creepy, transformed, like an evil intruder, a thief.

He went to the full-length mirror attached to the back of the door, and despite his anticipation, he caught his breath. To think that this mirror, right here in his very own bedroom, would ever reflect such a sight. Ghastly. Dreadful.

He stared through the vicious eyeholes. A Jew in a Klan uniform! He had to be one of a very select contingent—or maybe the whole contingent!

He looked like a dunce in the pointy hood. Ridiculous! But his chest and his middle—impressive. The robe did amazing things for his body; it made him look solid, practically svelte, and a tiny electrical buzz traveled through him. It lodged in his penis, which, shockingly, started to grow. Pretty soon it was firm. Not totally hard, but firm. Good God, Blumberg thought, what's this? Coincidence, maybe, nothing to do with the robe. He fervently hoped.

He took off the hood, then pulled the robe over his head. He looked at himself in his underwear, at the lump in his jockey shorts, and started to sweat. Coincidence, he told himself, and put the robe back on the bed.

As he started to fold the robe, his erection died, but his penis was throbbing with pleasure. Sweating quite heavily now, he stopped his folding and took off his shorts and put the robe back on.

Now the fabric was touching his glans and he firmed up again and the tip was rubbing the rough yellow cloth and now he was hard as a rock. Coincidence? Not on your life!

The major form of his marital slippage had started three years ago. In the middle of things he had popped out to find that he'd softened a bit. Reinsertion was tricky, for now he was bendable. This was a first. "What's happening?" Marilyn asked with concern, and he didn't know. He was able to finish, but rushed the job, fearing total deflation.

An aberration, he told himself, but it happened the following time and the time after that, and then to his great chagrin he found he was not getting thoroughly hard anymore. Hard enough to achieve penetration but pliable at the perimeter, and Marilyn was quite aware of this. One night she said, "I hope you are really really hard this time," and of course that totally did him in. From then on he found himself *thinking*—lethal during sex. Thinking and worrying. What in the world was the matter? What had gone wrong?

"You need more hormones," Marilyn said. "You need testosterone."

But that wasn't it. He hadn't lost drive, it was just that his organ wouldn't respond in the same old reliable way. No matter how horny he got, there was always peripheral sponginess. How could he stiffen it?

How had he ever? Erections had always been taken-for-granted mysteries: given the proper circumstances, they simply appeared in full bloom—like the one he had now. "Testosterone isn't the answer," he said. "I haven't lost interest, the problem is firmness."

"You need a pill," Marilyn said.

He doubted this, too, for at times he got hard as he ever had in his life: in the early morning he'd wake with it rigid as bone and lie there gripping it, telling himself he was fine.

"That isn't significant," Marilyn said. "One of my magazines had an article on it. Matinal firmness has nothing to do with performance."

Matinal? What was this matinal? Those magazines! But it proved to be true. Matinal, morning, whatever—no carryover.

Blumberg was baffled. Maybe he *had* lost interest in sex and just didn't know it. The more he considered this, the more it began to make sense. His interest in *everything* had declined. He used to be quite a baseball fan, now he rarely watched games on TV and never attended them. Athletes were all grouchy millionaires, so who cared? His job? He could take it or leave it. Same thing with movies and plays and restaurants. Take them away and yes, he would miss them a little, but not a whole lot. His batteries were running down, he could live without anything, really— even sex!

But he didn't *want* to, and one day in Boston, with sunglasses on, he stopped into one of those shops. This would give him the jump start he needed? Far from it! The *shtuppers* in all of the pictures were much too young! They could all be his children—if he had any children. No good!

So he went back to stamps, approaching the problem indirectly. If he could rekindle that innocent passion, maybe his other appetites would follow suit. He kept going to auctions, hoping, hoping…

According to Marilyn's know-it-all magazines, fifty percent of men over forty had problems getting it up. Had they suffered a generalized lack of desire, like him? Had the novelty worn off everything? Did they feel like an actor in *Death of a Salesman?* Feel they'd be stranded in deserts of sameness until some calamity struck? Time went faster and faster, and everything changed for the worse. No wonder this timid tumescence!

But now, good heavens, look at this! That recalcitrant outermost layer: solid gold! He took the robe off again, stared at his burning baton, astonished.

And realized he didn't know himself. He'd never have guessed such a thing would happen, never in all his life. He was a *stranger* to himself.

It was exciting.

His mouth was dry as he dressed again, guiding his undershorts over his bulge, which took five more minutes to die.

Marilyn showed him all her buys: a skirt, a blouse, some pantyhose and a pair of turquoise earrings. "A total of eighty-five dollars I saved," she said, and he thought: *I don't really know you. I don't really know what you think about God and death, I don't even know if you really like sex.* During their drinks before dinner he put on some Bach (he was a Bach man; she liked swing) then made a suggestion.

"So what's the occasion?" she said.

"No occasion, it's just that we haven't done things for so long."

His semi-softness had led to a marked reduction in frequency. When was their last time? Months ago. "Performance anxiety" (big spread about it in one of her magazines), had kept him from making advances. And Marilyn never made advances, she didn't feel it was nice. She did, at times, make sarcastic remarks, which compounded the situation no end.

"Sounds great," she said with a grin as she finished her drink. "If you think you're up to it."

Blumberg had laundered the robe during Marilyn's shopping jaunt. All mustiness was gone. It smelled perfectly fresh and clean, but still looked yellow. Maybe he should have used bleach, he thought, but that might have faded the patches.

Going upstairs before she did, he took the robe out of his drawer and smuggled it into the hallway bathroom. Filled with a fearful excitement, he showered, soaping his floppy tube. Hoping and praying (to what? to whom?) he slipped the robe over his head, and bingo! Straight out! He took the robe off again, put it away in a plastic bag, shoved it into the closet, then went to the bedroom and slithered between the sheets. Still good, still fine, still *wonderful.*

Then Marilyn entered, leaving the master bath. She was naked on top and wearing a pair of see-through panties that Blumberg remembered from better times. She slipped into bed beside him, he turned, and her eyes went wide. "What have we *here?*" she said in delighted amazement, and then they were kissing and groping and going at it. Good for a minute, two minutes, five minutes, and then, oh no, the softening started, he swivelled, was frankfurter flexible, finished it off. "Quick," Marilyn said. "Not bad, but quick." She squinted. "Hey, did you take anything? A pill?" He shook his head. "No pill," he said. "I told you before, I don't need a pill. Next time it'll last much longer." Marilyn smiled a little. "Mmm," she said.

His response to the robe was dreadful, disgusting—and mystifying. He hated the Klan, the Klan hated Jews and he was a Jew, it made no sense.

And yet... While watching the grainy gray horrors of films about Hitler, terrified, sickened, he also felt—yes, he had to admit it—thrilled. Something about the blind adulation the populace gave the man, the pomp, the coldblooded bestial cruelty past comprehension, struck some kind of primitive chord that he wished to deny with all his heart, but couldn't. He loathed himself for this reaction, but there it was. Surely he wasn't the only person who felt this degenerate rush. What other reason for so many TV specials about the Third Reich, all those books on the subject?

He looked up the Klan at the library where he worked, and learned that the klansmen called themselves "knights." The drop of blood on the uniform's shoulder? He couldn't find that in the books, but the sash was the sash of an officer, maybe a "wizard," not such a *shlepper* after all. The symbol adorning the front of his robe, the cross in the circle, was Christian. The Klan claimed that Christ was their leader. The cross was a symbol of faith, hope, love! For those who strung blacks up in trees, who denied there was ever a Holocaust! For Christians who hated Catholics!

Most people assumed that the Klan was confined to the South, but no, for years it had been all over the place—in Oregon, Indiana, you name it.

He looked up the Klan in Maine, its history. In 1923, the Klan swept the city elections in Portland, the town where this library was—the town where he worked and lived! Following these elections, the town's Catholic bishop received a letter which said:

"Perhaps you noticed that no Catholics got elected in the recent election in Portland. It is the eighteenth place in New England that the Klan has kept Catholics from holding office. Hereafter, no niggers, Catholics, nor Jews will ever hold office in Portland."

When Blumberg read this, his stomach churned. My God! He should burn the robe right now, today, destroy all the hateful things it stood for, yes, he should, and yet…

He tried watching a Red Sox game—and really enjoyed it. Those stamps he'd bought a while back? They proved to be pretty darned interesting after all. He nodded with a happy grin as Marilyn said, "I don't believe what I'm hearing. You made reservations for dinner?" "I think we should eat out at least once a week," he said. "I'm in heaven!" Marilyn said.

They were home from the theater, having a cordial, when Blumberg said, "Let's do it in the dark."

She stared at him. "The dark? But Hy, you've always said that you feel lost if you can't see."

"I won't feel lost tonight. Tonight I want the dark. I'll wait in the dark for you."

Marilyn's eyes lit up; she smiled. "A game," she said. "I thought our game-playing days were over. What's got into you lately?"

"I don't really know."

"Well, whatever it is, I like it," Marilyn said, then frowned. "What's this we're drinking?"

"Southern Comfort."

"Oh? Since when do we drink that?"

"It's good, don't you think?"

"Not sweet enough," Marilyn said, "I prefer amaretto." She smiled again. "A game. This calls for an outfit."

She liked to wear outfits. It made her feel sexy. She had special panties and negligees that were filmy, lacy, and never worn except on erotic occasions. Over the course of the last few years, she hadn't worn them at all.

"An outfit would be good," Blumberg said, "but I'll just have to feel it, we'll be in the dark."

"No light at all?"

"None."

"Weird. It's like when we first got married, and I was shy."

"Yes, that's the idea." Blumberg finished his drink. "But I'll wear an outfit too."

"You've never worn outfits."

"I'll wear one tonight."

"And I can't see it?"

"Not tonight. Some other time."

"How weird."

"I'll wait in the dark in the bed. You'll be in the bathroom. I'll call you in."

"Hey, kinky," Marilyn said, and drained her glass.

Blumberg showered then carried his plastic bag down the hall. In the bedroom he closed the door. He heard his wife scuffing around in the master bathroom, dressing and primping. He turned off the light. Pitch black. He felt around in his bag and took out the costume. Put on the robe, but not the hood. Standing there in the dark he grew instantly firm. He felt powerful, flooded with energy. *Man of steel!*

He took the hood to the bed and got under the sheet, not wilting the tiniest bit. *I'm doing this for both of us,* he told himself. *Not just for me, for both of us.* "I'm ready when you are," he called.

The door to the bathroom came open. A flash of black stockings, black garter belt, black pushup bra. Then black as she flicked off the lights. "Where are you?" she said.

"Right here, keep going straight," and then she was next to him under the sheet. "A game," she said. "I like it." She felt for his head and found his chin, slid her hand up his cheek. "Too bad you can't see me," she said as she gave him a peck on the ear, her breathing hot. "I bought this outfit a year ago and never used it. I got it for less than half price."

"I saw it a little," Blumberg said, "and now I'll feel it." He ran his hand over her back, touched the strap of the bra. His erection was raging.

"You're wearing…what kind of an outfit is this?" she said.

"It's a robe."

"A robe? What robe? Not a new one, you never buy anything new."

This was one of her standard knocks against him. "It isn't new," he said.

"I don't remember a robe with this texture."

"It's very old," he said. Against expectations, this dialogue hadn't diminished his firmness, not in the slightest. He rubbed her back.

41

"It feels like muslin."

"Muslin, yes. Or sackcloth, maybe."

"What color is it?"

"White."

"My outfit's black," said Marilyn. "I got it at—" A silence, then: "Oh my. Oh my oh *my*."

Oh my was right. What a fabulous stick! He was twenty years old again.

"This is fantastic!" Marilyn said. "This is incredible!"

Blumberg had hiked up the robe to set himself free and now was between her thighs. She moaned in a way that he hadn't heard in he couldn't remember how long. They kissed, hard, tongues conjoined. "Oh Hy," she said. "Oh God."

He was mounting her, robe above his hips, he was kissing her breasts. His organ, iron pipe, was in her fist. "Oh Hy, Hy, Hy," she said, "oh yes, oh now!" and he shifted and bullseyed in.

Catching her breath she groaned, "I never thought... I never imagined..."

He reached for the hood, which was near his right knee. Put it on. And then he was riding her hard and fast in the darkness, riding through thicket and field in the summer heat, his blood hot and rich with the promise of history, rifles and banners and hangmen's ropes, a warrior, conquering—

"What are you wearing *now?*" she said arching and digging his arms with her fingers. "My God, this is *wonderful*, what are you wearing *now?*"

"Just a robe," he said hotly, pistoning, hoarse. "A sackcloth robe."

"I mean on your head. There's something over your face."

"It's part of the robe," he said, and his mind held a blazing cross.

"Oh God this is simply fantastic!" she cried, and thrust and thrust and thrust so hard at his still unwavering staff. "Let me see it, I want to see."

"No you don't!"

"Yes I do, yes I do!" she gasped, "I *do* want to see, right now!" and her arm flew up skimming his ear and she clicked on the headboard lamp.

The room went white, her eyes went wide, her face was total shock. "Good God!" she cried. "Good God, oh Hymen, no, no, no!" She looked pale she looked sick she was starting to weep and she stiffened and froze, but Blumberg kept riding, riding, riding the glory road. "Don't say you don't like it!" he shouted. "Don't say you don't like it, you love it!"

# HUNGER

*reat, just what I need,* Dillon thought.

The guy ahead of him—the only other patron in the tiny store—was truly pathetic. He was bent and bald, with a stubble of mangy gray whiskers, a grubby blue short sleeve shirt with a missing right armpit, and watery eyes behind sagging glasses patched with electrical tape. To top it all off, he stank—the odor was sour and musty both. He fussed with his tattered wallet, his withered hands shaking.

With a sniff of disgust, Dillon looked at the rack of gum and candy bars. It had rained from Atlantic City to Pittsburgh, a tire had given out before Cleveland, a cop had made him move on when he tried to camp out in his car. He'd smoked the last of his cigarettes over an hour ago, had run in here to get a new pack, and—this is the way it was going—had gotten behind Mr. Slow.

"So how are the cats, Mr. Logan?" the man at the register said. He was middleaged, jowly, with dark blue suspenders.

The customer's voice was phlegmy and loose as he piped, "Getting old, I'm afraid."

"Aren't we all."

The customer didn't respond to this. A coupon slipped out of his wallet and fell to the floor.

"You drop something, Mr. Logan?"

"What?" The old man looked up with a frown. "Oh," he said, then he slowly bent down for the coupon. "Tissues," he said as he came up again. "I forgot them."

Taking the coupon the cashier said, "I'll be right back." He locked the register and walked away.

*Terrific,* Dillon thought.

The old man kept fooling around with his wallet, and when he at last latched onto something, Dillon's eyes narrowed. The bill those feeble fingers held bore the face of Benjamin Franklin.

"Here we go, Mr. Logan," the cashier said smiling, dropping the tissue box in the old man's cart. He rang up the item, deducting the coupon. "Twenty-three fourteen out of a hundred," he said as he took the money. "Oops, here's an extra." He held up a crisp new bill.

The old man stared at it. "What?"

"Two hundreds were stuck together."

"Oh."

The cashier counted out the change, placing it in the old man's palm on top of the extra hundred. Laying his wallet down on the counter, the old man picked up the coins in slow motion, depositing them in his pocket. He took up his wallet again and opened it wide and began to insert the bills.

Dillon watched. And there was another hundred, another, a fifty….

The old man at last got his things in order and shuffled off, dragging his cart.

"Sorry to keep you waiting," the cashier said.

"No problem, I just want a pack of Marlboros," Dillon said.

"Sure thing."

Dillon paid and went out the door.

The old man was lugging his cart down the sidewalk. Dillon tore open the Marlboros, lit one, got into his car and watched.

At the corner the guy stopped and looked both ways, craning his scrawny neck first left, then right, then all the way back to the left again before crossing.

The street was industrial, tired and bleak, in a lost hopeless pocket of urban decay. A car without tires, its windshield cracked, squatted next to the opposite curb. Except for the feeb, there was no one in sight.

Dillon smoked, thinking: Still Indiana, right? Yeah, had to be. He pressed on the gas and turned the key and started down the street.

Surely the guy didn't live far away, and the chances were very good that he lived alone. And he had *money*—possibly *lots* of money. Some of these characters lived like paupers and had thousands stashed in their cookie jars.

46

Dillon pulled to the side as a white truck with "Stanton's Prime Cuts" painted on it went by, and the old geezer rounded the corner.

The block was dead. A factory with its windows shattered took up the street's south side, while the north side held rubble-strewn lots and a trio of row houses covered with patterned asphalt: fake stone and fake brick.

Dillon parked on the corner, breathing out smoke and squashing his Marlboro butt in the car's ashtray. The dude hauled his cart up the granite step of the middle house—the one that was covered in fake yellow brick— then reached in his pocket. After a while he found the key and fumbled it into the lock. His door opened up and he hoisted his groceries inside.

Dillon lighted another Marlboro, thinking: Give him some time to take a leak, unpack, then go for it.

He finished the Marlboro, started another, and thought of Atlantic City; of how, in the very near future, a guy would show up out of nowhere, demanding the money. Five thousand bucks, and he'd better have it—or else.

He opened his door and got out of the car and flicked what was left of his Marlboro into the weeds in the empty lot on the corner. The air was damp and the lot smelled of plaster dust.

The houses on either side of the old coot's place were boarded up and the sidewalk was covered with garbage: smashed bottles, old rags, scraps of paper, a hubcap, some stained white acoustical tiles. He mounted the granite step and pushed the black button on the door jamb.

He heard no ring inside the house, and pushed again. Still nothing, so he knocked.

He waited awhile and knocked again. Come on, old man, he thought, don't make me break your damn door down.

A scratching sound, the click of the latch, and the door came open a crack. The man's face, puzzled, fearful, looking up.

In his mind Dillon saw himself shoving the door open, knocking the guy to the floor and grabbing the wallet. But Christ, it could kill the old fart. That, he certainly didn't need. No violence if he could help it. And maybe that wallet was only the tip of the iceberg, after all.

"I was thinking you might like some help around here," he said. "I could clean up your sidewalk. Your yard, your cellar, I'm fast and I'm cheap."

The old man stared with a dense, opaque look. "What?"

"Clean up," Dillon said a notch louder. "This mess on the sidewalk."

"Oh." The man squinted. "I saw you in Russell's, right?"

So he wasn't completely unconscious after all. "The store?" Dillon said. "Russell's Market."

"Yeah, I was there."

"I thought so."

Not good, Dillon thought. The cashier could tell cops important stuff if the geezer blabbed. "Your name's Mr. Logan, right?" he said.

"How'd you know that?" The wizened face was pinched and suspicious.

"The guy in the store called you that."

"Yeah, Logan's my name."

Dillon stuck out his hand. "Mine's Stanton. Bill Stanton."

The old man ignored Dillon's hand. He kept squinting. "So what do you want?"

"I do odd jobs."

"You live near here?"

"Across town."

"Where?"

"Lawrence Street."

"Never heard of it."

"I never heard of your street either until today," Dillon said looking down at the sidewalk. "It sure is a mess. Trash like this can attract rats, you know."

"Rats?" said Logan. He shook his frail head. "I got no rats, my cats make sure of that."

"Uh-huh," Dillon said.

Then the old man surprised him. "I got an old stove in the hallway," he said. "If you take it outside, I'll give you a dollar."

"A dollar. Sure," Dillon said.

Logan opened the door, and Dillon stepped into a vestibule tiled in brown. The odor he'd smelled in the store was heavy in here. Did this guy ever shower?

"This way," Logan said.

They entered the hall, where a low wattage bulb wrapped in cobwebs hung down on a cord. "That's it right there."

It was buried in bundles of old newspapers, and so was the hallway floor. "Gotta move all these papers to get to it," Dillon said. "So you want me to stick 'em outside?"

"While you're at it, sure," Logan said.

Dillon thought: While I'm at it. Clean out the hallway *and* move the stove for a buck. Quite a deal.

As he picked up some bundles of papers, the smell hit him hard. The place *reeked*. Cats, he thought. That's what that odor was, cats.

He carried the papers out to the sidewalk. Compared to the house, the

48

stale city air smelled sweet. In the hallway again he said, "You got a real fire hazard here. You oughta get rid of *all* these papers, you know?"

Logan didn't respond for a moment. Then, nodding, he said, "I suppose you're right. Well, I'll give you another dollar."

"For what's in the hallway?"

"No, no, for the living room too. And I got some out in the dining room and the kitchen."

The dingy living room was crammed so full there was barely space to walk. "It'd take me a couple of hours to get all this out," Dillon said. "I'll have to charge you five bucks."

"Make it four," Logan said.

Dillon looked at him hard. He imagined his fist smashing into that sallow face, those glasses splintering. "Four bucks," he said. "Not much for all that work."

"Well, take it or leave it," Logan said. "I have to check something out back, you decide what you want to do."

He made his way down the hall past the piles of paper. As Dillon watched, he thought: I've decided to take it, old man. I've decided to take it *all*.

He made five more trips to the sidewalk before he had cleaned out enough to be able to move the stove. He thought he'd get used to the sickening odor, but no, and now *he* stank; the cat smell covered his sweaty skin, was in his shirt, his hair. But where the hell *were* the things? He hadn't seen one of them yet, and you'd think that with a stench this bad the place would be crawling with them.

The stove was so old it was probably worth some money: a green enameled gas job on slender black legs. Dillon grabbed it and pulled.

Heavy sucker, for Christ's sake. He pulled on its opposite side and it moved a few inches—and something fell onto the floor.

Dillon stared at it. Money, a roll of bills. He reached down and snatched it up.

"Having problems?"

The old man was down at the end of the hall by the door that led into the kitchen. Slipping the roll of bills into his shirt, Dillon said, "This baby's heavy."

"Of course," Logan said. "If it wasn't, I'd move it myself."

"Right."

Inch by inch, Dillon wrestled the stove toward the door. Finally he got it outside on the step, then yanked it down onto the sidewalk and out to the curb. Out of breath, sweating hard and his shoulders aching, he stood with his back to the house and reached in his shirt.

He took the rubber band off the bills and unrolled them. Ten twenties. Two hundred bucks. If he had any luck this would just be the start. He went back inside.

He cleaned out the rest of the hallway while Logan watched. "I haven't seen this much floor in years," the old man said. "It sure makes a difference, all right."

Dillon found no more money. At the living room doorway he said, "Where's the light switch in here?"

"The bulb's dead," Logan said. "I don't use the living room much anymore, I pretty much stay in the kitchen. Just take out the papers now, don't touch those baskets."

"You don't have an extra bulb?"

"Maybe somewhere."

"Uh-huh."

Dillon had cleared out half the room before Logan said, "I'll be back in a while," and left.

The baskets were stacked at the foot of the bookshelves, most of them peach baskets made out of wood. Dillon went to them quickly, leaned down. The room was so dark he could hardly see. An iron without any cord, a few broken light fixtures, rusty stuck hinges, screwdrivers—just worthless junk. Three whole baskets of empty jars.

A toilet flushed, and Dillon stood up. On the dark marble mantel some lighter fluid, a bar of soap, and a carved wooden box. Dillon opened the box.

More bills. Two rolls. He shoved them into his pocket and closed the lid.

"How's it going?"

The old man was there in the doorway, his features in shadow.

"You sure have a mess here," Dillon said lifting more papers.

"I know," Logan said. "You save a little here, a little there, and the next thing you know..." He shrugged.

Dillon went through the hallway and out to the curb. The sidewalk held a wall of papers now.

As he looked at the house again, he gagged. His throat was itching, burning with that awful smell. For a minute he thought he should quit right now and be happy with what he had. Then he said to himself: Are you nuts? This guy is the next best thing to Fort Knox. Gagging again, he took a deep breath of foul air and went back inside.

"Just the newspapers," Logan said again. "I could probably do without some of the other stuff too, but I'd have to go through it first. You get old and forget what you have." He waved his shrivelled hand and said,

"You wouldn't know. You're young and strong and your mind's okay, you wouldn't know what I mean."

Dillon lifted more papers. His ribs and arms were aching now. When he went back into the house, Logan was gone.

Dillon went to the bookshelves. He leafed through the dusty volumes quickly, alert for the sound of Logan's slow feet. The books yielded nothing, nothing, nothing—then a bill floated onto the floor.

A hundred. All *right.* Dillon went through more books. A twenty, a ten and a fifty came out, and he stuffed them away in his pocket.

"So, Mr. Stanton, you like to read?"

Dillon broke into sudden sweat. "Oh, yeah," he said as he put the book back.

"Books are wonderful friends," Logan said. "Next to my cats, they're the best friends I have."

"Uh-huh," Dillon said. He bent over and lifted more papers.

"I'd hate to lose even a one of them," Logan said. "I'd miss them so. Funny, since I haven't been able to read in a long time now." He touched his glasses. "These things don't work anymore."

Dillon grunted and carried the newspapers out the door.

Logan watched as he finished the living room. But when Dillon attacked the dining room, the old man went off again.

A tureen on the dark ornate sideboard. Dillon went to it, lifting its china lid with the utmost caution. Paper clips and rubber bands and matches and stubs of old pencils, old gas bills, a few rolls of cellophane tape—and no money. He put the lid down again, holding his breath. It made a tiny clink as it touched the bowl.

He looked over his shoulder—no Logan—and opened the sideboard's top drawer.

He rummaged through playing cards, yellowed receipts, a lace table-cloth, white linen napkins. A handful of pennies. No bills. He shoved the drawer closed and opened the bottom drawer. No money. Behind the cabinet door on the right, more papers. He pushed them aside. No bills. Wiping sweat off his forehead, he opened the door on the left.

More papers, some plastic placemats—and then, beneath the place-mats, a metal box. Dillon opened it quickly, hands shaking.

His breath stopped. Good God. It was filled to the brim with hundreds. Quickly he shoved them down into his pockets, sweating. Thousands of dollars here, *thousands.* Closing the box, he put it back under the placemats and shut the door.

"Problems?"

Sudden cold sweat and his chest felt numb. Standing, rubbing his shoulder, Dillon said, "Yeah, pulled my back. I'm afraid that's all for today. I can come back tomorrow, though, if it eases up."

"Fine," Logan said. "I'll pay you tomorrow, then."

"I'd like to get paid for today's work now," Dillon said.

Logan nodded. "I understand. In case you can't make it tomorrow."

"Right."

"So how much you want?"

"Three dollars."

"Oh? You did three quarters of the job?"

Dillon narrowed his eyes and thought: *Come on, old man, don't push your luck.* He said, "I think three bucks is a bargain for what I did."

Logan didn't respond to this. He said, "Before you go, do one more thing for me."

"What's that?"

"There's a broken TV in the yard that I'd like you to take out front. It's small, not heavy, it won't hurt your back."

"Where is it?"

They walked through the kitchen, where fat flakes of cream-colored paint curled away from the ceiling and walls. The table was piled with magazines. A path through the newspapers led to the cast-iron sink, where a faucet dripped; another path led to the door, which was steel, like something you'd find in a warehouse or store. The window beside it was covered with metal mesh. Logan pushed back two bolts on the door, turned the knob.

The yard was bordered by high wooden walls that were smothered in dark lush vines. Its grass was knee-high, yellow and brown, and, down at the far end, a tangle of bushes with flat broad leaves obscured a wrought iron gate.

An old refrigerator stood against one wall, vines spilling across its door. Beside it, a rickety table, its legs lost in grass, held three cans of paint and the TV set.

"Just put it out front with the papers," Logan said.

Dillon entered the grass. He had just about reached the table, when Logan laughed. Then the kitchen door slammed and the bolts clicked shut.

Dillon whirled. "Hey!" He waded across to the door again, grabbed the knob. "Hey!"

Then Logan was at the window, behind the mesh.

"What the hell's going on?" Dillon said.

Logan held up a finger. "I knew," he said. "From the very first moment I saw you at Russell's, I said to myself: I've got one."

A nut, Dillon thought. The old man's a friggin psycho!

"And then when you walked in the the house and the cats went wild, I *really* knew."

"Open up this door," Dillon said.

"Oh I'm not always right," Logan said, "but with you I was certain. Your hunger was just so *obvious.*"

Sweat was pouring down Dillon's neck. "You open this goddamn door right now or I'll smash it down," he said.

"You can't," Logan said. "And you can't get the mesh off this window, either, don't think others haven't tried. What I need you to do now is go to the table and put my money on it."

A setup. The old man had set him up. But why? "What money?" Dillon said. "You didn't pay me yet."

Logan barked a curt laugh. "Put it all on the table right now, Mr. Stanton—if that's your name."

Dillon went to the window. Grabbing the metal mesh he said, "Now listen, Logan, and listen good. You call the cops and I'll get you. I'll come back someday and I'll get you, you understand?"

Logan's face was devoid of expression. "I won't call the cops, just do what I say. Put the money on the table. *Now.*"

Cursing under his breath, Dillon went through the tall yellow grass. He reached in his pockets and took out the bills and laid them next to the paint cans.

"All of it, Mr. Stanton."

"That *is* all of it, damn it."

"Good." Logan's shadow was barely visible through the mesh. "It never fails," he said. "When I ask them to take out the TV set, they never turn me down. Perhaps there's more money in there, they think. And then when they see the old ice box they think, I bet that's *jammed* with bills, it's the old guy's safe."

He laughed again. "They'll never have enough, you see, their hunger knows no bounds. You took ten thousand dollars of mine but you wanted more, and more, and *more.* And there *is* more. You know where I got all that money? You want to guess?"

"Deposit bottles?" Dillon said, sneering.

"Good to see you're retaining your sense of humor," Logan said. "No, I was a prospector, Mr. Stanton, up in the Arizona hills. I lived thirty years in those hills, and I know about hunger, I've seen what greed does to men. It was rugged up there, but I loved that life. When I got my cats I figured I'd stay forever, but no, it was not to be. My sister took sick and I had to come home. I was all she had left in the world. She died six years ago."

"I gave you your money back," Dillon said. "Let me out of here now."

"Let you out?" Logan said. "Without punishment? You think you can steal from me and not pay the price?"

"So you *are* going to call the cops," Dillon said.

"Oh no," Logan said, "I'm a man of my word. I promised you that I wouldn't do that, and I won't. You see, I don't trust the legal system—too many loopholes. And bringing police out here would be very unwise. My cats wouldn't like it, and what they don't like, I don't do."

He paused for a moment, then said, "Well, I pamper them, yes, I admit it. I worried about them so much when I moved back here. City air, my damp cellar, this cramped little yard. But they've thrived! And you know why? The extras! The once a year extras!"

"So why don't you clean up their shit?" Dillon said, "so your house doesn't smell like a zoo?"

Logan said: "But I *like* that smell. I love my cats and I *like* that smell. You see, they were born in captivity, bottle fed, given meat in a bowl, it's not good. If they don't have to hunt, they can lose their edge, their zest for life."

Dillon frowned. "What the hell are you talking about?"

"The kill!" Logan said. "I'm talking about the thrill of the chase and the kill!"

This time his laugh was hoarse, high, crazed. And a panel below his window slid open, a steel panel set in the brick foundation.

Darkness, then motion, a flash of tan. Then the head of a cat coming out of the cellar, a head both fierce and huge.

"Good God!" Dillon said, stumbling backward.

Another maniacal laugh, and, "You're not the only one who's hungry, Stanton! You're not the only one!"

Dillon ran through the tangled grass. It tripped him up; he fell; sprang instantly to his feet again and ran with his blood roaring loud in his ears. "For God's sake, Logan, no!" he cried.

He grabbed the rusted iron gate, and then they were on him.

# DREAM BOX

The popcorn had stopped exploding. Hanson turned the hotplate off; it sparked, smoke came out of its coils. The hotplate was on its last legs, like the rest of the crumbling hotel room, but Hanson didn't care. The only thing that *had* to work was his TV set.

He'd bought it the week before at a sidewalk sale, a real antique: the remote was gone, the buttons were loose, the picture was really sad, but at least it worked. When his old one quit and he'd gone without for three whole days, he'd felt so *nervous*. No TV for all that time. He hoped to God it never happened again.

He buttered and salted the popcorn and sat in his overstuffed chair. It groaned with his bulk. He checked the TV listings, ramming a handful of popcorn into his mouth; stray puffs rolled over his T-shirt and bulging gut. He reached out, pressed the power button, slumped again as the stage-coach driver got hit in the neck with an arrow.

Halfway through his second beer, a voice in the TV said, "Come on, jerk, what are you sitting there for when you could be getting something?"

"What would you know?" Hanson muttered, eyes glued to the screen. The burglars had jimmied the skylight and dropped inside. They approached the safe.

"What's that, old Dapper Dan?"

"I said what would you know, wise guy? You're just a bunch of wires and glass, you don't have to work, you don't have to eat, you ain't fifty years old with no stomach condition. So shut up and show me pictures."

A snicker. "I just might know more than you think."

"Yeah? Prove it." The safe had been cracked—in record time, but the guard—

"Go open your door," said the voice.

Hanson grumbled. "Will you shut up? I'm tryin' to watch this show!"

"You can watch shows anytime, jerk. Go open your door."

"Hey!" Hanson said. "Don't talk that way! Just who do you think you are?"

"You asked me to prove it, didn't you? Open your door."

"You gotta be kidding," Hanson said. "You think I'm nuts?" The burglars were fading, were hard to see, then the screen was a total blur. "Goddamn it, I knew this would happen. Fifteen bucks, too cheap, I shoulda known." Setting his beer down, he fooled with the rabbit ears. Frowned.

The rabbit ears vibrated strangely; they actually *buzzed.* He twisted them, spread them apart, pulled them out, pushed them in—but the picture didn't improve. And now it was bright, so bright that it hurt his eyes. He turned away.

"The door," the voice said sharply.

Hanson looked at the set again. That light! The next thing he knew, he was walking across the room.

The hall was empty.

"Room 28," said the voice. "That newspaper over there, on the mat."

"Hey," Hanson said, "you're in my room, so how can you see—?"

"Turn it over."

"Hah?"

"Your cauliflower ears plugged up? I said turn the paper over—so the headline faces the floor."

Squinting, Hanson stepped into the hall. Okay, I'll do it, what can I lose? he thought—and was suddenly caught in the grip of a dreamlike calm. His arm reached out, turned the paper face down.

Inside again, his trance dissolved. "What kind of a crazy thing was that to ask me to do?" he said, then thought: I've flipped! Only on my second beer, and talking to my TV set! And it's talking back!

"You did just fine," said the voice. "Now grab my ears, like you did before."

Hanson did, and the buzzing was stronger, oddly soothing.

"Let go now and just relax. Enjoy the show."

Hanson slouched in the overstuffed chair and eyed the set suspiciously. The screen was clear again. An attractively dressed young man was standing beside a bar in a gleaming, walnut-paneled room. Hanson opened another beer and took a swig. He watched. He frowned. That guy on the screen, he thought, he looks like—yeah! He looks like a rich, slimmed-down version of...*me.*

A knock at the door.

"Crap," Hanson grumbled, "just when things was gettin' good." He got up and opened the door—just a crack. There were all kindsa freaks around these days, you couldn't be too careful.

A bellhop in a dark blue uniform, a cart with silver platters. "Room service."

Hanson just stood there, staring, and then he laughed. "*Room service,*" he said. "At the Kenmore? Just what are you tryin' to pull?" He wanted to slam the door on the guy, but his arm seemed frozen, stuck.

"You *are* Mr. Hanson, right? This is room 25?"

"This is room 25 and I'm Hanson, but I didn't ask for no room service. The Kenmore don't even *have*—"

"Let him in," said the voice in the TV set, and like magic, his arm was free.

He opened the door and the bellhop entered, uncovered the food (my God it looked good!) poured wine and presented the check. Hanson stared. "Hey listen, I didn't order this spread and I ain't got the dough—"

The bellhop just smiled. Hanson followed his gaze, looking down at himself, and his huge beer belly was gone. He was wearing an elegant smoking jacket, just like the guy on TV. When he felt in its pocket, he found it was stuffed with bills.

"This is great!" Hanson said as he washed down the chateaubriand with a gulp of champagne. "But who sent it, and where did that dough come from? Room service here, at the Kenmore! I never knew they had no kitchen—and man, what grub! I'd love to tell the guys at the plant about this one, but who would believe it?"

Another knock. Swallowing the meat in his mouth, he thought, Damn, they found out they got the wrong room. Well, too late now, I *paid.* As he went to the door, his hand felt the bills. They were real, all right.

When he opened the door, his eyes bugged out. Two absolutely gorgeous babes. "Hi, Charlie, we're sorry we're late," one said. "You will forgive us, won't you, sweetheart?" Bright red hair and cool blue eyes. "Hi, honey," the other one said, the blonde, and planted a passionate kiss on his cheek. "How's my baby?"

Alarms rang in Hanson's head. How did these broads know his name? He looked down the hallway in both directions, expecting the worst, but no one was there. Hastily he locked the door as the women walked into his room.

"Oh look at this naughty Charlie," the redhead said, "he started without us. Well, guess it serves us right for being late."

When Hanson turned around, he gasped.

His room had been transformed: there were shelves of books and a stereo, a huge tank of tropical fish and a gleaming bar. "Well come on, Charlie," said the blonde, running her fingers through his hair, "make Carol a little drink."

"Oh," Hanson said, "yeah, right," and he moved to the bar. In the mirror above the rows of expensive booze he saw himself, and stared. For he was that man, that man on the TV screen. That thin and elegant Charlie Hanson, that was *him*.

"A drink for Carol and Rhonda and a bite to eat, and then we'll be ready for fun and games," the redhead said. She pressed against him. "Right, sweetie? Fun and games?"

"Right," Hanson stammered. "Oh, yeah, *right*."

He made the drinks. Words he had never known before flowed magically from his lips.

My God, what a dream! Hanson thought. The TV set was discussing Greek art; leaning forward, he turned it off. I musta dozed off as soon as I sat in the chair last night, he thought, I'm gettin' *old*. He laughed. The goddamn TV set was *talkin'* to me, *Jesus* what a dream.

As he shaved at the sink by the window, he thought, Well sure, it *musta* been a dream. Sure, look at this place, it's the same old dump. "Same ugly mug, no doubt about that," he said as he shaved his chin. "Same gut. And if I'da went through all *that*, I wouldn't be able to *move* this morning, and I feel great! The best! Not even no acid stomach. Crazy goddamn dream, but I slept like a log."

He dried his face and put on his shirt, made instant coffee and toast. Then, laughing to himself again, he left for work.

"So how'd you like it?"

Hanson sat straight in his chair.

"Last night," the TV said. "Did I prove myself?" A covey of chorus girls pranced on the screen.

"It really *happened*," Hanson said, staring into the girls. "It really *did*."

"Well of course. Did you think that hunk of clay you call a brain could dream up something like that on its own? So here's what you do tonight."

Hanson narrowed his eyes. "Just a second," he said. "What's the catch?"

"The catch?"

"Yeah. I do all this stuff and you treat me real good, and one day you want the big payoff, right?"

A laugh. "Come on, meathead, where'd you get that crap? There isn't any *catch*. All your jobs will be little things, just incidentals, things that I can't quite manage on my own. You'll receive a handsome reward for each favor performed. You'll stay the same dumb jerk you always were, but I won't take a thing away from you. Far from it, I'll give, give, give. But there is a condition—a very *important* condition."

"What's that?"

"Don't ask any questions. Agreed?"

Hanson's head was spinning. He stared at the screen.

"Perhaps if I refresh your memory," and steamy scenes of the night before went flashing through Hanson's mind. He nodded slowly. "Yeah," he said, "agreed, no questions. So what do you want me to do?"

"Walk up to the window. Open it. Pick up your ashtray and empty the butts outside. Good, excellent. Now grab my ears and hang on tight, meat-head..."

The night was incredible. Carol and Rhonda were back and he drank and played till the sun rose over the railroad tracks—now a sparkling river—and got no sleep at all. Even so, he felt better at work than he had in *years*. "Hey, look at Charlie," one of the boys said, "I think he's in love." Hanson laughed. If you only knew, he thought. If you only *knew*.

That night he turned on the TV set as soon as he got home, awaited his orders.

"Okay, here's the deal," said the box. "Go down to the lobby again, take the elevator, push button 3 on the way back up."

"And get off at the third floor?"

"No, no, some other jerk will get off there. Just push the button and come back here."

Hanson shrugged as he went to the door. "Okay, you're the doctor," he said.

When he got back, he went to the bathroom. The calm he'd felt in the elevator, standing beside the tall old man, had disappeared, and now he heard sirens. He opened the window, looked outside. An emergency wagon slammed to a stop, its blue lights slashing the street. "Third floor!" he heard a voice shout. "Hurry!"

The next few days were beyond belief. The babes were there in droves. He took them for midnight rides in his silver jet, to Broadway shows, to glittering parties, to restaurants in Paris and Rome. The night he spent in Monte Carlo, he won every game he played. Afterwards, they lay on the beach and drank till dawn, then gorged on a platter of strawberry crepes before he left for work.

"How can you do it?" Hanson asked. "I mean how can you make those dreams?"

"That's what I'm built for," the voice said, snorting. "Let's just leave it at that."

"But I mean—"

"These are questions you're asking, jerk. You remember our deal about questions?"

"Yeah, right, but I want to *know*. I mean why ain't it like that all the time, is it really *real?*"

"Does it feel like it's real?"

"When it happens, yeah, but then when it's over I can't believe it."

"So what's the difference?"

"Well—"

"Quit asking questions, jerk. Just enjoy yourself."

"Okay, okay," Hanson said, "but cut that 'jerk' stuff, I really hate it."

The TV snickered. "Who cares if you hate it, jerk, it's what you are."

He flew to Cannes with Crystal and Marlene. He was gone three days, but didn't miss any work. On the weekend he cruised the Virgin Islands. For these favors he had to:

1. Walk to the plant with a ten dollar bill in his shoe.

2. Feed a bag of popcorn to the pigeons in Pretzel Park.

3. Buy two pints of ice cream, one pistachio, one chocolate, at Milton's Corner Commissary. ("I never eat chocolate, it gives me the hives." "Just *buy* it, jerk. You can throw it in the sewer for all I care.")

"Why is this stuff so important to you?" Hanson said. He was worried tonight, but didn't know why; he had already downed two beers and was on his third.

"That's a *question,*" the TV said.

"Yeah, yeah, I know, but I mean…what *happens?*"

"What *happens,*" the TV mimicked. "Well, jerk, it's hard to say, one can never foresee the ultimate consequences of one's acts. I'm sure you've considered that numerous times, am I right, whiz kid?"

Hanson stared at the beer in his hand. "With the ice cream, for instance. Why did I have to buy two pints?"

The TV flashed sharp silver lines. "It had to do with the volume in his freezer, jerk. Enough! You want to have fun or not?"

Hanson ached for the transformation. He drained the rest of his beer in one gulp, sat back. I'm ready."

"Okay," the TV said, "so here's what you do…"

They were taking the furniture out of room 28.

Hanson said to the TV set, "That guy in 28, he…*died*."

The picture dimmed; horses clouded its glow with a flurry of hooves, then: "We all gotta go sometime."

"Yeah, right. But he wasn't old, maybe fifty, about my age, and he looked pretty good."

"You can't tell a book by its cover," the voice said. "Ready for fun?"

"I turned his newspaper over that time."

Yellow streaks and a buzzing sound. "So?"

"Well, I mean—"

"You think that *killed* him? Turning his *paper* over?"

"I just—"

"What a meathead you are. Okay, you dropped that orange in the mailbox, I owe you the night, grab my ears…"

Hanson was watching the morning news when the voice said, "Jerk. 42nd and Reed, you pass that corner, don't you?"

"So?" Hanson said.

"Pull the fire alarm on the pole."

"What? Hey, I can't do that! I can't turn in an alarm if there ain't no fire!"

Splashes of red on the TV screen. "Oh, there'll be a fire all right. Will you ever *learn?*"

Hanson was shaky and pale as he came through the door. He went to the TV quickly and turned it on. The screen began to shimmer orange, blue, the voice said, "Yes?"

"I have something to tell you," Hanson said. "The fire. The factory at 44th and Reed."

"Sure was a ferocious blaze."

"Yeah." Hanson got a beer from his fridge, tore off its ring and drank. He sat in his chair. "Three firemen were killed," he said.

"A wall collapsed."

"I turned in the alarm."

"Like I asked you to. Good work."

"But—three guys were killed!"

"Hey, fighting fires is a rough job, jerk."

"Yeah," Hanson said. "But somehow I *knew*. I mean even before I pulled the alarm, I knew three guys would die."

A purple snake squirmed on the screen as the voice said, "Oh? How interesting."

"Yeah," Hanson said. "And I went to the corner store today, and Milton—he's dead, had a heart attack."

"Yeah, well, he was sixty-eight."

"He was strong as a bull, never sick..." Hanson drank, shook his head. "It's nuts. How can taking some ice cream out of a freezer give a guy a *heart* attack?"

The snake hissed, bared its fangs. "Okay, jerk, you've gone too far. This is our last conversation."

Hanson stared at the set; put his beer on the floor. "Huh? What do you mean?"

"Your ears acting up again? It's the end, we're through. No catch, I don't want a thing, we're simply through. And, true to my word, you're still the same dumb jerk you always were."

"But I'm not!" Hanson said. "I'm not!"

A laugh. "Hey, what's your gripe, dreamboat? You oughta be grateful for what I did, I treated you special. You owe me a favor, if you recall. The fire makes up for that Venice jaunt, but that Stockholm trip with Elaine? Another go-now-pay-later job, remember?"

"Yeah," Hanson said. He was soaking with sweat.

"Well look, I'll forget it—as long as you just don't bug me. Okay, jerk, goodnight and goodbye."

The screen snapped, shrank, went gray. "No!" Hanson said. "Hey look, I didn't mean—" He fumbled with the on/off button, checked the plug, but the set was totally dead.

Two hours later, it came on again by itself. Hanson sat on the edge of his chair, put his beer on the floor. He was drunk.

"Yeah, I knew you'd come back," he said to the tenor's cavernous mouth. "You can't do your work without me, right? You need *me*, too. Look, I'm sorry about all those questions I asked, I was just kinda curious, see? I do all these goofy things for you, then a couple of times I find out something happened... It just makes you wonder, you know? But that's it. No more questions, I promise."

The singer kept singing. "So whattya say?" Hanson said. "Huh? Whattya say? Hey! Come on!"

«« —— »»

Two days later, pleading with a rerun, Hanson said, "I promised I wouldn't ask no questions, what more do you want? You're right, *I* didn't hurt nobody, *you* were to blame. Not that I'm blaming you, I mean—come on!"

"Well what about Carol, what about Rhonda? What about my Jag, my jet? That stuff was real, I didn't make it up. *You're* real! That trip to Honolulu I was gonna take! I *ain't* the same dumb jerk! You made me something different and you can't just leave me here like this! You can't!"

"Please," Hanson said, holding onto the rabbit ears. "Please." No vibration, none. "I can't stand it here anymore! I can't take this crummy dump and my crummy job! That favor you said I owe you—for Stockholm? I'll do it. Just tell me what you want me to do and I'll do it, no questions asked. Do you hear me? Hey!"

He walked the cold and lonely streets, unable to bear the quiz shows, westerns, mysteries and comedies that once had been his life. The TV hadn't spoken now for almost a week. "It just ain't *fair*," he said with his fists rammed into his jacket pockets. "All I done was ask a couple things, it just ain't *right!*" There was nothing but dullness, emptiness, loneliness left for him now if he couldn't return to that marvelous, elegant world. "I *earned* that yacht," he said aloud. "I *earned* that Jag. I want them back. I'll *get* them back!"

"Talk to me, talk to me, say something, damn it!" he yelled at the fat comedian. Kneeling in front of the set, he said, "I told you I won't ask questions! I told you I'd do that favor for you! Ask for anything, I'll do it! *Please!*"

Then suddenly that pleasant trance came over him and his arm, with a will of its own, put his beer on top of the set.

"Ah hah!" Hanson shouted, "that proves it, you're still in there! So talk!"

The set stayed silent. Sweat slimed Hanson's skin. Shaking his fist at the picture tube he said, "You sneaky bum! You're gonna talk! You hear? You understand?"

He grabbed the rabbit ears with both his hands, and there it was: the vibration again. "Ah hah!" he cried, and squeezed. His face was red, the veins in his neck were ropes. "I'll get you outta there, I'll *choke* you out!"

## Dream Box

The beer fell over, poured through the vents in the back of the set. A hiss, a snap, and a ball of blue lightning ripped Hanson's head. He shivered, twitched, collapsed on the floor. Stars whirled through his eyes and the last thing he heard in his life was: "Couldn't stop bugging me, could you, meathead? Thanks for the favor, jerk."

# CONVENTION

The ones he loved best were the little burnouts, the runaways with the hot salty taste of lust in their wild blood. He would pick them up late at night on the highways or dark city streets and away they'd go. And the tears, ah those sweet tender tears when he struck!

They were work, those young girls. They were quick and strong, and once they found out who he really was, did they ever put up a fight! The fighting was one of the things he liked best about them, that and the way they begged when they realized his strength. Oh please, oh no, you can't, you won't—

But he always did.

Those struggles were lovely. But every so often he needed a break from the spirited colts, the ones with the sharp little tongues and the tattooed breasts and the gutter grammar. Sometimes he wanted more class, erudition; something more mellow, sedate.

That was the mood he was in right now, and what luck! He could scarcely believe it. He'd spotted the piece in the early paper right before turning in. Scanning the news as he always did in that bittersweet hour before the dawn, tallying shootings and knifings and rapes, he'd found it:

A horror convention, that's what it said, at the Plaza Hotel downtown. Writers of horror stories would be there, and artists who painted book jackets and magazine covers. Fans, agents, editors…

In short, the exploiters—those who mocked his kind, who saw him as a source of sleazy thrills and titillation. *Them.*

His fantasies of editors enthralled him so, he had scarcely been able to sleep. Hundreds of people submitted to editors daily, and now one of *them* would submit to *him*. Delicious! On shiny black satin he'd tossed and turned.

He'd risen as soon as the sun went down, and by ten after seven was paying his fee at the desk at the Plaza Hotel.

"Just Vlad?" asked the kid who filled out the clip-on badge. He was maybe eighteen, with a chin full of pimples.

"Just Vlad."

"Cool," the kid said, writing. He looked up and grinned as he held out the badge. "I mean costumes, I mean, like, this isn't a fannish convention, but you are like totally *dude*."

"Indeed," Vlad said. He clipped the badge onto his cape, checked his program, and went to the elevators.

The transparent plexiglas bullet held odd-looking people with badges exactly like his: little bats on their borders. He sniffed. At the third floor he got off and went to the ballroom, where, under weak spotlights, an old goon was yakking about H.P. Lovecraft—an exploiter if ever there was one.

Vlad ignored the old buzzard, appraising the females who flanked him: the editors—all of a good age and pleasingly plump. He looked at the name cards that sat on the table: Ginny, Lucy, Joan, Melinda. Which one to choose? He grinned.

The Lovecraft talk was exceedingly boring, so Vlad left the ballroom and went to the bar. Some middleaged writers were hanging around swapping publishing stories, all dolorous. One of the anguished, a blonde dressed in black, looked appealing, but Vlad knew better, writers were bitter as bile. Those nice juicy editors, those with the power, *they* had the tang he craved.

He was ready to get up and seek them out when Ginny and Joan walked in and sat down at a table. Melinda and Lucy soon joined them. They all ordered drinks and engaged in loud spirited talk about nothing: clothing, food—ephemera. Vlad had expected better than this, and scowled.

Lucy sucked on a slice of lime. Ginny rattled the cubes in her glass.

"Oh no," Melinda said.

"What's wrong?" Joan said.

"That creep in the Dracula outfit is making his move."

"He's a writer," said Ginny, nodding gravely. "I can smell them a mile away."

"He just looks like a creep," Melinda said.

70

"Being a writer does not rule out being a creep," Ginny said.

"Do tell," Melinda said. "This bozo's been eyeing me ever since he arrived."

"Yeah, don't you wish," Lucy said. She dropped her lime in her empty glass as Melinda kicked her shin.

"Ladies!" Vlad said, eyebrows raised, eyes bright, "let me buy you a drink!"

They ignored him. Ignoring people was one of the things that editors were expert at, but Vlad wouldn't be denied. "We all like to *drink,* don't we, ladies?" he said flashing razor sharp canines.

"Oh boy," said Melinda under her breath. "I've heard truckloads of lousy Lugosi accents, but this is the absolute worst."

"Waitress!" Vlad shouted. "Another round for the lovely ladies!"

"No," Lucy protested, "we really can't—"

Ginny took hold of her wrist and said, "What the hell, if he's buying."

The waitress came over. "Same thing?" she asked.

They nodded; the waitress left. "My name is Vlad," Vlad said.

No one asked him to sit. "Vlad," Lucy said. "You don't hear that one much anymore, it's kind of like Adolf."

"So what's your *real* name?" Ginny asked.

"My real name is *Vlad*—the Impaler."

"Impaler?" Joan said with a laugh. "Don't you mean the *Impaled?*"

"I should say not!" Vlad snorted.

"You any relation to Ivan the Terrible?" Lucy said. "Or Pedro the Cruel?"

"None at all," Vlad said. "Pedro was before my time. I did know Ivan, though, he was such a dear friend. And you are Lucy, right?"

"Right. Lucy the Rejector."

"And you're Ginny—"

"The Tease."

"I see. And—"

"Joan the Hypercritical."

"I'll pass," Melinda said.

The waitress arrived with the drinks.

"None for you?" Lucy said.

"I'll do my drinking later on," Vlad said. He grinned and raised his arms.

All four women recoiled. "Good costume," Melinda said. "We're not supposed to wear costumes, but that's really something."

"I'm so glad you like it," Vlad said.

"You're a writer, of course," Ginny said.

"I? My writing consists of a daily journal. Sorry to disappoint you."

"It's no disappointment, believe me," said Lucy. The others concurred.

"Here's a question I've always wanted to ask," Ginny said with a little giggle. "Do vampires get tooth decay?"

"We get *no* decay," Vlad said. "Unless—"

"Unless?" Joan said.

"We do have a rather intense aversion to sunlight."

"And stakes," Joan said.

"Yes, certain stakes, but why discuss unpleasantness?"

"Indeed," Melinda said.

"The man's a writer, mark my words," Ginny said. She had already downed her drink, and stood. "Thanks, Vlad, I'll see you around. And I'll see all the rest of you shortly?"

"I'm leaving right now," Lucy said.

Melinda and Joan rose quickly too. "Thanks for the drink," Joan said.

"My pleasure," Vlad said.

He watched them cross to the elevators. One of the plexiglas cars came down and they stepped inside. It rose two floors, where others got on, then went way up where he couldn't see them. When it returned, he boarded it.

In its confines, the editors' scent was still heavy. At floor number 5 the doors opened up and a couple of men got in. They gave him a look, then continued their conversation.

"Talk about stupid covers," the shorter one said. "Not only is the skeleton dancing in blood, it's wearing a yarmulka."

"Jewish horror?" the other man said.

"Jewish horror is paying retail," the shorter man said.

Up, up went the sleek transparent pod, passing its twin, which had stopped at floor 9. Vlad looked over his shoulder. Down in the lobby the people were bite-sized morsels.

At floor 20, the capsule stopped. Another wave of the scent as the doors slid open. The two men got out and Vlad followed them.

Around a bend stood some people drinking. The men went past them and through a door.

The room was jammed and layered with smoke. In spite of this, the editor scent was strong.

Lucy, drink in her hand, was standing beside a couch. The sturdy man with straw-colored hair and gold-rimmed glasses beside her said, "Not right for us. You always say that, Lucy, but never say *why*. *Why* isn't it right?"

"Read the magazine," Lucy said.

72

"I *do* read the magazine," the man said. "And I think, "Ah-hah, this is perfect, exactly the thing. And what do you tell me? Not right." He rolled his eyes.

A tall dark man had cornered Ginny. "I sent it six months ago," he said. "Oh I probably didn't open it yet," Ginny said. "I'm very slow. Disgracefully slow, as a matter of fact. Hi, John, how's it going?" she said as she turned away. The tall man sighed.

Melinda was off in a corner, her back turned to Vlad. She was wearing a glittering purple blouse, black skirt, green socks, pink sneaks. Not supposed to wear costumes, she'd told him. *This* wasn't a *costume?*

He made his way toward her. "You see, what we want," she was telling a pretty young woman with freckled cheeks, "is something dark and shivery."

"Well seek no further!" Vlad said loudly.

Melinda jumped, clutching her throat. "You!" she said.

"Hello again," Vlad said with a grin, and the freckle-cheeked woman had fear in her eyes. "I…have to make a call," she said, moving into the crowd. "We'll talk again, Melinda—soon."

"Yes," Melinda said weakly, still holding her throat.

Vlad stared at her hard, still grinning. "I have that dark and shivery thing you seek," he said.

"You *are* a writer," Melinda said, at last letting go of her neck. "So Ginny was right after all."

"Oh no, she was wrong," Vlad said. "Dead wrong."

"I don't get it."

"You will."

"I'm not sure if I want to," Melinda said. With this, she moved off to where Joan held forth.

"Of course horror's not dead," Joan said. "It has its lows, but it always comes up again."

"Sounds like my husband," a pale woman said. A fat vein throbbed in her neck's creamy flesh. Vlad stared at it.

"Good costume," a near-sighted, gray-haired man said.

Vlad's only acknowledgment was a nod.

Joan said, "Oh, you think so? I don't. It's so *traditional,* so *conventional.* That's precisely the trouble with horror—it's ossified, rigid, bound up in *convention.* We need *innovation,* fresh air."

"Sometimes the old ways are best," Vlad said.

"Not at all," Joan said. "And you won't sell to *me* if that's how you think."

"I am not a *writer,*" Vlad said curtly.

"You have to be on the cutting edge to score with me," Joan said.

Who *wants* to score with you? Vlad thought, you're as sour as lemons. He looked up to see Lucy slip out the door.

By the time he made his way to the hall, she was gone. Her scent trailed away to the left; he followed it.

He found her at the elevator—alone. She had pushed the Up button. "Well," he said.

She turned, looking startled. "Oh, *you* again," she said. "Look, gimmicky stuff won't get you published. You have to have talent. You have to have skill. And most of all, you have to know what we want. Read the magazine."

"I am not—"

The door opened. She stepped inside.

"—a writer!" The door slid shut.

Cursing under his breath, Vlad scanned the hallway. No one in sight.

At the bend in the hall was a niche with a phone, and he went to it. Peering around the formica panel, he saw people leaving the party. Two men and a woman, engaged in a heated dispute, plastic cups in their hands, came near. He pressed his back into the phone as the trio went by.

"To be good, you have to be *obsessed,*" the woman said.

"Not at all," said the man on her right, a rotund, balding fellow with glasses. "You have to know how to use words, that's all. You have to know how to create a story, obsession has nothing to do with it."

"As a matter of fact, it can get in the way," said the other man (pear-shaped, bewhiskered).

"Well, yes, you can be *too* obsessed," the woman said, "but—"

Away they went without noticing him, and he thought: Obsessed! You know *nothing* about obsession!

He peered at the hallway again. The young woman with freckles was leaving the party. His appetite surged. But no, he was here for an editor, and an editor he would have.

A smug-looking man in a black silk shirt and a silver string tie strolled past with his nose in the air. A doctor? Lawyer? Something like that. His kind were especially tasteless. Vlad sniffed in disgust.

A brief lull. Then an older fellow in checkered pants, his scent like paper and ink. A publisher, probably. Goodbye and good riddance, Vlad thought as the guy ambled off. Beginning to feel a bit edgy now, he looked down the hallway again, and—yes!

Melinda! Alone, and heading his way with a vague, rather dreamy expression. How different that face would look in the throes of terror! Vlad's eyes opened wide with delight.

74

Melinda came scuffing across the rug, her sneakers like little pink boats. Vlad salivated, then: "Oh darn, I forgot the book," Melinda said, and turned and went back to the room.

Vlad gritted his teeth. He crouched in the phone niche, waiting. Thick minutes pulsed by.

—And then a familiar voice saying, "Give me a call in the morning, 2513, and we'll do breakfast."

Ginny's voice. Vlad peeked around the formica panel to see her blow kisses at somebody still in the party room. Quickly he left the niche and went down the hall.

At the elevator, he pushed the button. This was floor 20. If he could get up to 25 first, what a fine surprise Ginny would have! The numbers above the doors began lighting, 2, 3, 4—and stopped at 5. "Come on," Vlad said under his breath, "let's *go.*"

Another rise, to number 10. Again the elevator stopped. And Ginny was down by the phone now—with a man, a short, intense-looking, wiry guy with gray in his thick black hair.

"Damn," Vlad muttered, watching the numbers. 12, 13, come *on!*

Then 20, and ding! the doors slid open and out came a wan-looking man in an African robe. He sized up Vlad with an arrogant glance, then went on his way. Vlad stepped forward.

"Hey, hold that door," the wiry man said. He and Ginny rushed up and got into the car.

Vlad was fuming. "Floor?" he said.

"Twenty-two," said the wiry man. Vlad pressed the button as Ginny reached into her purse. She inserted a key in the brass control panel.

"Oh, one of the big shots," the wiry man said.

"Well, hardly," said Ginny.

"Yeah? *I've* never had a key."

"I'm sure you will someday."

"You mean if my numbers improve, right, Ginny? Is that what you mean? Well it ain't gonna happen with *your* crummy distribution!"

At this, Ginny yelped, "Distribution, that lame old excuse?"

"Hey, it's true," said the wiry man hotly. "No books on the shelves, no sales, it's as simple as that."

Vlad felt suddenly queasy. The car reeked of garlic! One or both of these people had eaten garlic! Not Ginny, he fervently hoped, but he couldn't tell.

Ding! The doors opened up. "We'll continue this later," the wiry man said.

"'Night," Ginny said, waving. The doors eased shut.

75

The garlic smell wasn't quite as strong, and Vlad felt a little bit better. The man was the one who had eaten that vile stuff.

Ginny stared straight ahead at the shiny brass panel. Vlad thought: I should take her right here, right now. Why not? The few people down in the lobby were too far away to see into this car...

The elevator stopped; the sleek doors parted. Ginny took hold of her key, but—it wouldn't come out of the panel. "Damn," she muttered, and gave it a yank.

"Allow me," Vlad said, swooping forward, his thick cape rustling.

He twisted the key with his slender white fingers as Ginny stepped into the hall. He jiggled and tugged, but it wouldn't come free.

Then Ginny cried, "Lucy!" and stood on her tiptoes and beckoned. "My key is stuck, do you know how—?"

The doors slid shut.

Vlad stared at his hand on the key. Outside, Lucy said, "Push the button, Ginny."

"Yeah."

On the panel a light went on, but the doors stayed closed. Vlad twisted the key hard, harder, with all his strength—and it snapped in two, broke off inside the panel.

"No!" Vlad said, and pushed the buttons frantically: "L," "1," "5," "10," "B." Nothing worked. He threw the remains of the key on the floor, grabbed the black rubber lip of the door. He pulled. No good.

"You still can't get it out?" Ginny asked from the hallway.

Vlad clenched his teeth. *If I could get it out, you fool, would I still be behind these doors?* Then he said to himself, *Did you forget? The woman is an* editor, *you'll have to spell things out for her.*

"The key broke off and I'm stuck," he said.

"Oh God," Ginny said, "I'm sorry. I'll call the desk right away and they'll send somebody."

"Please," Vlad said.

He waited and waited, but nobody came. His desire was urgent now. Down in the lobby two people sat talking, two middleaged men. They were starting to look pretty tasty. He cursed.

The other elevator, this one's twin, still worked, and up and down it went. It stopped across from him and Vlad saw Joan and the man with the straw-colored hair and gold-rimmed glasses. Joan's pale face was bland and bored, while the man was frantic, screaming and waving his arms.

"Hey!" Vlad shouted, banging the plexiglas. "Hey! I'm stuck in here!"

They paid no attention. The door came open and Joan got off. The man clapped his hand to his forehead and stared into space. After a minute the car took him down again.

The lobby was empty now; its lights were low. It was late, quite late, and where were the maintenance people? A cabinet beside the control panel held a phone. Vlad called the desk.

"This is the man who's stuck in the elevator. When are you going to help me?"

"Stuck?" said a woman's voice. "We didn't know you were stuck."

"What? No one reported it?"

"This is the first we heard about it."

Damn! Fool that he was, he had trusted that pair of editors! "Well get someone up here! I've been here a long time now."

"I'll see to it, sir."

"This is urgent!"

"Yes, sir."

He hung up.

It *was* urgent. For what was the time now, and when would the sun be up? In this plexiglas car he would have no shelter. Once he was freed, he would be just fine. Many a time he had hidden himself in the bowels of a hotel or office building and waited for daylight to fade as his victim lay in a dreamless sleep on a carpet or couch or bed. But if he were trapped in here…

Nobody came, and he called again. This time the woman was snippy. "I told you, sir, we'll send someone there just as soon as we possibly can. It's four A.M., we just have a skeleton crew at this hour, and one of the pipes broke downstairs."

Four A.M.! Vlad's throat seized up. He looked at the broken key on the floor, looked down at the empty lobby. Then, lifting his head, he realized something dreadful.

That speck of light on the hotel's ceiling was not a reflection, was not the bright wink of a tiny bulb, it was—a star! The hotel's roof was plexiglas too, and that was the morning star! He clutched his chest.

Then he heard them outside the door. "Sorry to take so long, sir," a deep voice said. "We'll have you out in a jiffy."

"Please! Hurry!"

"You bet."

They scraped and pried. A different voice, not the deep one, said, "Goddamn."

The hotel's roof was tinged with pink; the morning star was growing faint. Vlad shielded himself with his cape. "Hurry! Hurry!" he said.

"We're doing the best we can, sir," the deep voice said. More scraping, then, "We need that other bar."

"Down the shop?"

"Yeah."

"Be back in a bit."

Vlad's eyes went wide.

"We need a different tool, sir," the deep voice said. Across the way, Vlad saw a man in coveralls enter the functioning elevator. Down he went.

"You couldn't have thought of that before?" Vlad said.

"Hey, look, we aren't perfect."

"You don't understand!" Vlad said, and his eyes were burning. He banged on the brass control panel, tore at the doors.

"Hey, take it easy," the man outside said.

"Take it easy! You dolt! You fool!"

"Knock it off, pal, you hear me?"

The sky was a rosy peach. Vlad fell back gasping, arm over his face. Through the crook of his elbow he saw the cables across the way jiggle and yes, up it came, the elevator, holding the man in coveralls, who carried a prybar.

"Faster, faster!" Vlad urged.

The other elevator stopped; the man got out. And now, in the curve where roof met wall—the sun!

"No! No!" Vlad cried.

He buried himself in his cape, but no good: the glorious shining dawn seared through with blades of unbearable pain. He screamed.

"What a wimp," the man with the deep voice said. He grunted. "There, that's got it."

The two men looked into the car, astonished. A crumpled cape, a pair of shoes...

The man with the deep voice said, "What the hell...?" and looked at his partner, who shrugged.

At brunch, Melinda said, "No creep in a vampire suit—thank God."

Ginny, her mouth full of bagel, turned to Lucy. "Oops. He was stuck in the elevator, and—"

"We forgot all about him," Lucy said. "We started to talk about you-know-who and their dopey vampire novel, and just...forgot."

"You'll probably find one of his scripts in the slush when you get back," Joan said, sipping tea. "And it'll be real, real easy to turn it down. When it comes to scaring people, the guy's a dud."

Melinda frowned at her half-eaten bagel. "You weren't scared even the tiniest bit?"

"Not even the tiniest bit," Joan said. "He was just so *predictable,* just so *conventional.*"

"Yeah," Ginny said. "Those phony fangs."

"That slicked-back wig," Lucy said. "I mean really." She smiled. "Terrible how we forgot him, though. To keep someone waiting and waiting like that—"

"Inexcusable," Ginny said with a chuckle.

"Just awful," Melinda said.

"Outrageous," Joan said.

They laughed and laughed, and ate and ate, and discussed less amusing things.

# LUCKY SUNDAY

Gram yelled from the foot of the stairs: "My legs are killing me today! Don't make me come up there, young man!"

Her grandson Jimmy's cranky voice replied, "I'm almost dressed!"

"You better be," Gram said. "We have to leave in exactly five minutes."

"I *know*," Jimmy said.

He looked in the mirror again and scowled. He'd tied his tie three times and still hadn't gotten it right. Now the front part was way too short. Angrily he tore it off and started over again.

"Jimmy Jackson!" Gram hollered.

"I can't get my tie right!"

"Then get yourself down here! Right now!"

Jimmy came down the stairway, dragging his jacket, his tie draped over his neck. In the hallway, Gram looked cross. "One shoe's untied and your shirttail's out."

Jimmy knelt down and tied his shoe, then stuffed his shirt into his pants.

"That's better," Gram said. "Get over here now."

Standing behind him, she worked on his tie. "No time for another lesson," she said. "I just can't believe that an eight year old boy who has dressed up for church every week for two years hasn't learned how to fashion a knot. There. Turn around and look at me."

He did. Gram said, "It'll have to do. Now put your jacket on." He did this, too, and Gram said, "You actually look half-civilized. Where's your Bible?"

"Upstairs."

"Well don't just stand there, go get it!"

Jimmy went up and came down again, the black book tight in his hand. He wondered: If his parents were still alive, would they force him to go to church? He wondered this every Sunday.

Gram looked at her watch. "Behind schedule," she said. "We'll have to walk faster than usual, and me with these terrible knees."

They left the house and went down the porch without locking the door. People in Hamilton never locked doors. It was that kind of town—a decent town, Gram said.

On the dusty dirt road they met up with Evelyn, Gram's good friend. Evelyn had folds of fat at her neck; they were shiny with sweat. She was waving a fan at her face. "What a lovely suit," she said to Jimmy. "My, but you look grown up."

Jimmy scuffed at the dirt. Gram said, "It cost me an arm and a leg."

"It's beautiful, Doris," Evelyn said.

"Jimmy, pick up your feet, you're getting your shoes all dusty."

"The *road's* all dusty," Jimmy said. Then his Bible slipped out of his hands.

He scooped it up and Gram said, "Kiss it now, show your respect."

He wrinkled his nose, brushed dirt off the Bible, then touched it—just barely—with his lips.

"Sometimes I just don't know," Gram said.

They were passing Todd Mitchell's house, and Jimmy said, "How's come Todd don't go to church?"

"He will," Gram said. "He's younger'n you."

"He's six."

"He'll start going next year."

"He's lucky."

"Oh no," Gram said, "*You're* the one who is lucky. You're *special.*"

Evelyn looked up, away—at fields of stunted corn below blue sky. She said, "Never seen it this bad before my entire life. A third of the crop is already ruined, we don't get a good rain soon, we'll lose it all."

"Sure will," Gram said. "I can't understand why the Heavenly Father treats us so awful sometimes."

"No mystery to it," Evelyn said as she fanned her face. "We've sinned. I don't mean you and me, of course, but someone in Hamilton's sinned real bad."

"And all of us have to pay," Gram said.

"I'm hot," Jimmy said.

"Just keep it to yourself, young man," Gram said.

"But—"

"You think this is hot? You don't *know* hot."

Jimmy tugged at his collar. He wanted to tear it off, tear his tie and his shirt and his jacket off too, and run to the field down back of the Hamilton school. Todd would be there, and Eddie, and Luke. They'd go to the shade of the woods, to the fast-running crick, and turn over rocks and catch crawfish, and then they'd have crawfish wars. He'd splash clear ice-cold water on his face and they'd chop down saplings and make long spears and play they were Indians hunting deer—or hunting each other.

"Well, here we are—at last," Gram said.

The church was very plain outside, without any pillars or other such folderol, but it was the grandest building in town, aside from the court house. The two old women slowly and painfully mounted the steps to the white front door, which stood wide open in the heat. "Come on, don't lag," Gram said to Jimmy, "Lord, what I wouldn't give for your pair of knees."

Inside, it was even hotter. Thick light filtered through yellow glass and hung there perfectly still. Jimmy stopped in the aisle and Gram said, "Keep going, we're sitting up front today."

"But I don't want to," Jimmy said.

"I don't care what you want, that's where we're sitting."

Making a sour face, Jimmy followed the pair of old ladies. Evelyn heavily plopped herself into a seat three rows back, but Gram kept going, right to the very first pew. Nobody else was there. "Sit down," Gram said.

Jimmy had never before been this close to where everything happened, and stared with big eyes. As always, the huge double doors at the rear of the stage were closed. From where Jimmy usually sat, far back, you couldn't see the doors' details, all the carvings, the monkeys and snakes and tigers and other strange beasts he didn't recognize. They were kind of scary.

More people came in till the place was packed, and now the front door was shut. To the left of the stage a fan was whirring, just about making a dent in the hot yellow air. Jimmy was sweating hard and his neck was itching. He looked around and said to Gram, "There ain't no other kids today."

"Face front," Gram said.

"But how's come there ain't no kids?"

"There just ain't," Gram said.

Usually Lucy Crane was here, and Billy Hupp, but not today. Lucy was probably home playing dolls, and Billy was with the other boys down at the crick in the cool of the trees. He wished—

"Pay attention," Gram said, and then Reverend Barnes appeared.

He was tall and thin and dressed in black, and stood at the thing Gram called a podium. He asked everybody to rise, and he said a prayer. Then they sat, and the choir, standing in front of the big double doors, sang a hymn about Jesus the Lamb. Then Reverend Barnes started his sermon.

He spoke of the goodness of God and the mercy of Jesus His son. Then he talked about heat, and lack of rain, and dying crops, and called upon God to help.

And now Jimmy was feeling sleepy. The preacher was boring, the air was a blanket of itchy wool and his stomach was growling. He thought of the popsicles down at Wink's store. His eyelids were starting to close when he heard, "James Jackson, come forward."

*What? Me?* Jimmy thought, and his eyes snapped wide open. In utter confusion he looked at Gram.

"Go on, go on," she said. "Get up there. Hurry."

Jimmy stood, clutching his Bible, his heart in his throat. He went to the stage and mounted the steps.

Two men he had never seen before hurried forward and grabbed his arms. *What? Why?* Then Reverend Barnes, his eyes dark and piercing, was pointing straight at him and saying, "Hear us, oh Lord, receive our entreaty. Receive...our sacrifice!"

The huge double doors at the back of the stage came open, and—

Fire! Flames roaring and crackling and leaping as high as the ceiling. The men who held Jimmy now lifted him up and carried him right to the edge. He screamed. They threw him in. The doors clanged shut. "Let us pray," said Reverend Barnes in the sudden silence.

Out on the road again, Evelyn said, "You must be so terribly proud."

"I am," Gram said with a dab at her eyes. "He was just like a little man."

"He was indeed. So handsome in that suit."

Gram nodded, and a tear escaped and traveled her florid cheek. "I'll miss him so much," she said.

"Of course you will," Evelyn said. "We'll all miss Jimmy, he was a wonderful boy."

"So special," Gram said. She wiped at her stricken face with her hanky again, and Evelyn said, "By gum, those are rain clouds out there."

# NIGHT WATCH

You saw interesting things on the graveyard shift, things that daylight would seldom reveal. For example, decapitations. More heads rolled in the dark than in daytime because there were (1) more collisions at night, and (2) more *violent* collisions at night.

The night watch sights made a pretty spectacular photo gallery, and Drummond's apartment hallway was lined with this gore, all captured by him in the course of duty over the past eight years. None of these wonders, however, had ever appeared in the source of their funding, the *Clarion-Post*; for while readers were eager to see the vehicles, twisted and crushed, they didn't care to view the mangled occupants at breakfast time. Staring at severed heads could make it tough to get one's toast past the old Adam's apple.

More than one sweet (or not so sweet) young thing had turned green in Drummond's hall. It was sort of a test. Anybody who got through that gallery unscathed was his kind of woman.

It wasn't just heads that turned into missiles on impact, of course: limbs were also sent soaring, and even the odd big toe or ear or nose—or part best left unmentioned in a family daily. Drummond had once found a breast on top of a fire hydrant, perfectly centered. The photo of that was the last thing you saw before leaving his hallway.

Now this fellow here, on the side of the road, was missing an arm from the elbow down. His head was still present; however, his features were gone. Drummond went in for some closeups, then drifted away from

87

the scene: the cops, the flashing lights, the pool of blood. The driver's side of the car was wrapped around a utility pole. Weird how the guy had flown loose in a crash like that, but here he was, smeared on the road.

And here was the forearm, its elbow ragged, leaning against a boulder. Drummond bent down, took a quick look around, and slipped the gold watch off the wrist. It wasn't your usual arm, he noted: the whole thing was purple and green with tattoos, and so was the hand: there were triangles, spirals, eyeballs, snakes...you name it. He let the arm go and it settled against the rock again. As it did, its fingers contracted, and Drummond shivered.

There was loot in the graveyard shift. In confusion and darkness, plenty could disappear. Drummond had found this out early on, and over the years he'd acquired gold rings (two with diamonds and seven with rubies), a half dozen diamond pendants, a number of bracelets (both silver and gold), and other assorted items of turquoise, jade and pearl —all gifts that young ladies (and those with a world of experience, too) were highly appreciative of.

If his pay had been higher he might have felt guilty about his repeated indiscretions, but as it was....No raise in the the last two years, and was that any way to treat a guy who was willing to spend his nights chasing cops, blowing life into frozen fingers in bleak bitter darkness, and standing around in morgues?

They were lifting the body into the bag as Drummond came back to the streetlamp. He looked at the watch: a real beauty. Its gold hands said three twenty-two A.M., exactly the same as his cheapo digital. On its reverse it said, Rolex, 21 jewels. Real nice.

"The arm's over there," he said to a cop with his thumbs in his belt.

"What?"

"It's there, on the side of the road." He could see that the hand was now fully contracted, a claw.

"Oh, yeah, right. Thanks."

"You bet," Drummond said, and jotted a few more words on his pad, then tucked his pen back in his jacket. A genuine Waterman, old as the hills. Its previous owner—unidentifiable when found—had been in charge of loans at the First City Bank. A shame what he'd done to his nice blue Mercedes—right about this same time, too, 3:30 or so.

Drummond yawned and his stomach growled. Hard work like this always gave him an appetite.

Some bacon and eggs at the Stardust Diner would taste real good right now. He glanced at the cop staring down at the arm on the rock, and then went to his car.

«« — »»

"Drake Blackwell," Susan said.

"The one and only," Drummond said, looking up from his screen. The cursor blinked impatiently.

"I saw him perform when I was a kid—maybe nine or ten, at the circus. How old do they say he was?"

"Fifty-two." Drummond thought of the severed arm, the claw-like hand.

"Poor guy. You ever catch his act?"

"Nope. My father and grandfather did."

"Your *grandfather?*" Susan said.

"There was maybe another Blackwell?" Drummond said. "A Blackwell senior?"

"I guess. The Blackwell I saw could make himself disappear."

"Uh-huh." Drummond said. He poked at his keyboard. A sentence appeared on his screen.

"You ready for supper?" Susan asked.

"Not hungry."

"It's seven-fifteen."

"You're kidding," said Drummond, and looked at his watch—his new Rolex. "I only have five twenty-five," he said.

"You're wrong," Susan said with a nod at the clock on the wall.

It said seven-fifteen. Damn, a beautiful watch like this, and it didn't keep time. He took it off, set it forward and wound it, and put it back on again.

"Now that you know what time it is," Susan said, "are you hungry?"

"Not really. I'm gonna finish this story before my break."

"See you later, then."

The truth of it was, Drummond wasn't the least bit hungry—which was odd, since he hadn't eaten since noon. Even odder, he seemed to feel even less hungry as time went by. Right now he felt damn near full. He belched—and tasted the ham he'd eaten before he had come to work. That Stardust could make a meal that stuck to your ribs! Of course, he'd had ham and eggs, home fries, two blueberry muffins, a slice of peach pie... He'd been unbelievably hungry this morning, he didn't know why. Most days a coffee and danish would last him till lunch, but today he'd been starving.

He looked at his monitor, fooled with the final line. Drake Blackwell, one of the country's most famous magicians, dead in an auto accident. Old Drake had disappeared for good this time. Not a bad piece of writing, Drummond thought, and pressed two keys, and off the story went to the central office.

Then suddenly he was hungry. Not only hungry, ravenous! A minute ago he was stuffed, and now he could eat a horse. Weird. Very weird. He checked his new watch again.

Damn. He'd set it—what?—fifteen minutes ago? And now it had already lost more time—almost an hour!

He noticed the second hand then, and laughed out loud. Freddie Hopkins across the way looked up. "What's funny, Dan?"

"My goddamn watch is running backwards," Drummond said. "You ever see a watch do that before? Run backwards?"

"Never," Freddie said.

"Me neither," Drummond said, and his stomach growled. "I'm off to get something to eat. You covering, Fred?"

"Agnes and I will hold the fort," Fred said.

Drummond went to the cafeteria down on the corner and ordered some ham and eggs, the same thing he'd had for breakfast. For some odd reason he had a terrific craving for ham and eggs. He drank some coffee, ate his meal, then ordered some orange juice. Orange juice for dessert, that was a new one. It tasted great.

Back at the office he felt wiped out. Irregular hours had never bothered him, but now he was almost thirty-six, and it might be time to consider a slower pace. Leave the night watch to Freddie or one of the other kids.

He started a boring school budget story, quit and went home. He had promised to give Virginia a call, but instead he went right to sleep.

He woke up exhausted, as if he had never slept. He made some coffee, drank a cup, and checked Drake Blackwell's watch.

It said twelve fourteen. For a moment he almost believed it, then noticed the second hand glide from ten to nine.

The clock above the kitchen door said seven ten. Drummond took the watch off, set it, put it on the table—and the second hand resumed its backward sweep. What a crazy thing. Something Blackwell used in his act, no doubt, and totally useless—except to magicians. The good thing though—it was solid gold, and he might be able to pawn it.

He wasn't tired now, the coffee had worked. He went into the bathroom. And looking into the mirror, he saw the mole.

On his neck. It was back. He'd had it removed three months ago, and now it was back. The doctor had said it was gone for good. That crook, that quack! And now he'd have to go through *that* again.

When he brushed his teeth, he discovered his gold crown was gone. Good God, that crown had cost a fortune, how—? And where had it gotten to? Had he *swallowed* it? He examined the tooth in the mirror and saw it was one huge filling. But hadn't the dentist ground that filling down...?

He showered, frowning, thinking about the mole and the missing crown. He combed his hair, and the comb had more drag than usual. His hair was...thicker? Dream on, he thought.

The breakfast he made for himself was totally weird: steak, salad, and wine. Wine! For breakfast! He had a day's work ahead of him, what was he doing?

He looked at the crazy watch on the table and thought of his colleague, Marty Flynn. Practical joker Marty had been on assignment yesterday and hadn't seen the watch. He'll love it, Drummond thought, and slipped its band across his wrist. Next to it, he strapped his plastic digital.

"Are you losing weight?" Agnes asked.

"Don't I wish," Drummond said, looking down at his waist.

To his great surprise, he *did* seem a little bit thinner. Poking his crownless tooth with his tongue, he sat at his desk.

The screen of his word processor was blurry. He sat a bit closer. Better. He set to work on the school budget story again.

When Flynn came in, Drummond showed him the watch.

"For the man who yearns to live in the past," Flynn said. "I'll be damned. Looks expensive, too. Where'd you get it?"

"It's been in my family for years," Drummond said, "and always kept perfect time, till yesterday."

"Wild. Look at that second hand go!"

Drummond laughed and went back to his work. He felt fine, real good, but his eyes... He'd gotten these glasses just last month, and now they seemed wrong, too strong—what the hell was the story here?

As he finished a piece on a lucky guy who'd been mugged three times in a twenty-four hour stretch, he was struck by an urge to play tennis. What? He hadn't played tennis in over five years, hadn't even thought of playing ever since his wrist—

His wrist: some twinges there. Don't tell me that's coming back again, he thought, I've been so careful... Frowning, he touched his tooth with his tongue, put his hand on his waist—and broke into a quick, cold sweat.

In the mensroom he checked himself out in the mirror. Losing weight? He was losing weight, all right, he was downright skinny now, and his hair… It was thicker, it really was, his bald spot was almost gone. Touching the mole on his neck, he opened his mouth.

And his crownless molar had changed. There was less silver now, more white. The tooth was—growing back? But that was absurd, how could a tooth that was ground away and filled with metal grow back?

A hollowness spread through his stomach. He went to the front desk and said to Agnes, "I'm going to City Hall for a while," and took the elevator down.

In the corner drugstore, he stepped on the digital scale. Adjusting his glasses and squinting, he read the numbers: one sixty-eight. Good god, two days ago, at home, he'd been one ninety-three! He'd lost twenty-five pounds in just two days? Impossible! These digital scales were junk, this readout was wrong. It *had* to be.

He headed home. In his bathroom he nervously weighed himself: one hundred and sixty-two.


"Your eyes are just about where they were six years ago," Dr. Wiggins said. He was round-cheeked, pink, with wisps of yellowish hair raked over his scalp.

"But how is that possible?" Drummond said. "You gave me stronger lenses just last month."

"Strange," Wiggins said, "but true. You'll need to go back to weaker ones. *Much* weaker ones."

Drummond stood on the sidewalk, stunned by the sun, and said to himself: By the time my new glasses are ready, they'll be no good. My eyes will have changed again, gotten even better, because—

I'm getting younger.

That was the real, impossible truth. He was thinner, stronger, more energetic, his bald spot was gone, his tooth was restored. His wrist felt better but his ankle hurt, and now he knew why—he had twisted it climbing Mt. Washington, when? Almost eight years ago!

The watch. The watch he'd removed—had stolen—from Blackwell's arm. He looked at it there on his wrist, its second hand sweeping backward, smoothly, ruthlessly.

People passed on the sidewalk, floating through time. Drummond thought of the story he'd written on Blackwell. Fifty-two years of age when he died—or so the wire service said. But he had to be older than that—much older. Drummond remembered his grandfather talking about a Blackwell show he had seen years ago. And that arm on the side of the road had been wrinkled and drawn.

The watch…had kept Blackwell young somehow. And now it was haywire, out of whack. Perhaps when the arm flew off and struck that rock….

Drummond started to sweat again. His ankle hurt. He'd twisted it almost eight years ago. That meant he was twenty-seven now, not thirty-five? If this kept up, by tomorrow he'd be in his teens, and the day after that…

Wait a second, he thought, I once read a story about this kind of thing. The guy gets younger and younger until—

A seed of ice grew in his chest. Walking close to the buildings, he took off the watch, held it over a grate—and dropped it. Good riddance, he thought.

As he started to walk, his ankle felt better. All right, he thought. He laughed, ran his hand through his hair—through his thick, bushy hair. With alarm he went into the store he was passing, Crane's Emporium, and hurried up to a mirror.

Good God, his hair! It hadn't looked like this since… No! He was still getting younger!

In a hardware store he bought twine and a metal hook, tied the hook on the line and went back to the grate.

The watch was still there. Feeling utterly foolish, he lay on his stomach and fished for the watch with the line.

"So what are we trying for? Great white shark? Blue whale?"

Drummond looked at the officer's florid face. He felt suddenly very young, and rather scared. "Dropped my watch," he said.

"And just how did you manage that?"

"Took it off to wind it."

"Ah."

The policeman observed as Drummond kept fishing. Finally he managed to snag the band, pulled the watch through the grate.

"That's an old one," the cop said.

"Its been in my family for years," Drummond said as he put it away in his pocket. "Thanks for your help."

"Any time," said the cop.

Down the block and around the corner, Drummond looked at the watch. Backward swept the second hand. He went to the subway entrance and ran down the steps.

"You'd think so, but I don't see how. Mmm, strange."

"But you have to be able to get inside."

"Not if you can't get inside."

"But there must be a way to fix it."

"Mmm,. so it does. Well I've never seen one like this before. There's no way to open it up."

"It runs backward."

"What seems to be the problem?"

"Yes, I'd like you to fix this watch."

"Good afternoon, sir, may I help you?"

On the street again Drummond thought: What? What *happened* in there? His head was spinning, the light hurt his eyes. In his palm was the watch, with its hands moving backward, backward. And what if I smashed it to pieces? he thought. My age reversal would stop? Whatever age I am, I'd stay that age?

He figured he was twenty-one or twenty-two by now. To stay twenty-one—or resume his aging at twenty-one—he could live with that. He could surely do without that bald spot and gut for a decade or so.

But then he thought: what if breaking the watch doesn't work that way? What if breaking the watch stops time—stops all *my* time—for good?

He couldn't stop the watch, no way, that was a lousy idea. Then what—? Holy smokes, this was awful! And how could he ever explain it to Mom?

*Mom?* he thought. Mom was dead, had been dead for years. Then what was he thinking? How—? The second hand moved backward, faster. Faster? No!

Then he knew what he had to do.

He cruised skid row. In no time at all a foul-smelling scrawny old dude came up and said, "How bout loanin' old Jack a quarter, sonny." He was pleased as punch to receive a gold watch instead, and offered a swig from his paper bag, which Drummond declined, thinking, Couple of days from now, old man, that withered mouth of yours might just have a new set of teeth. As he walked down the subway steps, his ankle hurt.

In the subway car he picked up a dogeared *Clarion-Post,* and there was his piece on Blackwell. The print was clear, not blurred at all, he could see it perfectly fine. He ran his fingers through his hair—and felt the bald spot on his crown.

He smiled as he looked at the paper and thought, Well, Drake, you sneaky dog, you almost got me. Fifty-two years old like hell! You were double that—triple that, maybe. He thought of old Jack on Skid Row who was maybe, by now, not so old after all, but was Jack of the thickening hair and firming flesh. Jack the twenty year old would appear fairly soon, Jack the schoolboy, the infant, the...non-existent. He laughed.

When he got off the subway the pain in his ankle was gone—as was the urge to play tennis. He stopped into Crane's Emporium, went to the mirror, and saw the Dan Drummond he'd hoped to see: a bit on the heavy side, his hair getting thin, and no mole on his neck. He opened his mouth—and there was the crown again.

Back on the street, the air seemed thick. Pollution, he thought, and he stopped several times on his way to the *Clarion-Post* to catch his breath. These last several days had been hell, he was bushed, he'd send off the piece on the guy who'd been multiply mugged, then leave and hit the sack. Tomorrow he had the graveyard shift, he didn't have to report until late afternoon, he could sleep the whole day if he wanted to. And he wanted to!

The elevator reached his floor and he stumbled out into the hall. My God, did he need sleep! As he entered the office, Agnes said, "Well look what the cat dragged in."

"I *feel* like something the cat dragged in," Drummond said.

"Hey Dan," Freddie said from across the way, "good to see you again."

"How's it going?" said Marty Flynn.

"Very funny," said Drummond. "You guys have been known to take an occasional extended lunch break too."

They looked at him strangely, then Susan came over and shook his hand. "Can't stay away from the old place, huh? Nice seeing you, Dan."

"So you're a joker too, now," Drummond said. Then he started to cough—a deep racking cough that doubled him up.

"You feeling okay?" Marty asked.

"Yeah, fine," Drummond said as he fought for breath, and now his eyes were blurred again.

"So how do you like retirement?" Susan said.

"Enough, already," Drummond said.

"You go to Florida this year?"

"Oh boy."

"You must be bored not chasing ambulances," Marty said.

"You guys have to learn when to quit," Drummond said.

The three of them wore puzzled frowns. "Quit what?" Susan said.

A panicky feeling expanded in Drummond's chest. "Excuse me a minute," he said.

He went to the hallway, stepped into the mensroom, walked up to the mirror.

And stared at the rheumy-eyed man with the wrinkled neck, the mottled scalp, the thin fringe of gray at his ears.

When he coughed this time it hurt, and he brought up blood.

# A Fire in the Brain

A
s the young man stared at the river, a cold pale sun pushed its way through the clouds and silvered its slate-gray surface. Birds scolded busily overhead in the lindens that lined the banks. But what good is sun? the young man thought. Or birds and trees, what good is another spring?

All that effort, years of it, and they'd told him his work was deficient. His use of color was weak, they'd said, and his draftsmanship mediocre. Yes, they'd said, he could try for admission again when his talent (and one of the panel had actually smirked at this point!)—when his talent was further developed. But what was the function of art professors if not to develop talent? Furious, he had gone to his garret and thrust his portfolio into the stove, burned every last drawing and sketch.

*She* had rejected him first, two days before the professors. He was too moody, she said, too self-centered. Whenever they went to a tavern he brooded, he never had fun. Fun! So that was the point of existence? Amusements? Distractions? After she closed her door on him he stormed off and tried to draw, but…nothing. And now the professors had dealt him this terrible blow.

He stared at the distance, the buildings, the clouds. If he turned to his left he would see the academy's roof. The sight of it would bring another flood of rage, and so he did not turn. His very best, not good enough!

The sun had crawled into its hole again. The young man looked at the sullen water, thinking, Maybe its depths hold peace. In his nineteen years on the planet earth he had found no peace: not at home, at school, on the streets, in taverns—anywhere. But maybe there was peace in this cold gray river.

He started to walk again, blood bitter, a foul dark taste in his mouth. More useless trees and birds and cobblestones—more thoughts of *her.*

Up ahead now, a bridge spanned the water, and as he approached it, he noticed a gathering there.

Young men wearing uniforms. Not army uniforms—those of a school?

He walked closer, and realized that someone was giving a speech. This was some kind of ceremony? A graduation? Yes, of course. These men had succeeded at academics, and now would attempt to make their mark in the world.

The speaker was a sturdy-looking gentleman with silver hair and fine clothes. He looked optimistic, confident, and his voice was clear and strong.

The young man recognized him now. He had seen that face in the paper yesterday, had read the article: about the heroic captain so gravely wounded he'd nearly died. But he'd fought his way back to health and had taken a job as an aide to a politician. Over the years he had moved into higher and more demanding government posts, and now was an ambassador.

The young man came closer and stood at the edge of the crowd. There was something about the speaker's voice, his eyes, the way he used his hands, that captivated him.

"Consider the Russian writer, Dostoyevsy," the speaker said. "A person of frail constitution arrested for treason and nearly shot. Condemned to hard labor by the Czar, he became a severe epileptic. But nothing could stop him from writing. Not violent seizures, poverty, domestic woes. I say to you, it is perseverance that counts, determination, force of *will* that determines success. *Will* conquers all adversity."

The despairing artist, a hardened cynic despite his youth, was thunderstruck. He listened, mesmerized, to tales of other epileptics: Alexander, Caesar and Napoleon—who conquered worlds in spite of their disease.

"Consider the English poet Milton," the speaker said, "who, after the calamity of going blind at forty-three, went on to pen his masterwork, *Paradise Lost.* Beethoven wrote his great Ninth Symphony when deaf. And Handel, who gave us the gorgeous *Messiah?* He too was epileptic, he too lost his sight, but did he stop composing, stop conducting? No!"

The speaker's voice turned hoarse with passion as he told of those who, early aspirations thwarted, found another way to high achievement. A man who'd failed at business had become a great inventor. A teacher fired from his job became a famous architect. "When a stream is blocked," the speaker said, "it carves another channel. And once unblocked it can become"—a sweeping gesture of his arm— "as mighty as this river!"

Scanning the youthful faces before him he paused for a moment; then, eyes intense, he said: "Perhaps the door to opportunity seems locked. If so, go knock on another door. Eventually, one will open. Bear in mind there is always another way. There are infinite paths to success. Believe me when I tell you: No adversity, no stroke of drastic luck can stop determination! A strong will always triumphs, always! No matter what terrible blows life deals you, never, never, give up!"

The students raised their fists and wildly cheered.

The young man was electrified; a fire burned his brain. The speaker, with the force of words, just *words,* had totally transformed his life. Scant minutes ago, adrift in self-pity, he'd been on the verge of drowning himself in the Danube, and now...

He would not be defeated! No matter what the obstacle, he would conquer through force of *will!* No one would stop him! Not art professors, or fickle women, not bankers or Marxists or Jews! One triumph would follow another and he would bring glory to not just himself but to his entire race, to the German people! Yes! He would never give up!

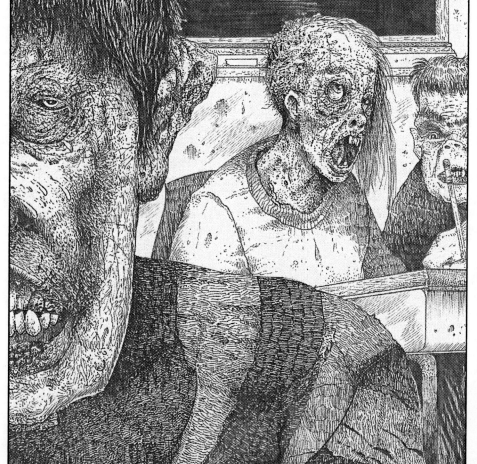

# TROLLS

Daddy had said: "You can't be serious, Beth. You actually think you're going to land a job at this late date? Fresh out of college, with no experience other than practice teaching, and you've waited till now to start looking?" He'd shaken his head in despair and left the kitchen.

And now as Beth looked through the tall dorm window, she thought: Well, Daddy, guess what? You're not always right after all.

It had been a close call, though, a very close call. By the third week in August, things had looked really bleak. She was trying to face up to building Big Macs for another year, but then—incredible!—she got the letter, interviewed, and here she was—a teacher!

Okay, so Radbourne wasn't a regular school, certainly not what she'd had in mind when she'd started her job search, but hey—it was better than Egg McMuffins and mopping floors—and might prove interesting. She'd only taken two courses in special ed, it wasn't her cup of tea, but who could tell, she might learn to like it. At any rate, a year at Radbourne would brighten her pallid resume—and it was a *job*. She'd be able to save for a car, pay her student loans.

And the campus was lovely—with rolling lawns and towering trees, yellow brick paths and wooden benches and globe-topped cast-iron lamp-posts. The buildings themselves, Victorian mansions with wraparound porches smothered in ivy and creepers, were in need of some tender loving care, but still, the impression was charming—as long as you didn't get too close. Barrington Hall, where she was lodged, was in decent (if gloomy) shape on the ground floor, where library, parlor and offices were, but its other three stories were sad: the walls hadn't been painted in years and were riddled with cracks, the faucets gave only a trickle of water, the green shades were faded and torn. And as for Beth's personal quarters...

A tiny cubicle with walls of mint-green beaded pine, a creaky dark varnished floor, one window, a small limp bed, a mismatched bureau, table and chair. The place made her college dorm look like the Ritz, but who cared, it was all her own—away from Daddy and Mum!

Kind of spooky, however, especially at night. The window sash behind the shade would chatter in the slightest breeze. And that door across from her bed, the defunct door to one of the storage rooms (the functioning door was out in the hall), really gave her the creeps. Buried so deeply in ancient paint that its hinges were blurs and its plugged-up keyhole was merely a dimple, that door was quite impossible to budge. Even so, it made her uneasy.

Yes, Radbourne was really a spooky place—but the view! She was up on the top floor, the window faced west, and the sunsets over the stand of pines behind Branch Hall, the schoolhouse, were spectacular. So far, she'd admired two of them; her third day here had been overcast, just like today. But even on gloomy days it was pleasant to sit in the chair in her room and look at the manicured lawns, the thick hedge of faded roses that bordered the narrow dirt lane, the students walking dreamily along the yellow paths.

She could hardly believe she had been here for only four days. The world of Daddy and Mum, of McDonald's, seemed so remote—though she was no more than an hour's drive away from her home town of Clinton.

Her first day at Radbourne—endless! She'd wondered more than once if she had what it took to make it here, and she'd fallen in bed exhausted. That scene on the tennis court, when the door to the gym flew open and a rush of students—dozens of odd-looking men and women— came up to her staring, grinning, drooling, shaking her arm like an old water pump as they said hello. Then the dining room: the squealing and moaning, the waving of fingers, the food falling out of slack mouths made her stomach churn. But not anymore; she was already used to all that. And now as she watched Jeff T. and Alice M. walk by below, she smiled to think of her fear on the tennis court. It already seemed so comical.

For the truth was that most of the students, no matter how threatening they looked, were quite nice. She had already made some friends, especially among the Down syndrome people. Freddie P. and Shirley S.— what sweethearts!

Freddie was twenty-five, three years older than Beth, but he looked every bit of forty, and acted no more than ten. Not a *normal* ten, however. He moved so clumsily and slowly, talked in such a halting way. He wasn't like any ten year old that *Beth* had ever known. But such good manners, so polite.

Shirley S., who was four years older than Freddie, had milky white skin and silky straight hair, large hands, splayed feet—and a smile that could light up a room. She was good at piano and played for Miss Hemphill, the school's director. Beth hadn't met Miss Hemphill yet, but had learned that she liked a piano selection or two and a glass of sherry (or two—or three) before dinner, which she ate in her ground floor chambers. Each evening as Beth combed her hair in the chipped wood-framed mirror atop the bureau, soft notes drifted up from Miss Hemphill's suite. Shirley played with a tender touch that made Beth sad; made her wish she were back at her parents' house or at college. But soon the melancholy notes would end and Beth would descend the steep wide stairs and cross the lawn to the dining room, and once she was there with the rest of the staff and the students, the sick lonely ache would fade.

Tonight, as at every meal so far, her tablemates were Sara—who, like Beth, had been hired just recently—and Pat and Diane, who had been with the school a bit longer, almost a month. They were all in their twenties. The whole staff was young. "Radbourne's just a stepping stone," Pat had said during Beth's first breakfast, "a place to get your feet wet." She'd lowered her husky voice and leaned forward. "With what they pay, I mean really, how can they keep anybody?" The others agreed, and Beth told herself that soon as something better showed up she'd be out of here. But for now this was fine; she was happy to have it.

The teachers had tables to themselves, though Mr. Critch, the principal, encouraged them to mix with the student body. Houseparents didn't have any choice: they *had* to eat with the students. Houseparents, by and large, were males, but Beth had seen nobody promising—yet. Considering the high turnover, though, the prospects looked pretty good.

Radbourne staff members didn't wait tables; the most able students did that, and did it quite well. Nobody had to write down orders or remember who got what (because everyone ate the same thing), but aside from that, the dining room work was a lot like work in the outside world, and some of the students had gone on to similar jobs in restaurants and lived in their own apartments. Radbourne was quite a progressive school, Mr. Critch had said with his tight little smile during Beth's interview.

A progressive school without any children, Beth soon learned. For the youngest student, Polly F., was Beth's age, twenty-two. There were quite a few middle-aged people, and several old-timers. One man, Harold G., was eighty-eight. He was the guy with the wicker basket who always smiled at Beth and said, "A.T & T., up seven eighths," or "IBM, down a quarter." He had lived here for sixty years. A weird old guy, but nice, like most of the students.

But not *all* the students. There were some Beth just couldn't relate to.

Like Garth, who was sitting across the way at the table below the window. She looked at him shoveling down his food. His nose was long, his mouth was wide, his eyes were small and sharp. She had him in morning activities class. So far he'd done nothing at all in that class, shown no interest in anything: puzzles, ceramics, drawing…

Adrian was another one. She was in afternoon activities, and could have passed for Garth's sister—same pointed nose, huge mouth. Same sour attitude.

Beth watched her eat and listened to Pat and Diane. They were talking about a store in the Westside Mall that had discount clothes, and wanted to know if she'd like to go shopping some time.

"Oh, sure," Beth said—though she didn't plan to add so much as a pair of socks to her wardrobe this year. She was going to save every penny she made, especially since pennies would be so scarce. And who needed new clothes here in nowhere land, where fashion was not, to say the least, a priority?

"Now who's got a car we can borrow?" Pat wondered aloud. "Maybe blue eyes?" She winked.

"Who's blue eyes?" asked Sara.

"Third table over," Diane said. "With curly blond hair?"

"Cute," Sara said. "He has a car?"

"One of the few houseparents who does," Pat said.

"So you're after him for his money," Diane said.

Pat laughed. "If that bomb of his can make it to Westside and back—"

"Dessert?"

It was Edwin M., a tall, brown-haired fellow with crooked pale eyes behind glasses with pink plastic frames.

Raising her heavy dark eyebrows, Pat said, "What is it tonight, Edwin?"

"Ch-chocolate pudding."

"Yum. I shouldn't, I really shouldn't. But of course I will."

The others decided that they would too.

"I've been at this place four weeks, and I've gained ten pounds," Diane said ruefully. "I've got to stop."

"Only ten?" Pat said. "I've put on twelve—in three and a half weeks. It must be the starches."

"Starches, protein, fat, who cares? As long as it's food, I'll eat it."

The others laughed, and Beth thought: *Got to watch myself.* The food, while not gourmet by any means, was better than they'd served at college, and there was a ton of it, all you could eat. And what else was there to do here *but* eat? Pat and Diane were decidedly chubby, and Beth would easily find herself needing an extra size or two if she wasn't careful.

Edwin returned with the four desserts, and set them before the young women. "Oh no, they look *good*," Pat said.

"I'll just have a bite," Diane said; and then with a nod of her pretty blond head she said, "Yeah, right."

They all laughed and dug in.

The following morning, Beth handed out modeling clay.

"Make a thnake," lisped Shirley S. with a lopsided grin.

"Sure, Shirley," Beth said, "that's a fine idea."

"Make a ball—*big* ball," said Freddie P., and Beth gave him the go-ahead. She helped Jimmy Q. and Blenda B., then said, "And how about you, Garth? What are you going to make?"

She flushed at her stupidity, remembering what she had learned last night: Garth couldn't talk. Neither could his look-alike, Adrian M. Some of the students just couldn't talk, and here she had thought they'd been holding out on her.

"A snake?" Beth said. Garth scowled. His eyebrows, black and bushy, formed a solid unbroken line. His eyes were deep-set, tiny, dark.

"A man?" Beth said. "It's easy to make a man, let me show you."

She pulled a chair over, sat in front of him, placed some more clay on his desk. He regarded it sourly, eyebrows furrowed. "Now watch me, watch what I do," Beth said. She kneaded the clay, then pulled it apart, shaped a torso, rolled arms, legs, head. She assembled the figure, then, taking a pencil, said, "Now we draw some eyes, a nose, a mouth, and—look—we have a man." She placed it beside Garth's lump of clay. "There. Now you try."

Garth scowled at the figure; retracted his upper lip, showing pointed teeth, and tore the appendages off the man; ripped the head off and squashed it flat. He stared at Beth defiantly.

"No, that's not good," she said. "I want you to *make* something, not destroy it."

He just kept staring at her hard. Deciding not to press the issue, she stood and said, "Well, let's see what Shirley's doing."

«« —»»

She arrived at the dining room late that evening. The only available space was with Mr. Critch, the principal, and two women. Feeling anxious, she sat across from Critch, who introduced the women: secretaries. Sally Z., the waitress, set a large steaming bowl of soup before Beth, who thanked her and then fell silent.

"How are you finding the work so far?" asked Critch as she took her first sip of the soup. He was sixty or so, with silvery hair that was thinning quite badly in back. His charcoal gray suit was expensive-looking, but worn.

Beth swallowed the hot soup quickly and said, "I've already learned so much."

"There is so much to learn," said Critch. "So much that the books don't teach you." With exquisite care he sliced some meat and lifted it to his mouth.

The secretaries daintily ate to the background noise of gnashing teeth, soft moaning, high squeals. Beth had another spoonful of soup, then said, "I was wondering about Garth and Adrian. What kind of syndrome are they?"

"Syndrome?" Critch said. He dabbed at his mouth with his napkin.

Beth blushed. "They look so much alike, I thought—I figured they were a syndrome. And Horace and Roland look like them too—don't you think?"

"They do?" Critch said. He glanced at the secretary on his left, a thin, lined woman named Marple, then looked back at Beth. "I never noticed any resemblance. However, now that you mention it... Hmm, interesting observation—but no syndrome, so far as I know."

Beth looked at the table that stood near the kitchen doors, where Garth and Adrian sat at opposite ends. They were both quite short, about four feet tall, but extremely stocky and solid-looking; had dark furry eyebrows and long snout-like noses, huge hands, couldn't talk... She looked across at Roland and Horace, who couldn't talk either. All four of them could have been siblings. And there, that other one, what was his name again? Brice?

It certainly seemed like a syndrome to her, and she suddenly thought: Wouldn't that be something? If Daddy's little ne'er-do-well, with her little old bachelor's degree, discovered a brand new *syndrome?*

"Billie Rae F. is a Treacher-Collins," Critch said, as he sliced more meat. "Note the narrow, pinched face. The palate is very high and arched, resulting in nasal speech. Intelligence often isn't affected, but in Billie Rae's case, it was."

"I haven't met Billie Rae yet," Beth said.

"She's at the the west wall," Critch said. "The young woman in the yellow dress."

"Oh, yes," Beth said—and there was another one! "Who's next to Freddie?" she asked.

Critch squinted. "That's Eldreth H."

Another one, absolutely. And Critch had never seen the resemblance? Weird.

As Critch and the women chatted, Beth looked at Freddie. A waiter came by with a tray of desserts. Eldreth gave hers to Freddie, who smacked his lips. Two desserts! He was thirty or forty pounds overweight, and they let him eat two desserts? Didn't anyone supervise diet at Radbourne School?

And now Sally Z. was standing beside her holding a tray and saying, "Bwownies and ice cweam?"

"Miss Lewis?" Critch said.

"Oh—I shouldn't," Beth said. But then said she would, and so did the others, Miss West, Mrs. Marple (who could certainly stand to gain a few pounds), and Critch himself. Folding his napkin with great precision, Critch said, "We're quite proud of our dining service."

"It's easy to see why," Beth said.

Mrs. Marple smiled. Miss West inspected a fingernail. Beth glanced at the various tables; at Sara and Pat and the new teacher, Marnie, eating dessert; at Shirley, eating, at Freddie—still eating!

And then she saw Garth.

Garth was not eating. He sat there, his arms hanging down at his sides as around him the others swallowed and chewed, his thick single eyebrow frowning. Frowning at her, at Beth. Yes, frowning at *her.*

That night she awoke from a dreadful nightmare and sat straight up in her bed. She listened, cold sweat on her skin.

There. She heard it again. It had been in her dream, but was real—a scream, far off somewhere. It stopped. She lay there, scarcely breathing, as again it rose into the night. She heard the sound of machinery then, a whining, metallic sound, and a pitiful faraway voice pleading, "No! Please! No!"

She got up and went to the window and lifted the shade. The night was totally black, without any moon. The lamps had gone out at ten o'clock, Radbourne's official bedtime, and now she could barely distinguish the pathways snaking across the lawn. No movement, nobody there. And now no sound.

She sat on the bed, her heart beating wildly; took a deep breath, let it out. She looked at the window, the bright high stars far off in the blue-black sky. Somebody coughed down the hall somewhere. Sara? Pat? Beth stared at the door to the hall, which was bolted, then looked at the door to the storage room, its mint-green panels gray in the feeble light. She finally lay down again, pulling the sheet up, and after a while she slept again, but not well.

"She already quit?" Beth said.

She was walking with Pat to her morning class. "Yep, she's gone," Pat said.

"Wow, that didn't last long."

"Hey, let's face it," Pat said, "this job is tough. You have to be right on top of things every second. At the end of a day here, I'm really wrung out. And I'm a high energy person."

"Yeah," Beth said.

"Diane was not a high energy person."

"Oh."

Beth was quiet a minute; then frowned at the yellow brick path and said, "Pat?"

"Yeah?"

"Did you hear all that screaming last night?"

Pat rolled her cowlike dark brown eyes. "Yeah, that's another thing," she said. "These folks have a nightmare, and bang, they go off the deep end. They think dreams are real, I guess—like those primitive tribes?"

"They were having a rough time, whoever they were."

"I'll say. It's that kind of stuff that gets you. I guess if you're here long enough, you can sleep right through it. To tell you the truth, though, I don't want to be here that long."

They'd reached the schoolhouse, and went inside. "Well, see you at lunch," Pat said.

"Yeah—and save me a seat," Beth said.

The morning did not go well. Freddie was not in a very good mood for some reason, and swiped a crayon from Yola R., a dour, white-haired woman with long ruddy cheeks and gray eyes.

"Give it back," Yola said.

"No."

"Yes! Give it back!"

"No!"

Yola, flushed and furious, sprayed spittle as she said, "You meatball!"

"No!" Freddie said, his eyes suddenly wide. "No meatball! Me...no meatball!"

Garth, who'd been sullen all morning, grinned at this; then laughed with a series of short loud grunts.

So that's what turns him on, Beth thought. A fight. "Freddie, give it back now," she said.

"Me...no meatball!" Freddie said, and Beth was surprised to see he was close to tears.

"No, you're no meatball," she said. "Give Yola her crayon now."

"No meatball," Freddie said, shaking his head as he handed the crayon back. "No meatball, no."

Exposing his jagged teeth, Garth laughed again.

"Garth, it's not funny," Beth said sharply.

Garth continued to grin. Beth glared at him, hands on her hips.

A piece of paper floated off Shirley's desk and landed beside Garth's chair. "Ooopth!" Shirley said.

"I'll get it," Beth said, and leaned over; was rising again when she felt a sharp pinch on her arm. "Garth!"

His grin was huge. "That's not funny!" Beth said. "Not at all! We don't pinch people here!"

Garth's grin dissolved. His eyes grew dark.

Pure hatred in those eyes, Beth thought, and she took a step backward, saying, "You do anything like that again, I'll report you to Mr. Critch—or Miss Hemphill, you understand?"

He continued to scowl, and she suddenly wondered: *Did* he understand? After all, he couldn't talk... The other students looked away—at the floor, at their desks—with sheepish eyes.

Beth gave Shirley her paper. To Blenda she said, "That's a very nice flower. A beautiful flower, good job."

"No meatball," Freddie said with another slow shake of his head. "Me...no meatball."

"Just forget that now," Beth said, and avoided looking at Garth again, and thought of Diane, who had already quit after only a month at this place. A month could be a long time when you had to face Garth and Adrian every day, she thought. A *real* long time.

The pay phone stood in the first floor hallway, next to Critch's door.

Beth looked at the massive squat-legged table with its dimly glowing brass globe lamp, at the heavy brown velvet drapes in the archway, the dull Persian runner on the varnished floor, and swallowed against the homesickness lodged in her throat. "Oh yes," she said, "quite challenging, I've already learned so much." "Just gorgeous—especially now that the leaves are beginning to turn." "No, not till Thanksgiving, I don't get any time off before then." "I love you, too. Say hi to Daddy. Bye."

As she placed the receiver back in its cradle, the loneliness hit her hard. She looked at the gilt-framed painting above the table: a landscape devoid of human figures, feathery and dark. The hallway suddenly seemed to contain no air. She left it, crossed the vestibule, and entered the library.

They *were* some kind of syndrome, she was sure of it. Garth, Adrian, Horace, Roland, Eldreth, Brice—and Grindle P. They looked alike and acted alike: stubborn, surly, and sometimes downright cruel. She had seen Grindle P. deliberately trip Amos A., sending him sprawling onto the yellow brick path, where he skinned both palms. And Brice had shoved Blenda into the drinking fountain, cutting her lower lip.

Beth wanted to check their files, their medical records, but that was forbidden; administration alone had access to those. What else could you expect from a place that wouldn't even tell you your students' last names? "Confidentiality is paramount at Radbourne," Critch had told her. "Many of our parents are quite…sensitive."

Denied the records, she spent three nights in the school's dank library, searching the ponderous volumes on disability, but found no pictures that looked like Garth or the rest. Mucopolysaccaroidosis (what a mouthful) came closest, but wasn't quite it. Maybe she *was* onto something new. If so, she wouldn't call it any tongue twister. Beth syndrome? Or maybe Troll syndrome. For that's what they looked like, those mythical, evil elves. Troll syndrome, yes indeed.

"Adrian? Are you kidding?" Sara said, placing her cup in its saucer. "She's done nothing in class for the whole three weeks I've been teaching. Nothing."

"Same here," Beth said, nodding, poking her meat with her fork. "I just can't seem to motivate her. Anything I show her, she refuses to even try."

"She pinched me once," Pat said; and Marnie, who'd been at Radbourne for only a few days, widened her big blue eyes.

"Garth pinched me once," Beth said, "but Adrian hasn't tried it yet."

"Garth," Sara said. "I'm glad I don't have him, he gives me the creeps."

"And Adrian doesn't?" Pat said.

"Well, yeah, she does, but not as bad as Garth."

Pat shrugged. "Horace, Roland, Adrian, Garth—they *all* give me the creeps."

"They're a syndrome," Beth said. "They have to be. I mean look at their faces, the way they behave, their lack of speech. And they all make that grunting noise."

"Isn't it gross?" Sara said. "They sound like a fish I once caught in the Delaware Bay."

"What kind of a fish was that?" Pat said.

"A grunt."

"Excuse me for asking."

"No, that's what they're called—really," Sara said, smiling.

Beth swallowed a piece of her meat and said in a soft voice, "I call them the trolls."

Pat giggled.

"I know," Beth said, "it's not professional, it's downright nasty in fact, but those folks are not nice."

"More coffee?" asked Edwin, their waiter, the pot in his hand.

They declined.

"More meat and eggs?"

"No thank you," Beth said.

In spite of her resolution, she'd already gained six pounds—in only two weeks! The others said they were finished too, and Edwin left.

"I'm fat, fat, fat," Pat said. "I think that's really why Diane quit, she was turning into a butterball."

"I can't quit, I need the job," Sara said. "But I can see burnout coming on fast in a place like this. Hard work, long hours, low pay—The Radbourne School has it all. And, as an extra added attraction, it's creepy. I feel like I'm being watched all the time."

Pat frowned. "By Critch?"

"Yeah, by Critch," Sara said, "but not *only* by Critch."

"Yes, I know what you mean," Beth said, "I feel it too. I've felt it ever since I first came here. I thought it was probably just me."

"It isn't just you," Pat said.

Marnie said, "No, I've been here for less than a week, and I feel it too."

They were silent a moment, and then Beth said, "Well, they give us plenty of food, at least."

Pat rolled her eyes. "Another problem to deal with!"

They finished and went outside. As they passed the building that housed the woodworking shop, Pat said, "My God it smells putrid out here."

Sara wrinkled her nose. "Yeah, what is that, the sewage system?"

"Whatever it is, I wish they'd fix it—fast."

The stench made Beth feel slightly ill, especially after all that food. As the four of them crossed to the schoolhouse, the feeling that Sara had talked about, that feeling of being watched, came over Beth. And then she saw why.

Far off, on the hill behind Kilby Hall, stood Garth, his thick arms at his sides. He was staring right at her.

She tried to deny what she felt, that quick stab of fear. Playing hooky today, Mr. Garth? she said to herself. Not a good idea. Mr. Critch isn't going to like that. In the schoolhouse she told the others she'd see them later, then went to her classroom.

And Garth was sitting there, clutching the edge of his desk, feet dangling above the floor.

So it hadn't been him on the hill after all, it must've been Horace or Roland or Brice. Proof positive they looked alike! "Good morning, everyone," she said, and those with the gift of speech returned the greeting—except for Freddie, whose cheeks were shiny with tears.

She went to him. "What is it, Freddie, don't you feel well?"

Looking up, Freddie swallowed with effort and said, "Him...call me meatball."

"Who?" Beth said. "You mean Yola again?" Freddie got "him" and "her" mixed up sometimes.

"N—not him," said Freddie. Then, eyes going wide, he pointed his stubby finger at Garth. "H—him!"

Beth frowned. "Garth? But Freddie, Garth doesn't talk."

"Him talk!" Freddie said. "Him...say meatball!"

"Garth?"

"Him say me meatball, yes!" Freddie said.

Frowning harder, Beth said, "Whoever called Freddie a nasty name, don't you ever do it again. If I catch you, I'll send you to Mr. Critch."

At this, Garth snickered. Freddie, his hooded eyes flashing, sputtered, "You bad! You bad!"

Shirley gasped. Blenda B. bit her knuckles and moaned. Yola, mouth going wide, scraped her fingernails down her flat cheeks.

"All right," Beth said, "enough. We're going to do some drawing now. Jimmy, pass out the crayons, please."

Jimmy, his eyes round and huge in his skinny pale face, got up from his chair and went to the shelf for the crayons. Garth snickered again. Furious now, Beth glared at him.

His eyes locked onto hers and stayed, and a chill went over her spine. Unable to bear his gaze, she turned away.

That evening, on her way back to Barrington Hall after dinner, she looked at the hill where Horace or Roland or Brice had stood staring down, and there, on its crest, she saw Adrian walking with Shirley. But not just walking—prodding her with a stick! Poking at her, herding her along. Shirley would turn every once in a while and utter a protest, lost at this distance, and then would submit again.

Bullies, Beth said to herself. They're bullies, all of them. She started up the hill to intervene; but Adrian flung down the stick and walked away as Shirley went into the dorm.

Beth, tired now at the end of the day, decided not to pursue. But she would tell Critch about this, absolutely, it had to be stopped.

The shouts woke her out of another disturbing dream. She could hear the words plainly this time: "Please! Please! Oh no, my God!"

It sounded like a woman's voice. But maybe it wasn't—for some of the male students' voices were almost falsetto, and some of the woman were baritones.

The whining sound she'd heard that other time began and the screaming stopped. Beth lay on her side, hunched up, and stared at the wall, at the door to the storage room, unable to sleep.

Freddie came forward and sat on the swing. "Okay," Beth said, "can you say it? *My* turn."

"M—my turn," Freddie said.

"Good for you," Beth said. "Whose turn is it, Freddie?"

"M—m—*my* turn."

"All right!" Beth said, and gave him a push. What a lump he was! Jimmy, that twig, had been a breeze, Shirley had been a lot harder, but Blenda and Yola had known how to swing by themselves, giving Beth a break. Freddie's ponderous body swung back and forth as he clung to the ropes, his mouth open, his eyes partly closed. "Is it fun?" Beth asked. Freddie gave no reply, and Beth let him slow down. When the pendulum stopped, she helped him off; he sat cross-legged on the grass.

Her heart gave a sharp little twist as she said, "Okay, Garth, now it's *your* turn."

Garth had stood on the sidelines, apart, as the others had swung. Now, craning his muscular neck toward Beth, wonder of wonders, he laughed!

"Your turn," Beth said again, puzzled. "Come on, you'll like it."

Garth nodded, his thick grin huge. He went to the swing and sat down.

Beth positioned herself behind him. "Hold tight," she said, and pushed.

His back was as hard and compact as stone, and her fingers recoiled. When again she made contact, he laughed with a bark-like grunt, and she said with a shiver, "Garth likes his turn, don't you, Garth?"

More mirthful grunting sounds. Freddie looked at him indirectly, appearing to cringe.

"Garth likes his turn," Beth said. Garth nodded heartily, laughing and grunting.

Beth backed away, the feel of Garth's loathesome flesh on her fingers, tingling. He slowed and stopped, sat grinning a minute, then stood up and pointed at Beth.

She frowned. "*My* turn?" she said. "You want *me* to swing?"

Garth nodded enthusiastically.

"Well, okay," Beth said, "okay," and she sat on the seat.

Garth went behind her and started to push. The feel of his hands on her back made her shoulder blades crawl. But this was amazing! She was actually breaking through to Garth? She was actually going to have some *rapport* with him?

She went higher—and higher. Garth pushed. And now she was going uncomfortably high and she said, "Okay, Garth, that's all, that's enough." He ignored her, though, sending her higher, up over the top of the bar; she was moving with frightening speed. "Garth! Stop!" she cried, but he pushed again. Her next descent, she scraped her shoes hard on the dirt and the swing spun sideways, crazily, twisting—went up again crooked, came down, she braked with her feet once again, and the swing at last stopped.

Garth was laughing without any sound, his mouth a black pit.

"No," Beth said, getting up from the seat, "That wasn't funny. That wasn't funny at *all*."

Garth's expression went sullen. He stood leaning forward, his arms at his sides, his hands in a simian curl.

"All right," Beth said, her heart beating hard, "it's time to go back to class."

Garth continued to stand there. "Let's go," Beth said.

Garth retracted his lip, showing crooked sharp teeth; then grinned again, and slowly began to walk.

There was somebody in the storage room.

Beth rolled over in bed. The clock's red numbers said 2:16. In the feeble light she could make out that door in the wall, and a fear of it suddenly flying open seized her. But no, that couldn't happen; it was painted in place, sealed tight.

She listened. Intermittent murmuring she couldn't understand. What in the world were they doing in there at this hour?

The creak of the storage room's hallway door, then footsteps descending the stairs. They were leaving, whoever they were. A silent space, then Beth heard them again, outside. She left the bed and went to the window and cautiously lifted the shade.

The moon was a pale green slit in the inky sky. She heard more indecipherable words, then saw three shadows huddled together beside the vine-choked porch. The shadows moved off in different directions, and Beth saw how short they were.

Three trolls! She squinted at the dark. Three trolls, and one was Garth! Her heart leapt to her throat—and the shape that was Garth turned and looked at her window.

She pulled away quickly, dropping the shade and pressing her back to the wall. Had he seen her? Her breath was loud in the tiny room. She waited awhile, then risked a quick glance outside again—and they were gone.

Three trolls, she thought. And they'd been *talking*.

"She's gone?" Beth said. "Just like that, without saying goodbye?"

Sara, fork in her meat, shrugged. "Yep."

"I thought we were her friends."

"I thought so too."

Beth poked at her meat. She pushed it aside and looked at Sara and said, "You aren't going to leave like that, I hope."

"Of course not."

"I'd like us to still be friends—on the outside, I mean."

Sara smiled. "You make Radbourne sound like a prison."

"Well sometimes I feel like it *is* a prison," Beth said, "and Pat's escaped."

Sara's smile turned wistful. "And she's not the only one. Did you notice who else has flown the coop?"

Beth looked around quickly. "Who?"

"A certain fellow with blue, blue eyes?"

"Don't tell me that."

"It's true. He's been replaced by the guy with the droopy moustache who's pouring Rick some milk."

"Oh, boy."

"My sentiments exactly," Sara said. Frowning at her plate, she said, "This meat is damn near raw."

"And full of fat," Beth said. She pushed some more of it aside and said, "I'll really miss Pat."

"Me too," Sara said. "You know, pretty soon, if this keeps up, we'll be the old timers here."

They looked at each other thoughtfully—then laughed.

A tremendous crash in the storage room sent her jolting awake with a gasp.

Pressing the sheet against her breasts, she listened, her eyes on the sharp streak of moonlight dividing the wall.

The hoot of an owl in the distance, and that was all. She waited, and then, once her heart had slowed down, put her head on her pillow again. As she stared at the wall, at the sickly light, at that ghostly painted-shut paneled door, her body began to shake. An hour went by before she could sleep, and her sleep was troubled and thin.

"I heard it too," Sara said as they crossed the lawn. "They told me it was the chairs."

"The chairs?" Beth said.

"Yeah, they hang onto everything here. When a chair falls apart, do they throw it out? No, they put it away in that storage room, till they get around to fixing it. They never do, of course. The room has hundreds of chairs and desks and tables piled up to the ceiling, and last night the chairs fell down."

"It scared me to death," Beth said.

"Me too," Sara said. As she reached for Branch Hall's heavy door, she said, "Have you seen Shirley S. this morning?"

"No, she wasn't at breakfast."

"She looks like those chairs fell on *her*," Sara said.

Shirley S. *was* in class—and looked awful. Her right eye was swollen and dark and her forearms were covered with bruises.

Beth went with her into the hallway. "Who hit you?" she said. "Who did this to you?"

"N—no," Shirley said with a shake of her head.

"Nobody hit you? What happened, then?"

"Fall down," Shirley said. "Fall down real bad."

"Shirley, look at me," Beth said, taking her chin. "Look at me now and tell the truth. Did Adrian do this to you?"

"No!" Shirley insisted. "Fall down!"

"Okay," Beth said, sighing, taking her hand from Shirley's face. "Okay, well, I'm sorry you hurt yourself."

"Y—yeth," Shirley said.

There were tears in her pale blue eyes.

Vines clotted the tiny window behind Mr. Critch's head. A potted palm spread dusty fronds toward the green-shaded lamp on the mammoth oak desk. Critch leaned back in his leather chair and said, "Specifically?"

"It's about Garth and Adrian," Beth said.

"Oh?" Critch's eyebrows went up.

"They bully the other residents. They physically harm them."

Pursing his lips and frowning, Critch said, "Miss Lewis, that can't be true, the houseparents would have alerted us."

"But it *is* true, I've seen it."

Critch swivelled a quarter turn in his chair. With a tone of impatience, he said, "Garth and Adrian are two of our oldest students, Miss Lewis— and very good Radbourne citizens."

Beth felt her jaw tighten up as she said, "Another thing—they talk."

"They do?" Critch said.

"They certainly do, I've heard them."

Looking slightly incredulous, Critch said, "Now that *is* news. They've had years of help with their speech, and to no avail—or so we thought. You've heard them talk. And when was that?"

"Two nights ago," Beth said. "They were standing outside my window."

"At night?"

"At night. It was late, very late, after two in the morning. First they were in the storage room, then they went outside."

Critch tilted his head. "Now what in the world would they want in the storage room—at that late hour?"

"I haven't the slightest idea," Beth said. "All I know is that they were there. And I know that they hurt other students. And Garth—he's even tried to hurt *me* at times. He pinched me once, and once he pushed me so high on the swing—"

"He pushed *you* on the swing?" Critch said.

Beth flushed. "I was teaching the concept of taking turns."

"I see," Critch said. He studied a cuticle for a moment, then said, "I'm sorry you don't like the work, Miss Lewis."

Stunned, Beth said, "Mr. Critch, that's not it. I *do* like the work, it's very rewarding. Most of my students are wonderful, it's just these few who spoil things."

Critch shrugged. "Some students are sometimes difficult—we are a special school, after all—but dealing with that is part of a teacher's job."

"I don't mean difficult," Beth said, "I mean *malicious.*"

"Most of our teachers learn to cope," Critch said.

Beth's skin went hot. "Most?" she said. "Is that why your turnover rate's so high?"

Critch paused, his expression perfectly bland, then said, "We want you to be happy, Miss Lewis. We want you to be successful."

"Thanks ever so much," Beth said, and she got up and left the room.

The pay phone was right there beside Critch's door. She wanted to call home, to talk to her mother and father, to hear their voices again. But no, not here, not now, with Critch sitting there in his office. No.

At the sound of piano music, she turned and looked down the hall. Past the squat-legged mahogany table a door was ajar; a strip of pale light creased the dark Persian runner. Miss Hemphill's quarters, Beth thought. That's Shirley playing.

She went toward the music, silently, slowly, and peeked through the crack in the door.

A brown leather chair with an old woman in it, a woman whose feet didn't touch the floor, who smiled and drank from a wine glass, her eyes half closed. A woman who looked—Beth caught her breath—a woman who looked like a troll!

Freddie was not in class the next morning. A note on Beth's desk—from Critch's office— informed her he'd switched to another school.

Sadness welled in her heart as she crumpled the note. Dear Freddie! Without him, it just wouldn't be the same. Radbourne was just too hard, she thought. Too many people you started to get to know, and then—with no warning—were gone. With thoughts of home in her heart, she handed out cardboard and yarn.

"Muh—mith Freddie," Shirley said, her red eyes moist.

"I miss him too," Beth said. "We all do, Shirley."

Well, not all. For while Jimmy, Blenda and Yola looked sad, Garth sat there smiling.

The screams tore her sleep apart and she lay rigid, curled on her side toward the painted-shut door in the wall. "Please! No!" she heard, so thin and distant, pitiful; then that whining, mechanical noise, and she thought: That was Sara's voice! Sara *screaming!* No, no, she told herself, it wasn't, it couldn't have been! But the thought made her cold all through. She clutched the covers, shivering, till the room's tall window filled with morning light.

《《—》》

Sara was not at the breakfast table.

"She quit," said Linda, one of the new houseparents.

Quit? Without saying goodbye? She had promised she wouldn't do that. And she *wouldn't*. Beth *knew* she wouldn't.

She fumbled her way through the day. Through all she did, she remembered those screams, those pitiful screams in the night.

There were meatballs for supper. She speared one, looked at it, put it down. Then, slipping the table knife into her purse, she went up to her room.

She sat on her bed and looked at the opposite wall, at that door to the storage room. It hadn't been Sara's voice, she told herself, it had just been a student, a student having a dream. Sara and Pat and Diane had quit, just *quit,* and so had the others, the blue-eyed young man and the others, and Freddie had switched to a different school—

She took the knife out of her purse and went to the storage room door. The keyhole was plugged with a filler as hard as stone. She attacked it, twisting the knife's blunt nose; grains of filler the color of sawdust fell onto the floor.

For over an hour, she worked with the knife as the light in the window died. Hurry! she urged herself. She had to finish before it got dark, while she could see into that room.

You will see only chairs, she told herself as she dug with the knife, her lips pressed tight. It's a room full of furniture, desks and chairs, old tables, that's all it is. She pushed harder, gritting her teeth—and the last of the filler gave way. Holding her breath, she pressed her eye to the opening.

Not chairs.

Not furniture, but bones. A roomful of bones—and skulls.

She put her hand over her mouth and stifled a scream as the table knife fell to the floor.

She would walk through the gate and keep walking. Right now. Pretend she was out for an evening stroll and slip through the gate—

But no: if they saw her she'd have no chance, none at all, the lane was a quarter mile long, and even once she reached the road there wasn't a house for another mile—

A taxi? And where would she call? From the phone outside Critch's office?

No, wait until dark, her chances would be much better—provided the trolls weren't roaming.

# TROLLS

She sat in the chair by the window, tense, her heart high and quick in her neck. She heard a radio playing somewhere, heard a laugh. The sky turned inky blue, then black. No moon. Good, good.

When at last it was quiet and very dark, had been quiet for over an hour, she went to her door and opened it slowly; winced at its tiny brief squeak. She stood in the hallway under the naked dim ceiling bulb, then turned and went to the stairs.

And there they were, on the landing, waiting.

Seven cavernous mouths. Seven throats making quick grunting sounds.

Garth moved forward a step. Flexing his knobby fingers slowly, he grinned, displaying his ragged sharp teeth. His eyes went wide. In gutteral but perfectly articulated syllables, he said: "It's your turn, Beth."

# THE PHAROAH'S CROWN

"I've seen them last almost forever," Dr. Waxman said as some drool escaped Parker's mouth and ran down his chin. "On the other hand, I've seen them give out in two days." Parker gagged. "Suction," Dr. Waxman said, and the hygienist set to work with her hose.

When the roar had stopped, Parker said, "Well what happens then?"

"If the endo crumbles?"

"Yes."

"We give it another try. If it doesn't work, we lose the tooth."

*We,* Parker thought. "So what would you recommend?"

"We cap it," Dr. Waxman said. "Gold crown."

"That sounds like big bucks."

Dr. Waxman looked pained. "It's not inexpensive, but think of the advantages. You can practically chew on stones. Once you've gone through the hassle of a root canal, doesn't it make good sense to protect your investment?"

*Investment,* Parker thought. He was starting to drool again. "Well…" he said.

The following week he had an impression made, and two weeks after that the crown was set in place. At home in his condo he checked the job in the mirror. He'd never liked gold teeth, and now he owned one—at considerable cost. It glowed far back near the hinge of his jaw, out of sight of the masses, the casual observer, the public. Thank God for that. He hated to call attention to himself. His ex-wife Gloria had called him the shyest man in the world. As if she had known all the men in the world, he thought with a sour sniff. There must have been a *few* she'd overlooked.

He closed his mouth, bit down. The metal clicked against the opposing molar. It felt too high—and weird, as if his tooth were trapped, imprisoned, suffocating.

He mixed himself a gin and tonic and sat on his couch, his hide-a-bed, one of the only pieces of furniture left from his Gloria days. That hotshot lawyer of hers had damn near wiped him out. She was to blame and *he* was wiped out—wasn't that some kick in the head? She had been on this very same hide-a-bed when he'd caught her, had come home early from work and found her with Adam Howard. Again he pictured her brazenly strutting across the floor in nothing but white silk stockings and lacy blue garter belt—items he'd never laid eyes on before—casually smoking as Howard had groped for his clothes. He went hot as he thought of that smirk on her hateful face. And the gall of her calling him "drab"! If he ever saw her again he would kill her, he swore he would!

He drank. Gin tingled against the tender gum surrounding the golden crown. The nub of tooth under there was dead, no worry about a sudden jolt from that. He could chew on the ice with impunity if he wanted to. And King Mohteb was pleased.

He swallowed a shred of lime and thought: What? Who? King...*who?*

He stared out the window, frowning. New buildings were going up by the river, tall concrete slabs; they looked ominous now in the dying light. Far off, on the water, the windows of one of the boats caught the sun and flashed red. Parker's heart sped up, he felt hot again, and he thought: that dental work sure does a number on you. Something about how you have to lie back like that. Saps all your strength. I'll hit the sack early tonight.

He had horrible dreams. His new tooth was glowing, ablaze. His breath was a dragon's breath, searing all in his path. King Mohteb grinned down from his throne as the fire spun into a circle, turned into the sun. The slabs ran red. Stone burned.

In the morning his mouth felt fine. The redness around the crown had faded away. When he brushed his teeth—no pain.

He was working hard on the Marshall report when the noises began. The fluorescents again, he thought. He hated fluorescents, especially the one on the ceiling above his desk, which would randomly flicker and buzz like a heavy bee. Sometimes a rap with his knuckle would quiet the thing, and Parker was ready to climb on his chair and bop the plastic panel diffusing the "cool white" tubes, when he noticed an odd undulation in the buzzing sound.

It wasn't the light, it was voices—a number of voices, low, in unison, a chant. Parker frowned, feeling slightly dizzy. "Hey Janet," he said to his closest coworker, "do you hear anything?"

"Like what?" Janet said with a squint, her eyes tiny behind her strong glasses.

"A buzzing, sort of," Parker said.

"I don't think so." She cocked her head. "No, nothing. Do you?"

"I thought I did for a minute. Thanks."

Parker stared at the Marshall report. He could still hear the voices, the rhythmical rise and fall, soft and low and yet urgent. His gum began to tingle and he poked it with his tongue. The crown felt warm and was vibrating ever so slightly like...like a radio speaker.

Parker opened his mouth and closed it again. Again, again.

The noise was coming from his crown.

"Every so often a filling will pick up radio waves," Dr. Waxman said. "It's quite uncommon, but it does occur."

"It's occurring to me," Parker said.

"What stations can you get?" Waxman asked with a jolly grin. "It's hell for a classical music fan to be stuck with rock and roll."

Parker wasn't amused. "Look, I want you to stop it, it's driving me nuts."

"Chances are it will just go away," Waxman said. "You had that endo for weeks without hearing voices, and it's probably temporary."

"The voices started when I got the crown."

"The crown isn't to blame. It isn't gold that picks up radio waves, it's silver."

"If it doesn't stop, I'll want the whole thing done over," Parker said. "I can't go around with voices in my mouth."

Dr. Waxman shrugged. "The job may not turn out as well next time. These root canals..."

"Om-ah-wat-toh-meh-ley-tep-cha... Amon, Amon, Amon..."

Parker was holding his head. The voices had persisted all afternoon, and now with three stiff gin and tonics under his belt and the sun long gone, they continued to drone.

He'd discovered a pattern to them. Certain syllables were repeated, especially that "Amon, Amon." The sounds were a language, not random noise as he'd thought at the start. But *what* language? Just his luck to pick up some *foreign* radio station, a broadcast in some tongue he'd never heard. He always got the bone in the burger, the cherry pit in the pie. As

Gloria had told him once, he would fall in a basket of roses and come up smelling like dung. Oh she'd been a supportive bitch, all right!

"Meh-lah-mah-tep-osh-beh-rah-tah… Amon…"

Parker slapped headphones over his ears and turned up the sound: The 1812 Overture: Crash! Boom! Blam! He drank and stared out at the river. And somewhere below the noise he could still hear "Im-leh-tak-met… "

This night's dream sent him jolting straight up in his bed, wide awake, his hand clutching his chest.

He had been in a dusty, arid land, a land of relentless sun. The sun had been a gold ball in his mouth, a ball surrounded by now too-familiar syllables: "Pah-leh-moh-ket…" He retreated from light and searing wind, was in dark chambers, smelled sharp incense, lifted the hem of his robe and was handed the sword. He tested its edge with his fingertip; its very touch drew blood. He smiled, and the sun fell out of his mouth, rolled to the altar.

The female sacrifice was naked, pleading, pale. King Mohteb glared from his golden throne. Parker ascended the steps to the slab. He raised the blade. Quick expert motion. The scream filled the air with red.

"It's still there," Parker said to the phone. "Three days now. It never stops."

"I'm still pretty sure it will," Dr. Waxman said. If you want me to look again…"

"I don't want you to *look,* I want you to take out the crown."

"The crown isn't the problem, I told you that."

"Well, take out the whole damn *tooth* then, I don't care."

"Mr. Parker, it wouldn't be wise. You just invested—"

"Hey! I can't sleep! I can just about *think!* I want an appointment! Now!"

"Very well," Dr. Waxman said, "I can see you on Friday at three. That will give you some time to reconsider."

Reconsider, right, Parker thought as he hung up the phone. It would give him some time to go looney, go totally nuts! To turn into the maniac that Gloria claimed he was when he finally caught on to her game. He'd bet the dregs of his checking account that she was behind all this. Still twisting the knife!

He stared out the window. The walls of the new construction protruded like giant gravestones, like monstrous teeth. It looked like the necropolis out there, the Valley of Tombs, King Mohteb—

126

He slapped his hands to his temples. "Stop!" he cried out loud. "Just stop! Right now!

Blood, so much blood; he could taste it in his mouth. He awoke to a slanting gold sword blade of sun and turned the alarm clock off. The buzzer died. The chant began. He groaned and sat up in his bed. How long had he slept? Two Hours? Three? He would die if this didn't stop, he would literally *die*. In the back of his mouth, the golden crown felt hot.

In the living room he snapped on the TV set. Amon. A coup in South America. Amon. The weather would be steaming hot. Amon. The Sox had lost again. Amon, Amon. He closed his eyes, saw red. The economic indicators rose. Amon. "And here's an interesting thing about gold, Steve, something I'll bet you didn't know. It's been recycled so many times throughout the centuries that nearly every wedding ring, every bar in the vaults at Fort Knox contains traces of gold from the bracelets, crowns, and amulets of the ancient Egyptian pharaohs."

"Out," Parker said.

"Just the crown," Dr. Waxman said.

"Just the crown."

Dr. Waxman sighed. "It seems such a shame."

"If this works, you can make another crown. I'll be glad to pay. I just don't want *this* crown."

"I did such a nice job."

"Out," Parker said.

The voices were gone. They were gone! Parker laughed with glee as he drove. Nothing to it. A two-minute hammer and chisel job, some silver amalgam to build up the stub, and that was it. It *had* been the crown all along.

At home he made himself an extra stiff drink to celebrate. When he looked out the window the buildings seemed fine again, were mere buildings, not teeth, not tombs. When he sat on the couch he heard traffic, and that was all. He laughed again. He drank. He bit on the ice and he heard something crack. When he opened his mouth and leaned forward, the shards of his broken root canal tumbled into his waiting palm.

"Yes, that's how it goes sometimes when they're unprotected," Dr.Waxman said. "Sometimes you lose the tooth. Now I'd like you to count from one to seven backward."

Parker looked at the tube in his arm. "Sev—" he said, then slid into the cool, dark vault.

The taste of blood. The white light of the gods shone down.

"Don't rinse till the gums stop bleeding," three hazy Dr. Waxmans said in a voice that blurred to other voices, a familiar drone. Parker narrowed his eyes and nodded slowly, just once. The cotton was gone from his cheeks but his mouth still felt fuzzy and full. Dr. Waxman was pale, unfocused, but Parker's mind was clear. The voices called him, each syllable diamond-bright. He'd been gone so long, so very long, and now it was time to return.

"Take it easy, now," Dr. Waxman grinned.

*Take it easy.* Parker tossed his head back and laughed. Dr. Waxman frowned.

The taste of blood. Outside, he hailed a cab. "To the airport," he said.

The guide was a low-caste clown, an incompetent peasant. "Then, after thousands of years of glory, this city was sacked by the Assyrians," he said with a casual wave at the columns that lay in the blistering sand. A gust of dusty wind swirled up, and a woman with wrinkled jowls and purplish spun-sugar hair began to cough. "That happened in 661 B.C. The Romans sacked the city in 29 B.C., and once-glorious Thebes was reduced to a few scattered villages."

Parker squinted and thought: You fool! The great god Amon lives! He looked up at the sun and grinned.

The fools never missed him. From his hiding place in the cliffs he watched the bus depart. Before its dust dispersed on the horizon, the voices began again.

Parker turned in their direction, to the cleft in the stone, and entered the cool of the crypt. The smell of incense filled the gray light. The chant grew strong.

At the corridor's first turn he donned his robe, and acknowledged the priests with a silent nod. At the second turn, they presented him with his sword. It was cool and gleaming, perfectly balanced. He tested its edge with his fingertip. It drew bright blood. As he entered the vault, the row of priests fell to their knees.

On his golden throne, King Mohteb stared with burning, shadowed eyes. Gloria, naked, bound to the altar, struggled in vain, bruising her skin on the stone. As Parker approached, she screamed.

Parker raised his blade. His eyes were suns, and the good taste of blood filled his mouth.

# RANDALL RODGERS REINVENTED

"When he woke to the sunbright room he blinked three times and said in a soft voice, "Randall, good heavens, what happened?" He looked at the window frame, glowing with light, and repeated, "Heavens."

He put on his glasses and looked at the clock on the nightstand next to the bed. Five of twelve! It was almost noon!

Disgraceful, he thought. He had never slept late like this before in his life—and he was eighty-two.

That terrible dream had been to blame: An IRS agent had grilled him for hours, shining a light in his eyes and questioning every deduction. "I deeply resent this," Randall had said. "I do not cheat!" "You're facing five years in the slammer, pal," the agent said, and the dream burst apart and now it was 12:03.

Randall frowned at the clock. No, you can't blame a dream, he thought. You've had plenty of nightmares before and never slept this late.

He propped himself up on his elbows. The room seemed to tilt, and then he remembered: he hadn't been up to snuff these past few days; as a matter of fact, he'd been feeling quite poorly. He'd picked up a bug of some kind? That's why he had overslept?

The room leveled out as he stared at the window, the chestnut tree's leaves, the powderblue sky—and then all at once he felt fine. As a matter of fact he felt great—light, strong. But now he was startled to see he was wearing an undershirt. Good grief, he'd forgotten to put on pajamas last night?

He looked at the dresser, at Margaret's picture, remembering how it had been with her. At first it was just little memory lapses, nothing to be concerned about; but then she had started to misunderstand and to say things wrong, and then came the wandering out of the house in the nude and trying to cook the roast in the washing machine, and everything went downhill so fast, and soon she was dead. Twelve years ago. He wondered if this was the start of that process for him. He lifted the covers.

Undershorts.

He heard something then, downstairs, and cocked his head. No doubt about it, someone had opened his kitchen door. But who? The only person who had the key was his son, Bill, who lived in New Jersey. So Bill was here? He had come without calling? Confused, Randall frowned, and below him the voices began.

He could only hear random words, not the gist of the conversation. Two males, and not voices he knew. "Big stuff," and "Reserve the grange," were two of the phrases he caught as the talk grew louder. The men, whoever they were, had walked down the hall and were now at the foot of the stairs. Randall reached for the phone on the nightstand and raised the receiver. No dial tone.

Dead phone and strange men in his house and he should have been scared to death, but he wasn't. Concerned, yes; frightened, no. "This is the real thing, Tiffany," the deeper of the voices said, then the higher voice said, "The library chair should bring in some bucks—original finish."

The nerve of them! Randall thought, sitting straight. How utterly brazen criminals were these days! His car was outside, they knew he was home—and didn't even care?

The men discussed the dining room set, the Wedgewood vases on the hutch, his grandfather's glass-front bookcase. "Wonder what we'll find up here," the deep voice said, and Randall heard the footsteps mount the stairs. "The son says the attic is full of junk. Well, one guy's junk is another guy's treasure, right?"

No lock on Randall's bedroom door, and the phone was dead. There was nothing to do but wait.

"Hey, a paymaster's desk," said the higher voice. They were standing outside the study now.

Randall had bought that desk from Captain Bright some forty years ago. The captain had been ninety-three at the time, and *he'd* bought the desk in his teens. And now these petty crooks were going to steal it? Under his breath Randall said, "Over my dead body!"

"That spinning wheel's in good shape."

"Not bad."

"Nice lamp."

"Let's see what's in here."

The knob of Randall's door was turned and there they were, a tall thin older man with green work pants and a beard, and a shorter man with rosy cheeks and a blue striped shirt that covered an ample paunch. Their eyes went wide as they fell on Randall.

"Good grief," said the tall man, the one with the higher voice. "What are *you* doing here?"

With a scowl Randall said, "What am *I* doing here?"

"This place is supposed to be empty," the short man said.

"My car's in the driveway," Randall said.

Both men wore frowns. "They told us the place was empty," the short one said. "Well, sorry to bother you, we'll do this room later."

"The devil you will!" Randall said. "You'll leave my house this minute!"

"*Your* house?" said the tall man.

"You heard me, gentlemen. Now leave!"

Shaking his head, the short man turned away. "I guess we better check this out," he said.

"Leave!" Randall said.

The men descended the stairs and were gone. Randall sniffed. *Do this room later! Indeed!*

He got out of bed with more zip than he'd had in years, and went downstairs and threw the bolts on the doors. He'd never bothered to use the bolts, but now, by gosh, he'd have to.

He brushed his teeth and showered, shaved. He nicked himself but it didn't hurt, and—interesting—it didn't bleed at all.

He put on clean underwear, a clean white shirt, and where was his blue serge suit? His other suits were there, and his jackets, but not the blue serge. Odd. Those criminals hadn't entered this room, they couldn't have stolen it. Well, he would wear his dark gray.

He felt so good that he left his car in the driveway and walked to town. It was now almost two o'clock but he wasn't hungry. He wondered why. Maybe he still had a touch of that bug. But he felt just fine.

Smiling, he went through the town office door. "Morning, Clara," he said to the woman who sat at the desk. "Is Tim upstairs?"

The round-faced clerk looked up and her jaw went slack. She dropped her pen on the blotter.

"Why Clara," said Randall, "you look like you've seen a ghost."

Clara seemed to be choking. Her face was the color of milk.

"Can I help you in any way?"

Clara shook her head quickly. "No, no," she whispered.

"You're sure?"

She nodded yes.

"Well, then, is Tim upstairs?"

Another nod.

"Thanks, Clara."

He went up the steps thinking, *Clara you don't look good.* She smoked, of course. It caught up to you after a while. Randall had never smoked, not even a pipe, never drank, and kept regular hours. Still, he had gotten that bug. Thank God he was over it now.

Tim Lewis, the chief of police, was absorbed in a crossword puzzle. Knocking on the door jamb gently, Randall said, "Hi, Tim, may I see you a minute?"

Tim Lewis looked up and his gray eyes widened. "Jesus," he said.

"This isn't a good time?" Randall said. "I can come back later."

Lewis kept staring, motionless.

"Is something wrong?"

Lewis opened his mouth, but nothing came out.

Randall looked at himself. Fully clothed, thank God. He'd forgotten to comb his hair?

"But Randall…" Lewis managed to say.

"Yes?"

"No. It can't be you."

Randall chuckled. "Well, Timmy, it certainly is."

"It just *can't* be."

Randall frowned. "Tim, why are you saying this?"

"Because, well, Randall, see, I mean… Because…you're dead."

You know, Randall thought as he walked back home, Tim just might be on to something. For one thing, he hadn't bled when he nicked himself. For another, he still wasn't hungry. He still didn't need to use the john. And then there was this matter of seeing things.

As he'd told Tim Lewis about the intruders, he'd seen Tim's thoughts. They were there in the air above his head. It was kind of like reading a comic strip. And that wasn't all he saw.

As an avid Baptist he'd always believed in demons, but never in all his eighty-two years had he seen one. Now, by gosh, they were everywhere: on curbs, on rooftops, on chimneys, on fences. Little things for the most part, monkey-like, dark and hairy, with long forked tails. Most of them simply sat around laughing and making unkind remarks about people, but every so often one did something mean, like ruffling the fur of a cat or tripping a child. Yes sir, Tim Lewis might be right, he might be dead, how else could he see such things?

In his living room, mail was piled on the couch. Time had passed that he couldn't account for, no doubt about it. A newspaper, more than a week old, lay on the floor. He checked the obituaries.

And there was his face, staring back from the page. "Well I'll be darned," Randall said, and then said, "Scat!" to the demon that sat on the TV set.

The two intruders, Timmy had said, were the Baker boys, from Baker auctioneers. They'd been given the key to the house by Bill, Randall's son, who was back in New Jersey now. Bill had told them to sell the entire estate. But that will never do, Randall thought, I need a place to live.

*Live?* he said to himself. Was that the right word? *No, stay.* I need a place to *stay.*

At six o'clock he walked to the pay phone in town and called New Jersey. "Bill? It's Dad."

The pause on the other end of the line was long. Then: "Whoever you are, this isn't funny."

"Bill, no, really, it's not a joke. Doesn't it sound like me?" No reply, so Randall said, "It's me, Chickadee."

Nobody else in the world knew that childhood name. In a failing voice, Bill said, "But...no, I just went to your funeral. The casket was closed, but... My God."

"I know, I can hardly believe it myself."

"But how could they make a mistake like that?"

"Oh Bill, no, see, I'm dead all right. It's just that I've come back."

"What?"

"I've come back, don't ask me how, and I'm going to need the house. For a while, at least."

"Dad, I don't understand. This is totally crazy. I can't... I'll have to come see you."

"Please do," Randall said. "You haven't visited since when? Three years ago? Will Mary be coming too?"

Randall stayed up all night, just thinking. When morning came, he was not in the least bit tired—and still not hungry, and had no bathroom urge.

He wondered about the bills on the couch. His pension had been cut off, no doubt, and where would he get the money to pay them? Did he still

135

RANDALL RODGERS REINVENTED

have his savings account? If not, he would have to borrow from Bill until...until what?

He thought for a minute. If somebody dead didn't pay a bill, what could happen to him? What could happen to him no matter *what* he did?

He thought about what he would need in this form of existence. Not food, not sleep, and would weather affect him? Cold and rain? Could he live outdoors in the ice and snow? Gosh, he'd done it again, used the wrong word—*live*. He wouldn't need health insurance, or, quite obviously, life insurance...

He washed his face, but his beard hadn't grown and he didn't need to shave. Would he ever need to again, in his whole—his whole *what?*

He dressed in a pair of yellow slacks and a dark blue jacket, then watched TV for a while. It bored him stiff. Who cared about any of this? The thought of an English muffin was comforting, though he had no appetite, and he walked down to Fanny's Diner.

There were demons all over the coffee machine, sticking their tongues out at people. When Randall came up to the counter, the customers there, a man in coveralls and an older woman, threw down some bills and left. Two men in a booth in a corner also left. Linda, the waitress, stared at Randall, then dropped her sponge and went through the kitchen doors.

Randall sat on a stool and waited for her to return. Ten minutes went by, then Vince Packer walked in.

Vince was county sheriff. Randall had known him for years and years. He was six feet two, with beefy broad shoulders and two white scars near his right eyebrow. He was wearing his uniform: crisp tan shirt, brown pants. He was wearing his gun.

The demon on top of the doughnut case was cackling and pointing now. "Shhh!" Randall scolded, then smiled and said, "Vince! Good to see you!"

The sheriff nodded, but didn't return the smile. "Hello, Randall," he said. "Linda called me and said you were here."

"I sure am," Randall said. "Can I buy you a coffee?"

"No thanks," Packer said with his hand on his gun. "Timmy told me about you yesterday."

"It's the darnedest thing," Randall said. "I can't figure it out."

"What's to figure, there's been a mistake," Packer said. "A *big* mistake."

"Well, yes," Randall said. "When you're dead, you're supposed to *stay* dead. At least that's what I always thought."

Parker snorted. "You aren't dead."

136

"But I am," Randall said. "I surely am. I don't need to eat, or sleep, or anything else. Watch this."

Leaning over the counter, he picked up a paring knife. "Watch." He drove the knife into his palm. No blood issued forth. "And it doesn't hurt. I daresay you could shoot me now and not do me a bit of harm."

Packer suddenly didn't look so hot. "Jesus Christ," he said.

"Amazing, huh?"

"It's a trick," Packer said. "You were never buried."

"They tell me I was," Randall said.

"They have to be wrong."

"Well let's go find out."

As Spooky Norris flung up more dirt, Packer said, "This just doesn't seem right."

"But it's *my* grave," said Randall. "I own the plot. And if I'm up here, I can't be down there."

Packer grunted.

The shovel struck wood. Excited, Spooky Norris worked faster. Spooky had dug graves for twenty-odd years, but he'd never done this before, unearthed a coffin. "There she is," he said, his scrawny head jerking back. "Jeez, I just got done fillin' her in a few days ago, this sure seems weird." He shoveled the last of the dirt away.

"Well open her up," Parker said.

"Uh-uh, not me," Spooky said with a nervous laugh, and he climbed up out of the hole.

"I'll do it," Randall said.

"Randall, no," Packer said, "you're too old for that."

"Oh no," Randall said, "I'm not old anymore. I may look old, but you just watch," and he scrambled down into the hole and stood by the casket. He felt for the catch, and up came the lid. Packer gasped. "Hah, just as I thought," Randall said.

Lying there on the coffin's plastic silk was his blue serge suit. "Well, I'll be needing this," he said, and scooped up the suit and climbed out of the hole. "I guess I should get that box out of there, it must have cost Bill a bundle."

Packer blanched. "Good God," he said.

"Have you ever in all your life?" said Randall. "Doesn't this just beat all?"

Tuesday was Golden Sea Lion day, and Randall, after he cleaned up and changed his clothes, drove down to the Wagon Wheel restaurant.

As soon as he walked through the door, the room fell silent. Dick Forrest got up from his table and went to the kitchen.

"Hi, fellows, it's good to see you again," Randall said.

From their seats at the tables, they stared. No one spoke. It was like they were made of wood.

"I think I've figured it out," Randall said. "'Whosoever believeth in me shall have life everlasting,' right?"

Bud Calloway shook his head. "But that doesn't mean here, Randall. Not here on earth."

"A couple of days ago, I'd have thought that too," Randall said. "But here I am."

"It isn't right," Lou Campbell said. "This isn't the way it should work."

"That's what I always figured," Randall said. "But who really *knows* how it works?"

"But nobody crucified you," Campbell said. "As a matter of fact, we treated you pretty darn good."

"I agree with you, Lou, I surely do. I can't really explain it. At any rate, it's good to see you all."

They just kept staring.

"Well, don't let me hold up the meeting," he said.

Bud Calloway said, "You can't stay here, Randall."

"Oh? Why?"

"Well, the fact of the matter is, we've never allowed dead members before and we're not gonna do it now."

"But fellows—"

Fred Grover said, "Sorry, Randall, Bud's right."

"Is it in the by-laws?"

Bud Calloway frowned. "No, we never had reason to put it in."

"Well, then?"

"We're revising the by-laws this evening," Fred Grover said.

Randall said: "What you really mean, Fred, and the rest of you, is—you're scared of me."

"No, that's not it," Pete Farrington said. He weighed two hundred forty-three pounds and was bald as an egg.

"But it is," Randall said. "I can see what you're thinking—see into your minds, as it were."

Pete Farrington scowled—then suddenly dropped to the floor. People gasped.

"He's okay," Randall said. "Just a bit light-headed, it happens during conversions."

The big man moaned. Bud Calloway knelt beside him. "Pete?"

Then suddenly Farrington sprang to his feet. Eyes bright, he said, "I'm going fishing!"

"Huh?" Calloway said. "You just passed out and you're going *fishing?*"

"Right!" Pete said, and he made for the door.

"That's the spirit!" said Randall. "Remember now, fish from the starboard side of the boat."

"You bet!" Pete said.

The door slammed shut and all was still. "It looks like you fellows are short on rolls," Randall said with a nod at the table. "But not to worry, you'll have enough soon." He left the room.

"Dad, why are you doing this?" Bill said.

They were both on the couch, at opposite ends. "I'm not," Randall said. "It just happened to me."

Bill stared down at the floor.

"I know what you're thinking," Randall said. "You're thinking, 'Dad, please, go down in the ground again.'"

"No," Bill said sharply, looking up.

"Oh yes," Randall said.

Looking down at the floor again, Bill said, "You always knew when I was lying."

"This time it's more than that," Randall said.

"I don't get it."

"Well I don't either," Randall said, "but the best I can figure, I'm a savior."

"You?" Bill said.

"I think so. I'll show you something."

He got up and went to the kitchen, returned with a glass of water. Setting the glass on the coffee table, he said, "Watch this."

He stared at the glass, and the water began to change, turned amber. Bright bubbles rose to a foaming head. "Take a taste," he said.

"Dad, really."

"Go on."

"I don't want a taste."

"It's not going to hurt you. All right, don't taste it, just smell it, then."

Bill sniffed at the glass. "Beer."

"Yes," Randall said, "It's the best I can do at this point, I'm still learning. The wine will come any day now, though, I can feel it."

Bill's face was a mask of dismay. "Dad, listen. We've had the funeral, we're executing the will..."

"I'm sorry, Bill, I really am."

"Mary says she won't visit. And Keith and Tina—"

"I love those kids. How are they?"

"Fine."

"Tina made Dean's list, didn't you tell me?"

"Yes. But this whole thing's upset her."

"I understand."

"They won't come to see you." Bill looked at the floor again. "Dad?"

"Yes, Bill?"

"Give it up."

Randall sighed. "Oh, if only I could. But I guess I've been chosen."

"Why *you* of all people?"

"Beats me. But I was an okay father, wasn't I? A decent man?"

"Of course."

"Well maybe that's why."

"But plenty of people were good," Bill said, "and none of them rose from the dead."

"I know."

"I think you better talk to Reverend Hopkinson," Bill said.

"Go back," Reverend Hopkinson said. He was hefty, with wavy gray hair and watery steel-rimmed glasses. He looked like an Episcopalian, not a Baptist.

Randall, frowning, his hands on his knees, said, "Is that what you'd tell Jesus Christ?"

Reverend Hopkinson smiled, displaying his large yellow teeth. "You're Randall Rodgers, retired from Zeus Electronics, not Jesus Christ, and you should go back."

"But I can't," Randall said. "I mean what do you want me to do, lie down in that coffin again and just *wait?* I wouldn't sleep, I know that much, I'm not tired."

"It's a problem, I realize," the minister said. "But somehow or other, there must be a way."

"I don't think so," said Randall. "I think what's going to happen is, I'll get called up to heaven—but not just yet, because I've got work to do."

"Oh? What kind of work?"

"I'm just starting to understand," Randall said—and saw a vision of Reverend Hopkinson siphoning off church funds for his personal use. "What you're doing's quite sinful," he said.

"What?" Hopkinson said.

"You know what I mean."

Reverend Hopkinson's cheeks became suddenly rosy. "No," he said, "I have no idea what you mean."

"Mmm," Randall said, rising.

"I urge you to reconsider," Hopkinson said.

"I urge you to also. I'll see you in church tomorrow."

"No!" Hopkinson said, his voice tinged with panic. "You shouldn't do that! You *mustn't* do that!"

"There's a small demon perched on your shoulder," Randall said.

He called Ed Pike and Don Mitchell, old friends he played cards with. They both cut him short and hung up. The library locked its doors when they saw him coming. The next time he went to the town office, no one was there.

Wherever he went, people hid—except for the children. They taunted him from a distance, in packs, urged on by their demons. "Zom-bie, zom-bie," they chanted, and some of them even threw sharp little stones, which, while they nicked his flesh, didn't hurt at all.

In his ramblings he saw lots of things: Willis Todd in the Sleepwell Motel, and not with his wife. He saw Henry Costanza, of "square deal" hype, sell a young girl a car with a ruined transmission. Saw Agatha Blunt in her beauty shop office, working on two sets of books.

The week went by slowly. He practiced the water-to-wine routine and got it down pat: progressed from a sour burgundy to a delicate beaujolais. He knocked quite a few of those devilish demons flat with an angry scowl.

When Tuesday came, he went to the Wagon Wheel restaurant. "Sorry, Randall," Bud Calloway said. "No room."

The same thing they'd told him at church. "Now fellows, this isn't fair," Randall said. "I served as your president three times. I headed the drive to raise funds for the new ball field. I chaired the library maintenance committee six years straight, and don't forget the ambulance fund, what I did for that. I may not be living, but I'm the same man, and I'd like to be treated the same."

"You're *not* the same," Dave Pendleton said, "and we don't want you here."

"All right, Dave, all right," Randall said with a nod. "But you know what? Those Holiday Paints you sell? They're crap, the absolute worst."

Before Christ arose from the tomb, he descended to Hell. Of course! Randall thought. That "dream" of the IRS! But after the resurrection, what happened? The Bible was vague about this. No preaching? No healing? No work to do? Christ just hung around for a while before he was called upstairs? He'd eaten some broiled fish...

But Randall still didn't have an appetite, which wasn't fun. It wasn't fun having no need for sleep. And the way he was treated by family and friends... Bill was letting him stay in the house until things were "settled." Letting him stay in his very own house, how kind. The kid had a heart of gold.

Randall had always been of *use*. He'd always had a role to play, but now? This water to wine bit was already getting old. Was this any way to make a—well, not a *living*...

Without appetites, it was boring. Without fear of death, who cared what went on in the world? And not only that, he'd always supposed that once he was dead he would be reunited with Margaret, his wife of forty-six years, and with Teddy, his older son, who'd been killed in the war. Instead, here he was where he'd always been, except nobody liked him now. His only real fun was with demons, knocking them flat.

He was passing the Pritchard farm on the edge of town, was watching the pigs, when it suddenly came to him. That part in the Bible where Jesus put demons in swine...

That demon up there on the fence, the one with the purple-green horns. Suppose instead of knocking him flat, you—

He tried it: concentrated hard—and the closest pig began squealing and running with terrified eyes, banging into the fence, falling down, its tan sides twitching, its muscles jerking and blood coming out of its nose.

Randall thought about Willis Todd in the Sleepwell Motel; about Henry Costanza selling bad cars; about Reverend Hopkinson lining his pockets. He thought about others whose minds he had read. Dave Pendleton, Ed Pike....

As the pig screeched and spasmed in mud, legs flailing, Randall walked back to town. There was spring in his step; he was humming a tune.

When he came through the door of the Wagon Wheel, they all looked up.

Randall grinned. In the silence he said, "Well, fellows, I understand it now, I know what I'm here for."

He held out his hand. And the water that sat in the rows of glasses suddenly turned dark red.

People gasped; stared at Randall with open mouths.

"You got it," Randall said, his smile huge. "Don't think I come to bring peace on earth, I come not to bring peace, but a sword."

# THE MAN IN BLACK

I encountered him only twice, both times on the strand.

In the summer of 1816, Shelley and I and my step-sister, Claire (who followed us everywhere) took a cottage on Lake Geneva's shore near the villa occupied by Lord Byron. Shelley and Byron became fast friends, and engaged in many an evening of heated debate on the subjects of poetry, philosophy, and politics, in which, to my great dismay, they were joined by Byron's physician, Polidori, a shallow and vain young man who considered himself their match—because of his medical training, no doubt. I, who was not quite nineteen at the time, felt equal to this buffoon, but far behind the other two, in spite of the fact that I had been raised in a highly demanding atmosphere, and I usually sat in silence along with Claire (who was madly obsessed with the roguish Byron), content to ride the eloquent twists and turns of thought of these passionate men, who seemed so much older and wiser. And Shelley at the time was but twenty-four!

The season began auspiciously, with sunny days of garden walks and rowing on the lake, but then the rain set in. One might have expected such weather to work in my lover's favour; the gloom negating the lure of the water and hills, he would turn to the core of genius inside and produce great reams of verse. But day after dreary day crept by, and nothing issued forth. "Oh, for a ray of sun!" he cried at the end of the first week of slate-dark skies. "A single ray!"

Byron was not affected thus. *Childe Harold* was going splendidly, and nothing could slow the pace of his fervent (and, some might say, twisted) brain. His cheer was unflagging, which tended to make Shelley sulk. Our evening intercourse became quite strained. To break this mood, we would read aloud from a volume of supernatural tales which Polidori (that arrogant fool) had found in the villa's library. One evening, after I'd taken my turn, Byron, tilting his handsome chin towards the ceiling and raising an index finger, said, "We shall each write a ghost story."

Few could oppose a command of Lord Byron, and none of us did that night: all swore an oath to write a tale with supernatural elements—even the pompous Polidori, even the scatter-brained Claire. A gleam came into Shelley's eye. He sees this as the way to break the paralytic grip that holds his muse in check, I thought. But I was wrong.

Almost from the time we met, Shelley had urged me to write, as the juvenilia I'd shyly shown him convinced him that I had talent. I was far from convinced myself, as his own superb efforts were so far above my productions that I was prepared to capitulate, and assume with contentment the role of wife and mother. But Byron's challenge inflamed Shelley's ardour to make me set pen to paper.

Each morning (oh how grey and desolate they were, with the rain beating down on the tiles of the roof, streaming over the panes of the casements), Shelley would say, "Have you thought of a story yet?" And I, in misery, would say, "Not yet," and blush with mortification. His story was going well, he claimed; he would show me a part of it soon.

One morning, my spirits depressed by the endless clouds and lack of inspiration, wishing with all my heart that Byron had never proposed his game, I went out alone to the shore of the lake, hoping that exercise would jog my muse, or, at the least, rouse my sluggish and fretful blood.

The air was a penetrating mist, which hid the snow-capped peaks, the farther shore, and most of the lake's expanse. My soul was claustrophobic, smothered in fog, and my stroll, instead of providing the elevation which I desired, served to oppress me further—the more so when I came upon a fish, dead, washed up on the sand.

It was beautiful, silver with tinges of green and gold, and of good size. I knew not what variety it was; I only knew it seemed a shame for it to die and lie here in the cold. I stared at it, my thoughts on how I too should end like this; how my dear Shelley, my dear friends should end like this—when suddenly a loud voice startled me:

"How soon the worm determines that the vital spark is gone!"

The man was small, a little taller than my height. His trousers and his coat were black, and somewhat frayed. I sensed he was close to Byron's age (which was twenty-eight) but had suffered the ravages of disease: his frame was bent, his brow was lined, his face was gaunt and pale.

"The worm," I said.

"Observe the eye. Oh, how it feasts!"

I regarded the fish again, but with more diligence, and yes, a worm— thin, white—was threaded through the creature's eye. I thought of the dream that had plagued me after the death of my infant daughter the year before. I dreamt that I had rubbed her chalky skin before the blazing hearth and her eyes had opened, gazed on me—and then I awoke once again to the terrible truth. The dream had returned to me last night when Shelley and Byron (and Polidori, who offered his "expert" views) had speculated on galvanism: if it might someday be applied to bring the dead to life.

"Oh, that the vital spark could be restored," I said, "and once again this fish could swim in all its beauty and its grace."

The small man stared at me, his eyebrows raised, his dark eyes shining bright. "Do not wish *that!*" he said. "Never, never wish *that!*"

Perplexed by this fervid response, I said, "And pray, why not?"

He proceeded to tell a fantastic tale: of a friend of his from the town of Zurich, a medical man, who had raised a corpse from the dead. He insisted this story was true, and more: insisted this creature constructed of parts from the tomb and the charnel house still roamed the world. His cheeks, so pale at his narrative's start, were brightly flushed by its end, and his eyes had the beady glitter and shift of a raven's. Mad, I concluded, and shivered from more than cold.

"The fish is dead, and must remain so, as all who die must remain in that state and return to dust," said the man in black. "Do you understand?"

I replied that I did, wanting ever so much to return to the cottage, my lover, the warmth of our hearth.

"Heinrich Berger," he said, extending his hand, and I took it; the fish could have been no colder.

"And you, my dear madame…are?"

Releasing his cold, dead hand I said, "Mrs. Shelley."

"Mrs. Shelley," he said with an odd, jerky twist of his head. "*Mrs.* Shelley. I see."

I sensed he knew it was a lie. My name was Mary Godwin still, as Shelley did not approve of marriage. More to the point, he already had a wife, who lived in London with their sons.

"I devoted myself to science," the small man said, "and neglected life's social side. And now, I fear, the pattern is solidified." He waved his hand impatiently. "Well, that is of no consequence, if only I—"

Then suddenly he craned his neck and said, "He's here! He's followed me! I shall never, never escape!"

I searched the fog, but saw nothing at all.

"He's here! Go, go, it isn't safe!"

With this, he turned his back to me, and raised his arms. "Begone!" he cried. "Begone, foul demon! Plague me no more! Return to the mouldering grave from whence you came!" Swinging towards me again he shouted, "Why do you stand here after I've warned you? Go! This minute! Now!" Then he strode forward into the fog, screaming horrible oaths. Soon he was swallowed up and I heard no more.

I shivered again and hugged myself and walked back up the strand. Every so often I glanced behind, but saw no man, and certainly no "demon." When I entered the cottage, Shelley looked up from his place by the hearth, smiled slightly, and asked: "Did your outing help? Have you thought of a story yet?"

His superior tone, his imperious high pale brow made me suddenly understand why his schoolmates had taken such great delight in tormenting him. I crossed to the fire and held out my hands, remembering my poor dead babe. I turned to the chair where Shelley sat, still with his haughty smile.

"I have thought of a story, yes," I said with a little smirk of my own.

Shelley quickly abandoned his story. Polidori, to our great surprise, managed a rather decent vampyre tale, while Byron (competing with his brash physician?) created a vampyre sketch of his own—and created a foetus in hapless Claire, whose condition dashed all desire to write—and even, at times, to live. Only I, of the five who had taken the oath that sodden, windblown night, wrote a book.

It was published more than two years later, thanks to great effort on Shelley's part. He had tried, while a student at Eton, to call up the Devil by chemical means, and the theme of my novel entranced him. He made me expand and embellish my early draught, then hounded Lackington & Hughes to bring it out.

Its first reviews were dreadful, but, despite these harsh pronouncements by the learned arbiters of taste, the public chose to enjoy it. *Frankenstein, or, The Modern Prometheus,* sold quite well—much better than any of Shelley's work—which created a certain friction between us. But Shelley was glad for the money, indeed, as Harriet, his wife, had drowned herself, and now he had charge of their two young sons as well as our own sweet William. Yes: I *was* now Mrs. Shelley.

I encountered the man in black again in 1822. By then we were living in Spezia, in the midst of savage native folk who howled at the moon at night. Often Shelley would join in their naked romps in the waves—his friends, the two Edwards (Trelawny and Williams), keeping a watchful eye on him, as (unbelievably for one who sailed so much) he could not swim.

Claire's daughter by Byron, Allegra, had died of typhus, and we had been forced to abandon Pisa, taking Claire, afraid that she might bring harm to the dissolute Lord, who lived nearby, as she managed to put the blame on him for Allegra's death. I was pregnant again, and not feeling well, when we moved. The doctor advised me to stay in my bed, but I refused; I found that a walk beside the Gulf would ease my pain and raise my spirits, and one penumbral afternoon, returning from such exercise, I suddenly heard from behind, "Mrs. Shelley." I turned.

He had aged to a shocking degree: his hair was white, his arms were sticks, his waxen skin sagged on his cheeks. He seemed to be clothed in the very same garb as the first time I'd met him, and now it was tattered and torn.

"It is you, I am not mistaken?" he said, his watery dark eyes shining.

"Mr. Berger," I said.

"*Doctor* Berger," he said. "Your memory is excellent." He took my hand. Again, it was so cold.

A pain ran through me then; I winced, and his eyebrows rose.

"A slight discomfort," I said. "I am pregnant, you see."

"Ah, yes," he nodded. "Your first?"

"My fifth," I said. "Three other children of mine have died, two since I saw you last."

"The curse!" cried Berger, clutching his vest. "I prayed that it would spare you, but, I see, to no avail! It is *him,* of course. Anyone who has even the slightest association with me can be caught in his spell. Oh! What have I done?"

"My children died of fevers," I said, "not of a curse."

This remark was completely ignored. "And how were you to know, when you transcribed the tale," said Berger, trembling now, "what horrors you would bring upon yourself?"

At this, I blushed. "The tale. You've read my book?"

"Of course."

I had altered his story, setting it in Geneva instead of Zurich, adding more characters, adding new scenes; and yet, it was *his* story. "I am truly surprised it has travelled so far," I said. "I expected it not to leave England."

"*He* learned of it," said the man in black. "It was *he* who brought me a copy, left it on my bedstand while I slept."

Poor Berger was still quite clearly mad. I contrived of a way to escape.

"He used to follow *me*," he said, his finger pointing to the sky, "but then I followed *him*. What difference? Either way we are bound to each other—till death! But now—" and here his grin grew wide, his stained teeth showed— "but now I have finally outwitted him, now I have trapped him. With luck..."

Then, tilting his head and staring at me with those red, wet eyes, he said, "Do not stay here. Though he is trapped, he has his ways. For the sake of the child that still survives and the child you carry, quit this place!"

I thanked mad Berger for his concern, then said I must rest, and bade him a quick farewell. As I made my way back to our villa, the dank and decrepit Casa Magni, his words reverberated in my brain, and I found myself constantly looking across my shoulder. I thought of the night before, when Shelley, out on the terrace with Williams and me, had suddenly cried, "Look! There it is!" and pointed to the sea. He insisted he saw the dead Allegra perched on a moonlit island, clapping her hands. But Williams and I saw no island, saw nothing but waves; and now, as I looked behind, the man was gone, and only a handful of moon-mad natives occupied the sands.

I reached our odious abode, and all at once my strength abandoned me. Shelley ran over and clasped my hand and pressed it to his breast. "A chill," I said, and straightaway took to my bed.

The pains commenced soon after: wracking, horrible pains that would not allow sleep. Feverish, I tossed and turned, my mind obsessed with thoughts of the man in black. On the fifth night, the bleeding began.

Claire and Jane Williams did what they could, applying towels to stanch the hemorrhage, yet still I bled. We were far from a doctor; one had been summoned hours before, but had failed to appear. I lapsed into coma and, in the depths of that shadowy state, encountered my precious dead children again. Oh happy reunion! I shrieked with joy as we embraced, then felt the cold. Such cold! For Shelley had somehow procured some ice; its application stopped the flow; by the time the doctor arrived, I was back from the brink.

For several days, I was terribly weak. At times I feared I should perish and go to that better place where my mother, who'd died giving life to me, dwelled. I nurtured a piece of her rationalist soul in my all too unworthy breast, and gave no credence to demons and curses and spells. And yet, another child of mine was lost—and I thought of the man in black.

I had barely begun to regain my strength, when Shelley announced that he and Williams were sailing across the Gulf to meet their friend Leigh Hunt. No, he could not desert me! I cried, and lapsed into histrionics worthy of Claire. He reasoned with me soothingly; assured me he would soon return; explained that he could not leave Hunt, who'd just arrived, alone in a foreign land. He had hired a young but experienced sailor, Charles Vivian, to help with his week-old boat. His argument calmed me; I said he should go. But when on the following dawn I saw him ready to take to the wide black sea, I was shaken by fear, and once again begged him to stay. Now, though, he would not be swayed.

The days were long, the nights were longer still; with natives dancing 'round their fires and howling like wolves as I tried to rest. The skies turned dark, the waves turned wild, my heart was sick with fright. Then a letter arrived from Hunt—confirming that Shelley had started back at the very height of the storm!

Trelawny was the first to hear the news: three bodies had been washed ashore far distant from one another. In accordance with local law, they were buried in quicklime.

It was good Trelawny who arranged for the exhumation; he who built the funeral pyres, each on a separate shore. It was he who notified Byron and Hunt—who attended the burning—and he who collected the ashes and placed them in casks of his own design. It was he who rescued my husband's heart from the eager, merciless flames.

Disconsolate and inconsolable, I hid in my room in the horrible Casa Magni with hardly a thought (with what shame I admit to this) for my only surviving child, small Percy, who, thanks to Claire, was cared for well. (For once Claire had made herself useful.)

For weeks I was sunk in a pit so dark I scarcely desired to live. Trelawny, Hunt, Lord Byron, even Jane—whose husband died along with mine—I had Claire turn away. Why I did not bring an end to it all with a draught of laudanum, as Fanny, my older sister had, remains a mystery. I felt, though, even in the blackest gloom, that I was destined for some great and noble task; and one bleak morn, while gazing at my husband's heart in the jar on my bedroom shelf, the nature of that task grew clear: through his work, he must live again. Whatever time remained to me would be spent in securing his fame.

One sleepless night, as I lay with the ceaseless pulse of the murderous waves in my ears, I was jolted straight up in my bed by a thump at my door. Claire, of course. The lateness of the hour could only mean one thing: she was caught once again in the grips of hysteria.

"Claire, please," I said. "I have no strength—"

With a creak of its hinges, the door swung inward, then crashed to a stop. A huge black shadow filled the hall. With my heart in my throat, I turned up the wick on my lamp. The shadow, stooping to avoid the jamb, came forward, into my room.

It was eight feet tall at the very least and its shoulders were four feet wide. Its flesh was grey, its lips were black, its eyes oozed yellow slime. It raised its arms; its limbs were clothed in rags. "I have waited so long, so very long," it said in a rough wet voice.

My mind had not been strong for weeks, and now I knew: I was mad, as mad as the man in black! My brain had conspired to make my contrivance real! I gripped my shoulder, squeezed it hard; it hurt. Yes, I was awake.

I smelled him then; he reeked of death; I clutched my throat. He said: "I love you. Now you will be mine."

"Foul vision, let me be!" I cried. My heart was wild now.

"I am no vision," he replied. "I am the one you love. For only one who loves me could have told my tale so well." He showed his cracked and jagged teeth; he issued forth a hiss. "The last remaining obstacle between us is no more," he said. "My creator is gone!"

"Your creator," I said.

"Doctor Berger," he said.

I gasped.

"Yes, Berger was your 'Frankenstein,'" he said. "He had no 'friend,' *he* gave me breath—but did not make me whole. And I, his flawed creation, took the breath from *him*."

"You killed him!" I said.

At this, he grinned. It was dreadful to see.

"He thought he had outwitted me," the harsh voice said. "As my creator, he had powers over me, and lured me to an island and stranded me there. But I have powers too. I knew the boat would someday come, and I was right. The three of them were no match for my strength and I hurled them into the sea."

"My husband!" I cried.

"Your husband and both of his friends!" said the monster. "I stole their spark, then sailed for shore and caught my creator unaware, before he could weave his spell." At this, he held out his massive hands and made a twisting thrust.

"You killed...them all," I said. "You killed...my love!"

"And took his spark. And now you must love *me*!"

"Love *you*!" I cried. "You killed my world!"

"I *am* that world," said the fiend in a rasping voice. "For I contain your husband, babes—"

"My babes!" I said.

"I contain all you love!" said the demon, grinning again. "And now you must come to me!"

I grabbed the lamp and held it out, praying with all my heart that the light would banish this apparition. No: it remained. I thrust the flame at the creature's wet, dull eyes. They widened with alarm; he sucked in breath; he shielded his face with his hand.

"You killed the greatest poet in the world!"

The fiend drew back, his arm still raised. In a voice akin to a wind on the moors, he said, "But I *contain* that poetry. I hold inside me all you love, and I love *you! * Love is the vital spark! It makes us whole! Without it we wither! Without it we die!"

My heart was filled with hatred and revenge, and yet this creature's words were so infused with pathos that, for an instant, my fury wavered. Sensing my conflict, he advanced again.

The stench of the grave rushed forth on his breath. "You gave me a second birth," he said. "A *noble* birth, in your book! You, who had never met me, understood!"

I gagged, I groaned; I pressed the lamp against his wrist. He shrieked with pain.

"Begone!" I cried.

"No, no!" he wailed. He tore his hair and gnashed his teeth. "You love me! You do! You must!"

Again I singed him; smelt his flesh; the dark room stank of death. "Begone!"

He howled, he fled, his feet like thunder on the stairs; the whole house shook.

I quickly went to Percy's room. The babe still slept, unharmed. I set the lamp beside his bed and sank to my knees, hands clasped.

The sea banged loudly on the shore, but otherwise, the house was still. My nervous disposition made me prone to vain imaginings; had all this been a dream? My heart beat on, then seemed to cease. I fell into a faint.

I awoke in the morning to screams: hysterical Claire. At once I ran to her and found her pale and gasping at the door that led to the terrace. She pointed down, and there, on the stones, was the source of her consternation.

A severed finger, purple, oozing putrifactive blood, and I too caught my breath. The finger was huge and could only belong to— I had not dreamt!

I locked the door and led poor Claire to the table. There we sat, trembling, hand in hand, as I told her my gruesome tale. A knock on the door made us frantic. To our vast relief it was good Trelawny—with grisly news.

Feet, hands, arms, legs in a state of mordant decay and of monstrous size had appeared on the strand overnight. They seemed to belong to different persons—to a race of giants, he said. In addition, the corpse of a Zurich physician had been discovered, his neck snapped so badly it lolled on his shoulders. A terrible shipwreck was suspected, as for days now the sea had been rough, but so far no fragments of any boat had been found.

I thought of the monster; heard once again his pathetic wail. "There was no wreck," I said to my noble friend, "unless it was the wreck of a tortured soul."

With a puzzled frown, Trelawny said, "I'm sorry, Mary, but I do not understand."

I flung both hands against my breast. "The vital spark," I said with tearful eyes, "the vital spark is *love*."

# TRANSFORMATIONS

The cold wind blew harder, cutting through Winston Boyle's coat as he hurried along the street. He clutched the manila folder tightly so nothing would blow away. Laughing bitterly to himself, he thought: *So it blows away. So the whole thing blows away, what does it matter?*

Forty-eight poems in sixteen years—only three lousy poems a year—and no matter how many times he revised them, he just couldn't get them right. He'd had acceptances from tiny magazines with names like *Sod* and *Bumblebee*, but what did it prove? Anyone with persistence enough could get a few poems published.

He opened the bookstore door and went inside. Thick warmth and rows of paperbacks: gothics, westerns, sagas, science fiction... The old jealousy stabbed him, the yearning to see his name on these shelves. At the age of eighteen, when he started to write, he'd been sure it would happen: his work would be heralded, book after book would be published and sold. But now at the age of thirty-four he had an aborted novel, a handful of feeble stories, and forty-eight poems that nobody cared about.

It was ten after nine, and except for the owner, the store was empty. A pudgy, short, balding man named—Barlow? Benbow?—he stared into space as he tore the wrappers off stacks of fresh magazines. Winston approached the counter, clearing his throat. "Good morning," he said. "I'd like to make a few copies."

The owner tapped the bottom edge of some magazines on the counter,

157

lining them up. "We just got a new machine last night," he said with a touch of annoyance, "so I'll have to show you how to work it."

He went to the rack near the wall, inserted the magazines, then padded across the rug. Winston followed him silently, vaguely embarrassed.

"Standard eight-and-a-half-by-eleven sheet," the owner said as he lifted the copier's black plastic top, "you place it between the elevens, put its edge against the frame... Here, give me a page."

Winston opened his folder, came out with the poem called "Seasons," and gave it to Barlow/Benbow, hoping he wouldn't read it.

Showing no interest in it at all, the owner slid the poem against the glass. "Right between the elevens, and touching the frame. Then we put the flap down"—he did so — "and...how many copies you want?"

"Six," Winston said.

"Six," Barlow/Benbow touched a key, and a red "06" appeared in a black rectangle. "To copy you press this button. This darkens and lightens and this enlarges, but I guess you won't need that. This orange thing lights if you need more paper. If it jams, this red one lights. Any trouble, just holler."

"Thanks," Winston said.

The owner went back to the counter; a customer came through the door. Winston glanced through his poems quickly and his stomach plunged. Not good enough. All that effort, years of it, and still—not good enough. He *knew* what he wanted to write, he *felt* what he wanted to write, why didn't it ever come out on paper the way it was born in his head! Why was he cursed with all this desire and so little talent?

He looked at the manuscript. Barely enough for a book, a book no one would publish. Well, no harm trying. No harm giving his malformed babies one more chance. He'd send six poems to six different publishers, asking if they'd like to see more. If they said no—time to pack it away.

He pushed the button. A light, a whirring sound, a click, and a copy dropped into the tray. It looked marvelous, sharp and clean. More flashes and clicks, and all six copies were done.

Much nicer than the old machine, Winston thought. So fast, and the print is so... Frowning, he stared at the page.

The poem he held in his hand was called "Transformations"—but he'd never *written* a poem called "Transformations." Barlow or Benbow had put the poem called "Seasons" in the machine. What the devil was going on?

Winston picked up the poem that lay on the glass and turned it over: "Weather."

"Weather"?

He looked at the copy, "Transformations," again and began to read. When he finished, his mind was reeling.

This *was* his poem—but not as he had written it, as he had *conceived* it! Astonished, he read it again—and almost wept, it was so fantastic. The choice of words, the rhythm, the imagery, all were excellent, and the title—absolutely right. Not "Seasons," but "Transformations"! Why hadn't *he* thought of that?

He looked at "Weather" now, and *this* was his poem too—a palid, feeble, first draft version of "Seasons." The machine had somehow extracted the good from his poem and amplified it.

As he placed the next page on the glass, the poem "Highway," his hands were shaking. He lowered the plastic flap, changed the quantity to "01" and pressed the button.

The light went on, the motor whirred, the copy slid into the tray. Trembling all over, Winston retrieved it: *"Destiny."*

He read it, scarcely daring to breathe: exultation and terror seized him. The poem was more than good, it was magical, the perfect blend of language and idea. And the poem under the flap was now called "Road"—and was pathetic.

A woman came into the store and began to browse. A man bought a paper. Behind the counter Barlow/Benbow unpacked books. With a tight throat, Winston lowered the flap on another poem, pressed the button…

The copy came out. Incredible! Stunned, he read all three poems again. Why, editors would *fight* to publish these! There was no time to lose! He would run all his poems through the copier! And his stories, too, and—

A sudden thought brought him up short: *If it works for me, why won't it work for others?* Well it will, he thought. Of *course* it will. He broke into a sweat.

Quickly he crossed the rug and went up to the counter. Barlow/Benbow looked at him. "Problems?"

"No, none at all, it's fine," Winston said. "As a matter of fact, it's the best I've ever seen. So good that I'd like to buy it."

Barlow/Benbow laughed.

"I mean it," Winston said, his pulse loud in his ears. "Mr.—"

"Bartle."

"Mr. Bartle, I really want to buy your machine."

Slapping a stock card into a book, Bartle shrugged. "It's not mine to sell," he said. "I lease it from a company downtown. I'll give you their name and number. I'm sure they'll be glad to sell you a copier just like this one here."

"I don't want a copier just *like* this one," Winston said, "I want *this* copier. Another one—the very same model—might not be exactly right."

"But they just brought this one in last night, I don't want to go to the trouble—"

The woman at the magazine rack turned and stared. Winston's sweat came freely now. "This copier's the one I want," he said in a confidential tone, and I'll tell you what. If you can arrange for me to buy it from the leasing firm, I'll pay you a thousand dollars."

Bartle sniffed, "You're kidding."

"I couldn't be more serious.

"You got yourself a deal."

"Terrific. And one more thing. Now that it's mine, I don't want anyone else to use it."

"I'll disconnect it right away," Bartle said with a grin.

When the men from Horn Duplicator came that afternoon, Winston could scarcely contain himself. He hovered around them anxiously as they rolled the copier through his door, maneuvered it into place in the cramped living room. He chafed impatiently as they showed him how to load it, change its fluids, clean it. He gave them each a hefty tip and they left all smiles. He closed the door behind them, took a deep breath, and hurried to the machine.

The "Quantity" space showed a squared-off "01" and the "Ready" indicator glowed bright green. Winston ran his hand over the panel; the plastic was cool and smooth. A thousand down and another grand to Bartle and he'd pulled it off; the machine was his! Making the payments would pose no problem at all. That novel he hadn't been able to sell? The copy machine would make it a winner, and soon he'd have *plenty* of money, tons, he could quit his lousy job—

But suppose, he thought with a sinking heart, suppose they had pulled a fast one. Suppose they had brought him a different copier, thinking he wouldn't notice. Quickly he lifted the plastic flap, put a poem face down on the glass.

The light flashed on, the motor whirred, the paper came out of the slot. He picked it up, hardly daring to look.

The poem, "Wings," was now called "Flight." Winston read it four times. So good, so incredibly good, and he thought: why can't *I* write like this! It irked him that a machine... But of course what he had here was no mere collection of nuts and bolts, what he had here was—what? It scared him to think about it.

An idea came to him then and he went to his desk, opened a drawer, pulled out a manila envelope: the poems he'd struggled with and finally decided were hopeless. What would happen if one of *them*...?

He lifted the flap and took out "Wings" (now "Birds," he noticed) and put in "Honey," a poem that over the years had given him fits. He pressed the copy button, watched intently as the paper squeezed into the tray.

The copy, "Sweets," was much better than "Honey"—but not really good. So he lifted the flap, replaced "Honey" with "Sweets," pressed again.

Now the poem was called "Desire"—and was perfect! My God, Winston thought, even the junk! Even the garbage that's been in my drawer all these years! I just run it through twice—or as many times as it takes to produce—the literature of genius!

Another thought struck him. He went to his bedroom.

His collection of butterflies, long abandoned, sat on the closet shelf. Suppose, he thought, as he picked up a tiger swallowtail—and a wing broke off. So much the better, he thought, and went back to the copy machine.

With quivering fingers, he placed the torn wing on the glass. Closed the flap, pressed the button. And there in the tray was a butterfly—lifeless, but whole.

Winston's heart skipped a beat. When he raised the black flap he found nothing but colorful dust.

He lifted the butterfly out of the tray. And what if I copy this *copy?* he thought. What then? He felt dizzy. Not yet, he thought. My poems, my stories... Not this, not yet.

Winston skipped dinner, drunk with delight. He was copying poem 38, "Hope," when the doorbell rang.

The tall man was dressed all in black: black coat, black shoes, black tie; his hair jet black, slicked back, and his eyes luminescent and probing. They made Winston cold in his bones.

"Mr. Boyle?" A voice smooth as steel. "Mr. Horn, Horn Duplicator. May I come in?"

Winston's heart felt sick as the man stepped inside. Closing the door against the night, he said with a nervous smile, "It's working fine. No problems at all."

Horn went to the copier. Winston followed. Horn ran his long fingers across the controls. "No problems," he said. "I'm so happy to hear that, Mr. Boyle. I'd be very disturbed if you'd hurt this machine."

"I'm extremly pleased with it." Winston said, and his mouth went suddenly dry.

The tall man said, "I'm sure you are," then glared with silver eyes. "But you see, Mr. Boyle, there's a complication."

"What kind of a complication?"

"This machine was never for sale."

Winston's heartbeat quickened. "But I signed an agreement. A thousand down and two hundred thirty-two dollars and sixty-nine cents a month for—"

"I'm fully aware of the terms," said Horn, his eyes glinting like knives. "It's our standard contract for the C-11 copier. But *this* is not a C-11, this copier's one of a kind. It's my personal machine."

"You're a writer," Winston said.

An icy grin. "No, Mr. Boyle, I'm... a businessman. This copier is used by an exclusive clientele that pays quite handsomely—some might even say excessively—for what it has to offer; to mediocre architects, uninspired scholars, over-the-hill composers—you'd recognize most of the names, I'm sure. They want and need this machine, Mr. Boyle. But not only that, *I* need this machine—for certain pet projects of my own."

The sweat was thick on Winston's nose. "But I signed a contract." he said.

"Quite true," said Horn. "A grievous error. Even an organization as old and efficient as ours makes mistakes every now and again—though rarely of this magnitude. Those responsible for the slip-up have been...taken care of."

His smile this time froze Winston's blood. "I signed a *contract*," he repeated.

"So you did, and a contract must be honored. But I have a proposition for you."

"Which is?"

"You return my machine and I'll give you a new one, free—and a lifetime supply of paper, toner, cartridges, free service—"

"I want *this* machine," Winston said, his neck slimy with sweat. "And you know why."

"Indeed I do." Those eyes: like a roadside animal's eyes in the night. "But there's more to my offer—much more. Give me those thirty-eight poems you've copied. I'll send them to a publisher I know, a user of this machine, and a year from now you'll be this country's most respected poet."

"How did you know about my poems?" Winston asked. "And how can you guarantee—?"

"I just know about things," said Horn. "Let's leave it at that. As for guarantees..." His laughter echoed hard in the tiny room. "I'm *famous* for my guarantees."

Voice breaking, Winston said, "You can actually promise—"

"Yes. You will be *revered,* in just one year."

Winston's pulse was thick and his thoughts were racing. "Well, " he said, "if you can guarantee that—and you really want the machine—you can guarantee more."

The silver eyes glared. "Such as?"

"That my poems will live forever—as long as poetry is read."

Horn stared. "You drive a hard bargain, Mr. Boyle."

Winston trembled all over. Noise flooded his ears. "Take it or leave it," he said.

Horn sneered. "Mr. Boyle—"

"I said take it or leave it!"

"I'll take it!" Horn snapped. Running his tongue across his teeth, he reached inside his coat and brought out a vellum scroll. "Kindly look this over," he said with a hiss.

Astounded, Winston read the contract.

"Well?"

"It's acceptable," Winston said.

Out of nowhere, a pen appeared in Horn's hand. "Then sign," he said.

Winston's arm was shaking. "Not yet," he said. "Not yet, I want another guarantee. Write into the contract, 'Winston Boyle shall be unharmed.'"

Horn's lips curled back; his bright eyes flashed; then his features relaxed and he grinned. "Tell you what," he said. "I'll do better than that. Not only will Winston Boyle be unharmed, he'll be able to write great poems all on his own, with no effort at all. He won't even *need* this machine."

Winston's temples were pounding, his cheeks were hot. To be able to write great poems *without* the machine! He'd rank with poetry's immortals! "Put it in the contract," he said.

"It's in," Horn said.

Winston looked at the paper again. The clause had been added.

"Deal?" Horn said.

"Deal," Winston replied in a whisper.

"Then sign."

With trembling fingers, Winston signed his name.

Horn took the contract, grinning. He tucked it away in his coat and extended his hand. "Let's shake."

Winston hesitated. But the contract was signed, a deal was a deal, even a deal with—

Horn's hand seared him, hot as flame. He jerked back in panic but the grip held, trapped him, flooded him with pain. "Deal," Horn said, pulling Winston down with incredible ease. With his free hand he lifted the copier's flap and pressed Winston's face on the glass.

A blinding flash and Winston screamed. The echo swallowed all light in his brain. He felt the glass slide forward, back, felt his essence flatten, stretch like melted cheese.

When his vision cleared, he saw himself next to Horn. No, not himself, but a duplicate Winston Boyle, a *revised* Winston Boyle; tall, handsome, with a charming smile—and a sheaf of familiar papers under his arm.

"Winston Boyle is a marvelous writer," said Horn, "but you, Mr. Byle, are not. You can barely construct a coherent sentence, I'm afraid."

"Mr. Byle?" Winston said. "Mr. *Byle?*" His head suddenly hurt; he felt weak.

Horn laughed. "How famous Winston Boyle will be! Your paths will never cross again, Mr. Byle, so take a good look—at the century's greatest poet!"

Winston blinked. In a flash the door opened and closed again and Horn, the machine, and the new Winston Boyle were gone.

Mr. *Byle?* Winston said to himself, and reached for his wallet.

His driver's license confirmed it: Winston Byle. His face in the photo: wrinkled, gray.

He collapsed on the couch, exhausted, and all words failed.

# A SPECIAL BREED

"That," said Dr. Charles Meade, "is a story for another time." He sat at the head of the dining room table, dapper in dark blue blazer and red bowtie. On his right sat Roger Pell, a rising star in the brokerage firm of Tilden & Cross. With his pink complexion and straw-colored hair Pell looked young for his age, which was thirty-six. "Dr. Meade, that's not fair," he said with feigned indignation. "You can't leave us hanging like that."

"I'm afraid that is just what I'm going to do," Meade said.

Lydia Dilworth, who sat on Meade's left, said, "All in favor of hearing the story raise their hands." Her husband, Bob, across the table, did, and so did Nicholas Hunt, beside her. "We won't leave this house till you tell us," Hunt said. He and Ardeth, his wife, had known Meade for almost a year. The others had never been here before. They were friends of the Hunts.

Smiling, Meade tilted his handsome gray head. "Fine with me if you stay," he said. "I have plenty of room and plenty of food, and I love company—especially such sophisticated company as this."

"Now Charles, flattery won't get you off the hook," Hunt said, his face bright and rosy with drink. "You know you can't tempt us like that and not follow through." He looked at the others. "A genius at telling stories—as we've already witnessed tonight—and he teases us like this just to build suspense."

Meade held up a hand. "No, no, that isn't it, the story's simply not appropriate right now. It contains what some might call material of an adult nature."

"Well, no adults here," said Lydia Dilworth, smiling with perfect teeth. "So I guess the story *will* have to wait for another time."

"Well I *can't* wait," said Ardeth Hunt. She was large and blond, with bright red lips. "Promise you'll tell us later, after the meal."

"Yes, promise us," Lydia Dilworth said.

The doctor grinned. "I make no promises. But maybe, if you all behave yourselves..."

"No problem with that," said Nicholas Hunt, placing his napkin on his head, and everyone laughed—except for Carrie Pell, who simply frowned.

The doctor said, "All right, now, everyone, eat up, I don't want leftovers. Henry?"

The old manservant approached the table, lifted the lid of the silver tureen and began to circulate. As Lydia Dilworth helped herself she said, "This dish is simply fabulous, I can't resist, though God only knows I should. What is it called?"

"It's called my secret recipe," the doctor said.

"Leeks, celery, potatoes, carrots... What herbs do you use? What gives it that special flavor?"

"That's the secret!" Meade said with a laugh.

The servant stopped at Ardeth Hunt. "Well, just a *little* more," she said.

"I want to see it disappear," said Dr. Meade, grinning again.

"I'll do my best to help," Bob Dilworth said.

Dessert was a glazed peach tart that everyone raved about. Coffee was followed by liqueurs. Nicholas Hunt was on his second amaretto when he said, "Now, Charles, your story."

The doctor was silent a moment, then said, "No, I don't think so."

"Charles," Ardeth Hunt complained, "come on, we're *dying* to hear it."

"I'm not so sure—"

"*Aren't* we dying to hear it, everyone?"

"I know *I* am," said Roger Pell.

"You must," Bob Dilworth said.

The doctor sighed. "Well then, if you insist. Henry?"

The manservant poured him another Drambuie, and he began.

"This incident happened long ago," he said, "near the end of my surgical residency. One late winter night they brought in a man whose car had hit a pole. No alcohol involved, just a patch of black ice, bad luck. The man was young, just twenty-two, in excellent health, with sandy hair and pale blue eyes, eyes I will never forget as long as I live. I remember his first name, too: it was Robert. Sadly, his thigh had been crushed and we had to remove his leg.

"I assisted with the procedure. The attending surgeon that night was one I had never worked with before: a man in his forties, small and trim, with a black moustache and a touch of gray at his temples. He was breezy in manner, but highly skilled. After the patient was in the recovery room and we'd cleaned ourselves up, the surgeon—whose name I will not divulge, although he departed this planet long ago—went to the O.R.'s refrigerator. He opened the door, and there was the leg we'd removed, wrapped in cloth. 'Shame to let it go to waste,' he said.

"I looked at him, startled. 'What do you mean?' I said.

"'Just think of all the starving people in this world,' he said. 'There is nothing wrong with the flesh of this leg, not a thing, no infection...'

"'But what kind of person would ever—?'

"'I would,' he said. 'And I have.'

"'You can't be serious,' I said.

"'Oh, but I am,' he said. 'Shall I prove it to you?'

"I thought he was jesting, of course. He was trying out one of the tricks that 'real' doctors play on residents. All of us rookies were forced to endure such foolishness, and I resented it. I decided to call his bluff and said, 'Yes, I want you to prove it to me.'

"Another surgical team had taken our place, and shortly I found myself in my senior colleague's car—a new Mercedes—with the leg in the trunk. I wondered how far he was going to carry this morbid joke, but didn't speak as he drove.

"Once inside his apartment, we went to the kitchen. A chopping block sat on the counter. My colleague unwrapped the mangled leg and centered it on the block. 'Stand back,' he said. Then, taking a cleaver out of a drawer, with one swift blow he chopped off the foot. The sound of the blade striking bone made me flinch—the reaction my colleague had hoped for, I feared. Adjusting the leg, he swung once more, and severed the knee from the calf, again displaying the expertise of the butcher, not the surgeon. Cynics would say there's no difference, of course; whatever, both blows had been perfect. He smiled at me. 'Step one,' he said.

"Next he sharpened a long thin butcher knife and went to work on the calf, skinning it first, then slicing the meat from the bone. Why had he bothered to chop off the foot and knee? I wondered, and had to conclude it was just for effect. 'Filet Ro-bare,' he said as he worked, giving a

French pronunciation to the name. 'Ah, Robert, you are so young, the very best.'

"With a gleam in his eye—the gleam of a maniac, I thought—he looked at me. 'You certainly understand,' he said, 'that surgeons are different, we live on a higher plane. How many people can cut into human flesh without a touch of squeamishness? Saw open a chest and fondle a bloodsoaked heart? Plunge their hands into hot intestines and search for a tumor? No, you and I, my friend, are a special breed. with special skills and special attitudes—and special tastes.'

"He placed the strips of calf in a roasting pan and soaked them in marinade, then wrapped the remains of the leg in old newspaper. 'Now for a drink,' he said.

"I needed one—badly. I'd seen a tremendous amount in my years of medical training and thought myself hardened, but this was beyond the pale. I considered bolting—just running out, but was sure that the moment I grabbed my coat and went for the door my colleague would start to laugh like mad at the monstrous prank he had pulled. I stayed put on the living room couch.

We drank. I looked at the artifacts on the walls—strange hangings and tools and masks—as he started to talk of tribal customs in varous parts of the world: New Guinea, Africa, the Philippines. He spoke of how the consumption of human flesh was acceptable practice in these tribes: sometimes they ate their enemies, sometimes flesh was part of religious ritual. All I said was, 'Cannibals.'

"He nodded, smiled, and went to the kitchen. Soon he returned, and sat again.

"'Words,' he said, 'can be prisons. The concepts we learn in our youth can impair our growth. Imagine how free we would be without the constraints of our culture. Imagine what we would see, what we would feel. What we would *taste*. Many tribes eat live beetles and grubs. We find this repulsive. Why? Because of our training—*indoctrination*. Our minds have been stunted and bent.'

"As he spoke, the aroma of roasting flesh filled the room. I had eaten practically nothing all day and was almost faint from hunger—or maybe fear. My heart was beating thickly in my neck as I realized: I liked the smell. I *loved* the smell.

"The surgeon left me once again and soon I was called to the kitchen. He'd dimmed the lights and the small kitchen table held place settings, candles, and glasses of dark red wine—and a platter. A platter with roasted potatoes, carrots, celery, leeks—and roasted meat.

"We sat. He raised his glass and said, 'To freedom of the mind.' I simply nodded, touching my glass to his. He drank, then picked up his knife and fork and sliced into his meat. Smiling at me, he ate.

"I pictured the lad who had owned this leg for twenty-two years, lying in pain in his hospital bed at this very moment, mourning his loss. Before he had been anesthetized, I'd held his hand and told him my name. 'I'm Robert,' he'd said with effort between clenched teeth. Something I was about to eat had *talked* to me.

"As I thought of this, my stomach turned—but gingerly I tried a piece of carrot. It had a delicious flavor, utterly unique. As I chewed, my colleague said, 'Now suppose that I told you the meat on your plate was lamb. Would you or would you not eat it with gusto?'

"I said that I would. 'Then…it's lamb,' he said.

"But—"

"'Maybe I pulled a switch when you weren't present,' the surgeon said. He was into his second strip of meat, and I hadn't touched my first. But then I steeled myself, trying to block the thought of the accident victim from rising again, and cut the flesh and brought it to my mouth. *It's lamb*, I told myself, *just lamb*. I took it in, and chewed.

"And it was wonderful: succulent, tender, its flavor was out of this world—but it wasn't the flavor of lamb.

"My colleague was holding his wine glass and smiling. 'So?' he said.

"'It's excellent,' I said. 'But what—?'

"'You might expect the meat of a human calf to be rather tough,' he said, 'but no, my secret marinade takes care of that.' He smiled again and tapped his head. 'Our thoughts determine everything,' he said.

"So I'd done it, had crossed the forbidden line. And now I continued to eat. Why not? After that first bite of flesh, could my crime increase? I ate, I drank. Oh yes, I drank, all right, and thought of the tribes that ate beetles and grubs—and human flesh. I thought of cultures where men took fifty wives, and told myself I was still Charles Meade, the same Charles Meade I had been a half hour ago.

"But of course I did not convince myself. That taste! Once you have eaten human flesh, you want it again and again, you crave it with every cell in your body. You feel that you can't live without its ineffable sweetness. Forever, I'm afraid.

"Now imagine my horror when, after a sleepless night, the very first person I met as I walked through the hospital's doors the next day was my senior colleague. 'Our patient is doing fine,' he said with a sunny smile. 'Are you going to see him now?' The thought of it made my stomach heave, and I'm sure that Robert, the person I'd dined upon, could not understand why the doctor who'd held his hand never once stopped by.

"A few weeks later I finished my training and never laid eyes on that surgeon again. But of course I never forgot his smiling face as he gave his toast: 'To freedom of the mind.' And ever since, whenever I did an amputation, I saw the severed limb as a source of food."

The doctor fell silent now, and nobody spoke. Roger Pell cleared his throat, and the sound was loud. After a sip of Drambuie, the doctor said, "So that's my story, the story you wanted to hear."

The quiet in the room was absolute. Then Nicholas Hunt, his complexion no longer rosy, said in a voice that was almost a whisper, "Good God."

"I gave you fair warning," the doctor said.

Bob Dilworth nodded, looking stunned, and Lydia Dilworth, ashen, said, "Did you ever—? You said that once you taste it—"

"No questions, please," the doctor said. He smiled, and then with a gleam in his eyes he said, "Would anyone care for another aperatif? Oh, by the way, the meat in the meal tonight was lamb."

"It wasn't lamb," said Carrie Pell outside in the freezing dark. She was walking with Roger to their car.

"Of course it was lamb," Roger said.

"It *wasn't*," Carrie said. "I know the taste of lamb, and—oh my God…"

"Carrie, don't be ridiculous, why would he ever—"

"For godsake, Roger, don't you see? You know what lamb tastes like. You know what its texture's like, and—"

"Carrie—"

"He set us up."

"No, no, we *made* him tell the story. We *begged* him to tell it."

"Because he set us up. He planned to tell it all along and teased us with it, fed us, fed us—" She finished her thought with a shudder.

Under the streetlight, tiny silver flakes of snow came down like soft pieces of glass. Roger was thinking the roads might be greasy when Carrie burst out with: "The man is a monster! That look in his eyes when he told us we'd eaten lamb! He's a beast!"

Roger blew frosty breath and said, "Come on, he doesn't even practice anymore, where would he even—?"

Clutching her stomach, Carrie said, "I'm sick."

"Carrie, no!" Roger said. "No, it's all in your mind!"

She held herself tighter, doubled up, and vomited hard on the gleaming snow.

172

His voice with a frantic edge to it now, Roger said, "*Please,* Carrie, it's in your *mind,* don't *do* this to yourself!"

She retched again, whimpering, sobbing, unable to speak.

# RECOVERY

I t's not easy to get a job when you're hurt like I've been hurt, Jerry tells me. I'm lucky to be here, he says. I know he's right, but sometimes, after hours and hours of this, I wonder. My feet ache so much and my arms are like lead, the pain in the back of my skull splinters into my eyes. And it gets so cold. My face is always stiff. You'd think they'd give us warmer clothes, but all we get is Dickies grays. Nobody complains, so I don't either. I mean, if the women can stand it, I can stand it. And like Jerry always says, it could be worse.

The fish never stop, pour out of the chute by the thousands. We cut off their heads and tails and fins, we slit their stomachs, scrape the guts out, send them on their way. At the end of the line, when they're washed down clean, the women pack them into cans. The packers amaze me, the way they rock back and forth like that, keeping time like that. The cans fill like magic under their fingers and go to the sealer, the steamer, then into the crates. We work as a unit, all of us, just parts of a big machine.

Nobody talks. Even on the van that picks us up in the dark and takes us home before sunrise, nobody talks. I can't get used to it. Before the accident I loved to talk. But it's hard now to form the words just right, it's hard for the others, too, so they don't even try. To me, that's wrong. I mean how can you ever get well if you don't even try? There's a pretty girl down at the end of the line, pale and blond, I've said hi to her several times in the van, but she never answers, just stares straight ahead like the rest. Jerry says that's how folks are on the night crew. He says I'll get used to it, but I wonder.

I don't know which plant I'm in, or how long I've been working here. Jerry told me, I think, but I forgot. You get hit on the head as bad as me and you're never the same again. For example, I can't smell the fish. Before I was hurt, I could smell the fish on the street when I drove through this section of town, and now, with my hands and arms all covered with scales and blood, I can't smell it at all. I can't seem to see right, either, the colors are weak and thin. Half of the time I feel like I'm underwater. Another thing, my appetite's messed up. I'm hungry—always hungry—but don't want to eat. The very thought of eating makes me sick.

The strangest thing of all, though, is—I don't bleed. You can't do this work without cutting yourself, but when I do, no blood. Same thing with the others, they don't bleed either. It's because of the cold, Jerry says. I'm not sure that makes sense.

I used to fix cars, but I don't remember it much. When I got out of high school I worked down to Miller's Garage, and then later I switched to Tolman's. Body work. A lot of it's done by feel: you run your hands over a panel to make sure it's smooth. I can't do that now cause my fingers are numb. I talked to Jerry about it, asked him if the feeling would come back, but he said he didn't know. He told me I'd have to talk to my doctor. But where is my doctor, when did I see him last?

And where's Lucy? We used to go out every night, almost. I think she came to see me in intensive care, but I can't remember. I miss her real bad. Sometimes I think the hunger I feel is for her, not for food. But Jerry says I can't see her yet, it's not time. When I ask when it will be time, he doesn't answer.

That's the way Jerry is. He takes good care of me, I can't complain, but he's strange. He's big, maybe six foot four, and over two hundred pounds, like a football player. He never smiles and he's always watching. Well, that's his job. It's a big one, making sure all goes right in this place. I wouldn't have the energy for that. Before the accident, I had lots of energy, used to stay up all weekend, but now my eyes keep closing—they're all gummy and smeary, I can't seem to get enough sleep. And my legs get so weak that sometimes I feel like I'm just going to fall on the cooncrete floor in the muck there and never get up. When I ask for a break, Jerry tells me I already had one. When I say that I can't remember it, he tells me that's part of my problem.

All I remember about that night is Lucy, her telling me not to drive—and me telling her I was fine. Just a couple of beers, I said, no problem at all. What a fool I was. If people could only go back and live one day over, just one. But what's done is done. I'm sure every one of us here would like to return to a certain day, but we have to keep going ahead. It was raining that night, I remember that, but the rest is all blurred. Just as well, I don't want to remember.

The fish keep coming. We cut off their heads, fins, tails. It's a river of silver slime we work in, elbow deep. There's a constant clanging, like somebody pounding steel plate with a maul, but I've never been able to tell where it's coming from. The lights are so bright, it's so cold, and my knees are killing me, my back...

The headache is awful, but Jerry won't give me a pill, not even an aspirin. Won't do any good, he says. No clocks in here, and when I ask Jerry the time he simply shrugs.

I keep plugging away, and my mind slips off: to hot summer days down on Lucia Beach, Sunday picnics at Alford Lake, snowmobiling on Appleton Ridge, or driving with Lucy. I miss her so much, and I dream that I'm with her again, then Jerry will poke me awake and I'm shocked by the glare of a thousand herring, the flood, no end of it. How many weeks has it been since I've seen the sun?

I look at the girl at the end of the line, the blonde. Her face is so tired, so pale. This isn't good for us and we know it, but Jerry's right, we're lucky to have the work. Even perfectly normal people can't get jobs these days, and we shouldn't complain. But I feel so terribly heavy.

I stare at the blonde, my eyes dull. A gray snow seems to be falling, covering everything, that's how tired I am. And then, for the first time ever, the blonde looks back. Her eyes are as pale as the scales on the fish, and are filled with such loss that my spine goes cold. I turn away and look at the herring, sick. Will this night never end?

A brown grease oozes out of the conveyer. Jerry tells me to clean it up. I leave my post and get some newspapers out of the pile, spread them over the floor, wipe the struts with a rag. When I look at the floor I am startled to see—myself, my picture, staring up.

The paper is dated July 13th, and the picture is on the front page. A hurt fills my throat and I choke. "Look," I say, and the word is an effort to form. It gets harder and harder to talk, which isn't right, I'm supposed to be getting better. "I was hurt...even worse...than...you told me. They thought...I was dead."

Jerry's eyes are flat. "Keep reading," he says.

I do. Killed instantly, it says, when I hit another car, one driven by Alice Meyers, twenty-two—who was also killed. I turn the page, but no photo of Alice Meyers.

The fish keep coming down the chute. They daze my eyes. Killed someone? Why hadn't they told me? But maybe the paper was wrong about that. It was wrong about me, and maybe Alice—

July 13th. "What…day…is it…now?" I ask, and my tongue feels huge.

For the first time ever, Jerry smiles. "I'll take over," he says. "You get back to your station."

I do, exhausted. shaking. Once I get my strength back and figure things out, I'll quit this place. I don't like Jerry, don't like him at all.

We are back in the van. Some are already sleeping. There are leaves on the trees and chicory blooms by the side of the road, but it's cold.

Thoughts jostle and burst in my mind. I feel sick to my stomach. I have to find out about Alice Meyers. How had the newspaper made such an awful mistake about my accident?

I am next to the window, and Jerry is sitting beside me. The driver moves off. As always, nobody speaks, they just stare straight ahead. I look out the window. Far to the east, across the bay, a blade of yellow morning cuts the sky.

It hurts my eyes. They fill with snow. I slump against the window and breathe on the glass.The glass is cold, but no moisture collects on its surface.

A bright flash of panic runs through me. I breathe on the glass once again; it stays perfectly clear. I look up at Jerry. His gaze is hard.

Across the aisle, the blonde young woman has turned to look at me—accusingly, I think. Her scar begins below her ear and travels along her cheek, rings her pale white throat. Her silver eyes are pools of longing and pain.

I turn to the window, chilled to the bone. We are passing the drugstore now. People wait in the dark for the Portland bus. And among them is Lucy, a travel bag by her side.

My heart contracts. I press my hands and face against the glass and cry her name, but no sound issues forth.

Jerry seizes my hair and pulls me down, away from the window. Once again I cry out and the words don't come, are nothing, less than air. The van slides silently past the drugstore. Nobody pays attention: it's like we don't even exist. Lucy's image grows faint at the edge of my eye.

I try to scream. My mouth is choked with fog, with silver scales.

Under Jerry's strong hands I sink into endless dawn.

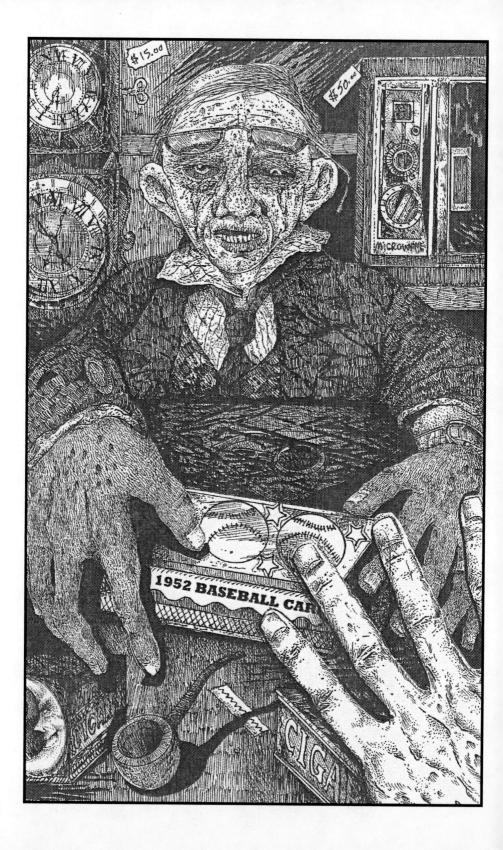

# IT'S IN THE CARDS

Cooper couldn't believe it: the pack was empty. He fished inside it with a frantic finger, cursing under his breath. Just this morning he'd promised himself to cut down, and another whole pack was gone.

Well today had been rough, real rough. And on top of it all, this heat! On Monday he'd quit these filthy things, no ifs, no ands, no buts. *No butts,* he thought with a little sniff, then started to cough again. He tossed the empty pack at the green wire basket strapped to the lamppost. It hit the side of the basket and fell to the gutter. He left it there.

Up ahead, past the jewelry store, he saw what he needed: "Small's Novelties: Tobacco, Candy, Sundries." He hurried up to the grimy entrance and opened the cracked glass door.

The air in the cramped gray space was as stale as old fur; his lungs felt squeezed. Monday he'd stop cold turkey, he told himself. Tony Nason had done it, and anything *that* jerk had done couldn't be *too* hard.

Sweat blossomed on Cooper's face as he thought: God, why don't they open a window in here?

He looked around. The place didn't *have* any windows, that's why—and what a mess! How could anyone work in such chaos? The counters were piled with papers and boxes. In the wooden display cases, trinkets, souvenirs, tee shirts and magic tricks crowded against the dull hazy glass as if trying their best to escape. Pennants hung from the ceiling beside dusty baskets and silver balloons with ears. The shelves lining the walls overflowed with cigars, tobacco, pipes...

"Can I help you?"

The man's head floated in all the junk like one of the balloons. Had it been there all along?

"Marlboros, hard pack," Cooper said.

The man—short, squat, thick glasses and shiny scalp—reached under the counter without even looking and brought out the cigarettes. He laid a matchbook on the pack. "Will that be all?"

How Cooper despised that question. If he'd *wanted* more, he'd have *asked* for more. How much did you have to buy before you weren't assailed with that stupid *Will that be all?*

He paid. The man rang up the sale on a machine that looked like it belonged in the Smithsonian. "Thanks," Cooper mumbled, dropping his change in his pocket. Dying for air, he turned to go, sweat beading his forehead, and tore the red strip off the cellophane sealing the pack. As his eyes hit the junk on the counter, he suddenly stopped.

The object of his fascination sat between boxes of Rollos and Milky Ways. Come on, he thought, this is some kind of joke.

For one thing, the box was in such good shape. It was covered with dust, but it looked so *new.* Then he understood: a reproduction, an imitation, a *fake.* Sticking the Marlboro pack in his shirt he smiled and said, "That's something."

The face of the man at the counter was slack, impassive. "What?"

"These baseball cards. They put out the whole thing like that? The whole box?"

The man shook his head, his expression still bland. "I don't understand," he said.

"These '1952' baseball cards," Cooper said with an edge to his voice. "Yes?"

"They're reproductions, right?"

The short man, looking quite uncomfortable, slowly shook his head no. Behind his thick glasses, his eyes were opaque.

Cooper frowned." They're *not* reproductions?" he said. "And they're for sale?"

"Of course," the short man said with a shrug. His face was practically colorless now.

Cooper's sweat was copious. "How...how much do they cost?"

"It's right on the box. Five cents a pack."

Five cents a pack! Cooper damn near laughed. For 1952 baseball cards? My God, there might be a Mickey Mantle in there. That card alone would be worth...he wasn't sure just how much, but he knew it was...*thousands.* "I'd...like to buy them," he said, his mouth suddenly dry. "I mean all of them, all you've got."

The proprietor's eyebrows went up. He scurried around the counter to where the cards sat. "No, no," he said, "they're old, the gum's gone stale, it's hard as a rock."

Cooper smiled. "I don't really care," he said, "I just want the cards, not the gum. For my boy. He's eight. He loves the things, he has shoe-boxes full."

The short man's pate was sheened with sweat. "The cards are probably stained," he said. "Sitting there all these years, the gum has bled into them. Stuck to them, maybe."

"Ten cents a pack," Cooper said, reaching into his pocket.

The man shook his head. "I've got new ones," he said. "I'll sell you those—good price. How can your boy eat that stale old gum? You'd actually have him put something like that in his mouth?"

What was this guy, some kind of moron? "Look, you said they're for sale. Did you say they're for sale?"

The man's Adam's apple bulged. "Yes."

"So?"

Another sick smile. "It's not that simple." He wet his lips; they gleamed in the murky light. "I'll tell you what. I'll give you a whole box of new ones, half price."

"I don't *want* the new ones, my kid *has* the new ones, what I want is *these*," Cooper said as he jerked his thumb at the box. "I want them *all.*"

The proprietor's eyebrows went up. "Just buy one pack," he said. "Okay? If you like it, come back and buy more."

"I can open it here and tell you right now if I like it," Cooper said.

The man threw his hands up. "No, no, you can't!" he said. "If you're going to do that, I just can't sell. You have to take the cards home and open them there—inside your house."

Insane. Not a moron, insane, Cooper thought. "Okay, sell me just one pack. If I like it, I'll come back for more."

The man nodded, ashen. His hands were shaking hard as he picked up the cards. "Five cents," he said. "And remember—don't open them till you get home. Till you get in the house."

Cooper laughed to himself and handed the man a nickel. "Thanks," he said. "I'll be back."

"I know," the man said with a nod.

Compared to the store, the street was as fresh as an ocean breeze. What a lunatic, Cooper thought breaking into a grin. But okay, he'd play the game. If he had to buy the cards one pack at a time, one day at a time, well, that's what he'd do. As he looked at the package a thrill went through him. *Don't open them till you get home—till you get in the house.* Okay, a deal's a deal. He took out one of his cigarettes, lit it, inhaled. My God but it tasted good!

In his driveway he just couldn't wait any longer. He turned off the car, took the pack of cards out of his pocket, unfolded the waxy bright wrapper. A face appeared, and a name.

Harold "Peewee" Reese, Brooklyn Dodgers—in perfect condition. A rush of excitement hit him. He turned the card over. Number 333. High numbers were rare, he'd read that somewhere. He fanned out the other cards. Dick Gernert, Joe Adcock, Cal Abrams and Ewell "The Buggywhip" Blackwell, looking as if they had just been printed. The flat pink pieces of gum were hard as glass, and shattered in his hand.

That nut owned a goldmine! At least forty packs of these things, and who *knew* what was buried there? A Willie Mays? A Satchel Paige? He stuck a small shard of the gum in his mouth. The old flavor, still there, and he laughed. He'd pulled off some deals in his lifetime, but this was absurd. Wait'll Jackie saw these.

He got out of the car. The light was quickly leaving the sky, and he checked his watch. Good God, already that late? He hoped Sue wouldn't be mad.

She stood at the kitchen sink with her back turned toward him. "Sue, you just won't believe this," he said.

She rinsed the bowl and turned to him, and he caught his breath. "Sue..."

She looked like she'd aged twenty years. Her face was lined, her eyes were red, and her hair...it was almost completely gray! Frowning, Cooper stepped forward and gave her a tentative kiss. Her lips were cold—and smelled of booze. "I won't believe *what?*" she said.

"It can wait," Cooper said. "You look like you've had a rough day."

Brushing her hair back sharply, she said, "That's just what I needed to hear."

Whoa, Cooper thought. What *is* this? "Where's Jackie?" he asked.

"Where the hell do you think?"

"What's *that* supposed to mean?"

She glared. "What's the matter with you tonight?"

"What's the matter with *me?*"

She sighed disgustedly and turned to the sink again. "Hint," she said. "Try his room."

"Thanks a lot," Cooper said.

He went down the hallway. Jesus, something was drastically wrong here. Sue *drinking?* She looked so *bad.* Whatever the trouble was, they'd have to get it out in the open—fast.

He stopped at the door to his son's room. "Jackie? You in there?"

No answer. He knocked. "Jackie, wait'll you see what I got."

Dead quiet. He turned the knob.

The door came open. Someone was there in the failing light, somebody in a wheelchair, head slumped to the side. Cooper's throat seized up. His voice was a whisper. "Jackie!"

The child responded by twisting his neck and rolling his hooded eyes. Drool escaped from his lips, joined the pool on the wheelchair's tray.

The scar on Jackie's head began at the hairline, crossed the forehead, dropped down beside his left eye and encircled his jaw. Cooper tried to speak again, but no words came out. The baseball cards blazed in his hand.

He stumbled out of the room and made his way down the hall. "I'll be back," he told Sue as he crossed through the kitchen.

"Be back! Where the hell are you going, we're ready to eat!"

"I'll explain it all later," Cooper said, and hurried out of the house.

Small's Novelties was closed. Cooper banged on the glass, his heart pounding fiercely. "Come on," he said between clenched teeth. "*Come on!*"

Feeble light, then the shade on the door was pulled aside, revealing the short man's face. The door came open and Cooper stepped into the store.

The man closed the door and locked it. He stared at Cooper and said, "You asked for them. I tried to convince you not to buy, but—"

Cooper grabbed the man's arm. "What the hell have you done?" he said.

The man stared at him coldly. "Let go of me. *Now,*" he said.

Cooper did. He was shaking all over. "My Jackie," he said in a whisper. "My son."

"An accident," the short man said. "Your wife was at fault. I had nothing to do with that. I had nothing to do with any of this," he said with a sweep of his arm. "It's all in the cards."

"What the hell are you talking about?"

"The cards," the man said in an urgent tone. "You couldn't wait till you got in the house, could you? Nobody can. *I* couldn't."

"And if I had waited?"

"It wouldn't have been as bad," the man said, and then, with his eyebrows raised: "You kept all the cards, I hope, you didn't destroy them."

"Here," Cooper said, reaching into his shirt. "Goddamn it, *here.*"

The bulb on the cord overhead flickered twice as the man took the cards. "Ewell Blackwell," he said. "Joe Adcock. It could've been worse. Much worse."

"How?" Cooper said.

"You don't want to know," the man said, looking up. "And you wanted to buy them all!"

Cooper took a deep breath. The room was incredibly hot and close; sweat poured down his temples and cheeks. "My son," he said.

"You can make him well," the short man said, "if you're willing to play the game."

"Game?" Cooper said. "What game?"

The man's thick glasses caught the light. "With the baseball cards. We flip."

It's a dream, Cooper thought. It's a nightmare, it isn't real.

"Oh, it's real, all right," the proprietor said. "If we win, your son's okay."

Thoughts collided in Cooper's mind. He said, "If *we* win?"

"Yes, we're on the same team—in a way. It's a matter of odds."

"And what if we lose?"

"Things stay like they are—for both of us."

Cooper wiped at the sweat on his forehead.

"What *is* this place?"

"Good question. I wish I had an answer, but I don't."

"How the hell did you get here, then?"

The proprietor sniffed. "An even better question. Everything's going along just fine, we think, then suddenly: How did I get here? How did I end up a banker, a plumber, a prostitute?" He looked up sharply. "I got here because of greed. And you?"

"I ran out of cigarettes," Cooper said. "I came in to buy some. That's all."

The proprietor shook his head. "Oh no, my friend, nobody comes here by accident. The Walker project? The Cunningham merger?"

Cooper had made a less than legitimate killing on both those deals. "How the hell do you know—?"

"Like I told you, it's all in the cards. Are you ready to play?"

Cooper swallowed. He thought of the wheelchair, of Jackie, Sue. "I'm ready," he said.

"Okay," the proprietor said, "then here's how it works. We get seven cards each and take turns flipping. If both cards land the same side up, we earn a point. Four points and we win the game. You hold the cards like this—the long way, and snap your wrist backwards."

"I've done it a million times."

"I know," the man said with a smile. He went to the counter and rummaged around in some junk, then came back with a handful of different cards. "I'm the dealer," he said. "I give you one card at a time, and the cards are...weighted."

Cooper frowned at him. "Weighted?"

"Your players have all been the victims of rather bad luck, and are likely to land face down. Mine, however, are superstars, and are weighted the opposite way." His smile was bitter. "That's how it works. You aren't the first one to play me, of course, I've been here for quite some time." He looked at the cards in his hand for a second, then thrust one at Cooper, who took it and said, "Eddie Waitkus."

The short man repeated the name. "Yes, shot in a hotel room in Chicago, and never quite right again. Flip."

Cooper did. The card caught the light from the overhead bulb as it spun. It landed on the dark wood floor—face down.

The short man sniffed. "As always," he said. "All right, my turn."

The man tossed his card, a Whitey Ford, and it also fell face down. The man's eyebrows shot up. "Whitey Ford face down!" he said. "I don't believe it! Fantastic! We've got a point! Good, good, here's your next one, Herb Score, a great pitcher—felled by a line drive right in the face and never regained his form. Wait, I go first this time."

His Stan "The Man" Musial landed face up. Cooper flipped and Score's face hit the floor.

"As expected," the short man said. "Three more like that and we're finished."

Bob Feller vs. Pete Reiser ("Beaned, ran into walls"), Warren Spahn vs. Bobby Shantz ("Walt Masterson broke his wrist with a fastball"), were both—incredibly—matches.

"Three to one," the short man said, "this has never happened before." He was sweating profusely now. He looked at the light bulb a moment, then said, "I go first this time," and flipped a Yogi Berra—right side up. He handed Cooper a card and said, "Curt Simmons. Cut off his toe with a power mower. It ruined his windup, his stride."

Cooper flipped. Simmons landed face down.

Licking his lips, the short man said, "Three to two," and gave Cooper another card.

Another mismatch. "Even up," the proprietor said, his voice thick with despair. "Even up, this is it, our last shot. I go first again." He looked at his card. "Oh my God," he said. "Ted Williams." He swallowed hard, flipped; the card landed face up. "Of course," he said. "What else?"

With a sigh he gave Cooper his final card. "Oh no," he said. It was almost a moan. "Howie Fox. Shot to death in a Texas bar."

Cooper stared at the ballplayer's rugged grim face. He cupped the card in his palm, took a breath and extended his arm. *Jackie, Jackie, Jackie,* he thought, and flipped. The card spun over and over and fell, struck the floor on its edge, balanced, tipped—and came down face up.

Cooper couldn't believe his eyes.

The short man punched the air with his stubby arms. "We won!" he cried. "We won! I'm free!"

"My son—"

"Is fine. Your wife is fine."

"Thank God," Cooper said, drenched with sweat.

The short man fished in his pocket. "Okay, here's the key," he said.

"Key?" Cooper said. "To what?"

"The door, of course."

"Well what would I want with that?"

The man stared at him hard. "Lock up every night. To leave the place open will mean your death." He went to the wall, took a suit jacket down, slipped it on. "When people ask about the cards, you have to discourage them from buying. If you don't, you won't get a game. Only the ones who persist—who *must* have them—deserve them. I really don't have to explain, you'll see how it works soon enough." He shook his bald head, sighing deeply. "My twenty-fourth game. Twenty-three losses in—God, what year is this? Well"—he nodded—"goodbye," and he went through the door, closing it hard behind him.

Cooper ran after him. "Hey! Wait a minute!"

He opened the door. Blinding light, sheer white, and heat— He staggered back.

The man said, "These are for sale?"

"They're for sale," Cooper said, "but you don't want to buy them."

"Oh," the man grinned, "but I do."

Cooper started to sweat. Closing time, and a good one, a live one: the guy had maneuvered his partner out of the firm last week and the partner had suffered a heart attack.

"These cards are too old," Cooper said with a shrug. "I meant to get rid of them years ago."

"I'll be glad to dispose of them for you," the man said, still smiling.

"No, no," Cooper said, "the gum's stale, it's as hard as a rock."

"I don't care about that. What I want is the cards."

"But somebody might eat the gum. It might make them sick."

"I'll open the cards right here and throw out the gum."

"No, you can't do that. I can't let you do that."

"Why not?"

"I just can't."

The man shrugged and said, "Well, seems crazy to me, but whatever you say." He reached in his pocket and pulled out his business card. "If you change your mind, I'm interested," he said, and turned away.

*No!* Cooper screamed in his head as he watched the man leave. *No, please, come back!* But the door banged shut.

Another one gone. Another one! He'd only had five games in—God, how long?

He looked at the box of cards on the counter and wondered what year this was. He thought of a dark-haired woman, a boy who loved baseball. How old were they now, where were they, and what were they doing?

Licking his lips and wiping the sweat from the top of his shiny bald head, Cooper pushed up his glasses and hurried to lock the door.

# SEED

She'd hated this place four months ago, and today she hated it even more. At least the air had been clear and bright that other time, but today the sky was a dark gray lid on the dripping trees as she steered her little Ford down the rutted lane.

It was late in her workday, and ground fog was snaking its way through the trunks of the trees. What a spot. Even in summer, in bright dry weather, it had a dank desolate feeling. Kathy was hoping this visit would go smoothly, quickly, and she could get out of here fast, before the fog thickened. She wouldn't go back to the office, an hour away, she'd head straight home, but even her home was a forty-five minute drive—a hazardous trip in the fog, especially with so many deer on the roads in the fall.

It was early November, and daylight died quickly this time of the year, especially on overcast gloomy days, and the woods on both sides of the lane were already dark. The trees were spruce and pine and fir, all evergreens, and their needles were wet and black. Kathy wondered again: Why would anyone choose to live all the way back in these woods? Because they were misfits, that had to be it. They hated humanity, wanted to hide.

The Ford bumped along, splashing into a puddle. The lane had been spongy in spots in the summer and now it was worse, and Kathy feared getting stuck. If it happened, she'd use her cell phone, but who knew how long it would take Triple A to get out here. She pictured herself all alone on this lane in the dark, just waiting, surrounded by foxes and bobcats and bears.

The car hit more water but kept on going, and soon it came to the halfway point: the cemetery, a family plot with no more than a dozen stones, each of them tilted and streaked with lichen and moss. No kin of Mrs. Flint were buried here, she'd only moved to Maine two years ago. Probably nobody knew anymore who these dead people were.

Now a stand of stark trees, their branches barren, their bark gone gray, as if death had seeped out of the graveyard and killed their roots. Kathy shuddered and reached for the dashboard and turned up the heat.

Pretty soon the big snows would come. There had already been a couple of dustings, both of which had depressed her. She liked her job and her colleagues okay, but the weather in Maine…it was just so different from back in New Jersey, where she'd grown up. The spring came so terribly slowly, the summer—while often quite lovely—was painfully short, the winter was long and hard. Four years of this and she hadn't adapted, and maybe now that she'd split with Paul, it was time for another change. A change of climate, a change of work—a better job where she wasn't constantly coaxing people to do what was in their best interests.

The car finally left the dark woods and entered a clearing. Kathy could just about see the old trailer ahead in the gathering fog. It sat at the end of the narrow path that led through a field on the right and a dense stand of brush on the left. She parked by the field, grabbed her briefcase and locked her doors. Silly habit, she thought. City habit. Who would mess with her car out here? A moose? A crow gave a mocking croak as she started to walk.

Kathy thought about Mrs. Flint, who had gotten the wrong idea last time and had not been nice. She'd insisted that Kathy was trying to "put her away." A common misconception that Kathy encountered time and again in the course of her work. She always explained that her agency's goal was just the opposite of that: it tried to increase people's independence, teach them the skills they needed to stay in their homes.

Mrs. Flint, though, had not seemed to grasp this. "I ain't goin' into no nursin' home no matter what," she'd said. "I take care of myself real good, and if I have trouble, my boy helps me out."

"I work for a home health agency," Kathy had said, "not a nursing home. If you have any problems with cooking or cleaning or personal care, our staff will come out here and help you."

"I'm doin' okay," Mrs. Flint had said. "Me and my boy, we can handle what comes along."

Four months had gone by since she'd made that pronouncement, and during those months she had lost her right foot and her vision had badly declined. Dr. Cunningham's nurse, Jane, was very concerned. Mrs. Flint had been losing weight for weeks, and, failing to see the hallway threshold, she'd fallen and badly bruised her hip. "Lucky she didn't break it," Jane said as she re-referred. "And once the air turns cool she'll crank up her wood-burning stove again. She claims her son will feed it, but I'd feel better if somebody went there and checked things out. Nobody here knows her son. And this weight loss, I don't think she's eating right. Not that she ever did, of course."

So Kathy had called Mrs. Flint again, but again the old woman insisted she didn't need help. "I'm doin' good. They cut that gangrene off and my leg healed up right quick."

This wasn't what Jane had told her, but Kathy said, "I'm glad to hear that, Mrs. Flint. And what about doing things around the house, you have any problems with that?"

"Oh no, no, no, I'm doin' fine. I got my boy to help, you know, so I'm in good shape."

"So you don't want another visit from me?"

"Can't see how it would help."

"Okay then, I won't come out, but if you ever feel you need anything, don't hesitate to call. You still have my card?"

"Yep, got it right here by the phone."

"I mean it now, don't hesitate. And I'll call you again in a couple of weeks just to check on things."

"You don't need to do that."

"I'm sure that your doctor will want me to."

The old lady grumbled "Doctors," but said no more.

"Nice talking to you again," Kathy said. "Glad to hear that you're doing so well."

"Uh-huh," Mrs. Flint said, and then she hung up.

Kathy had called Dr. Cunningham's nurse again: "She insists she's okay. She won't see me."

"Some folks are incredibly stubborn," Jane said with exasperation. "Well maybe that's why they live so long. The most you can do with that type of person is plant a few seeds, get them thinking about their options. The next time she comes for a checkup, I'll try to convince her it's in her best interest to meet with you. Her next appointment is two weeks away, however."

But then, only three days later, Kathy's cell phone rang as she drove along Wilton Road.

"Hello, this Kathy—the social worker?"

"Mrs. Flint?"

"That's right. Now listen, I changed my mind, I want you to see me again."

Kathy smiled to herself as she thought, *Well what do you know, the seeds that I planted have started to sprout.* "Of course, Mrs. Flint, I'd be glad to," she said. "I'm on the road today and can stop by later this afternoon if that's convenient." *Strike while the iron is hot.*

"Yeah, that'll be fine, I'll be here."

"After four? Between four and four thirty?"

"That's good."

"See you then," Kathy said.

And now, as she walked down the muddy path to the trailer, she wondered what prompted the old woman's call. Something probably pretty drastic. She had to be using her woodstove now, and maybe she'd burned herself. Or maybe she'd fallen again or was finding it hard to get dressed.

Kathy came to the end of the path, and the scruffy front yard looked the same as it had last time, in the summer. No, actually even worse, with the grass all tangled and yellow now. It was cluttered with all kinds of stuff: an old washing machine, an outboard motor, a banged-up bathtub, aluminum lawn chairs without any webbing, a bike with no wheels...

The trailer was blue, a lot of it chipped and faded to gray, and a window a few feet away on the left was broken and covered with plastic sheeting. The pebbled aluminum door's two hinges were rusty and hanging loose. As Kathy mounted the wooden steps—they were splintered and shaky—she thought, *My God but it must be cold in here in the winter.* She knocked three times.

"Come in!" yelled Mrs. Flint's raspy voice, and Kathy worked the latch.

The door stuttered open. She crossed the threshhold and entered the miniscule living room/dining room/kitchen. No lamps were on—indeed, there appeared to be no lamps—and all was dim and gray. When she closed the door behind her, it banished half the light.

As before, the place was a mess; each horizontal surface overflowed. The sink on Kathy's right was filled with dishes and so was the counter; the centrally located table was covered with papers and boxes and cans. The ratty upholstered chair near the hallway, over on the left, was heaped with matted clothes that looked filthy and wet. The room had a sour musty smell and Kathy's throat closed off.

Mrs. Flint sat just a few feet away in front of the daybed that served

194

as her couch. Last time, she'd sat on that bed, but now she was in a wheel-chair. The cuffs of her dirty gray pants were turned up and Kathy's eyes instantly went to the stump: it was puckered and raw, and the flesh above it was dark.

"Yeah, ain't it a beauty?" said Mrs. Flint. "My boy coulda done as good a job with his axe!"

Kathy's only response to this was to clear her throat.

One side of the old woman's face was in shadow; the other side caught some light from the window behind her head. It looked sunken and gaunt. She certainly *had* lost weight since back in the summer. With a curt little nod at Kathy she said, "Take a load off your feet."

Except for the daybed, rumpled and stained, there was only one place to sit—on one of the two wooden chairs at the littered table. That's where Kathy had sat last time, but now both chairs were piled with newspapers. What should she do, should she move them? If so, move them where? She was ready to ask, when Mrs. Flint said, "Just set them papers on the floor."

Kathy did it—the papers felt sticky and damp—and she sat. Contrary to her expectations, the wood-burning stove was not in use and the seat of the chair was cold. A deep shiver went through her.

"Be winter real soon," said Mrs. Flint, "but I'm all set. My Bucky been cuttin' wood like you wouldn't believe. Does it all with his axe, no chainsaw, he hates the noise, and by God but that boy can chop! We already got five cord out there, plenty enough for a tiny place like this."

"That's good," Kathy said.

"And I handle my stove just fine."

Kathy reached in her briefcase and took out her pad. No space on the table, none at all, so she set the pad on her knees.

"Huh, already startin' to write," said Mrs. Flint. "I musta said somethin' important."

"I have a few questions to ask," Kathy said. "If I don't write the answers down, I'll forget them."

"Yeah, questions," the old lady said. "Always questions. About how I'm eatin', right?"

"Well, actually, yes, I *would* like to know about that."

"I'm eatin' fine."

"I'm glad to hear that. Sometimes people with missing teeth have problems meeting nutritional needs."

"Not me, I eat what I want."

Kathy wrote on her pad, and Mrs. Flint said, "You don't believe me."

"Of course I do," Kathy said. "But I want you to know that our agency helps people get false teeth."

"False teeth," the old woman said with a sniff. "Hell, I already got 'em. They're in that drawer over there, ain't a damn bit of good."

"Would you like to try—"

"New ones? Forget it. No set of choppers has ever done squat for me."

Kathy wrote on her pad, then looked up. "The last time I came, I asked you about your hearing—"

"And it ain't no better. But hearin' aids won't help, they're layin' in the drawer alongside the teeth." She frowned. "I told you that last time."

"That's right, you did."

"And you wrote it down."

"Yes—"

The old woman narrowed her eyes. "Look, get this straight. Not you or nobody else gonna put me away."

With a sigh Kathy said, "Mrs. Flint, we discussed this the last time I came. I told you that's not what I'm here for."

"I know what you told me, that don't mean it's true." Then slapping her truncated leg she said, "See, this is what they do. They chop off pieces bit by bit till you have to go into a home."

Kathy said, "Mrs. Flint, you had gangrene—"

A sudden sharp groan of metal and Kathy jumped. The door had come open. She turned and looked over her shoulder.

A shape filled the doorway, hulking and huge—a man with his face in shadow. She saw his coveralls, his boots. His mammoth hands hung loosely at his sides. Mrs. Flint had a scowl on her face as she said, "You done?"

The man didn't speak for a couple of seconds then said, "Not yet." His speech was low, rough, indistinct.

"What's takin' you so long?"

"It's bigger."

"What is? The car?"

"Uh-huh."

"Well how much longer?"

"Not too much." The syllables were muffled, hard to understand.

"You been at it for two days now."

"Don't holler, Mumma."

"I ain't hollerin', I'm just askin'. It's gettin' dark, and you have to hurry."

"I'm thirsty, Mumma."

"Well go get a drink then, don't dawdle."

The man had to duck to get into the room. He lumbered across the floor and the whole place shook. At the kitchen sink he filled a glass, gulped the water noisily down. Then wiping his mouth with the back of his hand he turned and looked at Kathy.

And now in the light from the open door, she could see his face. It was frightening—broad and flat, its eyes set wide apart and one of them halfway closed. A patchy beard, thick purple lips. A grunting sound escaped those lips and Kathy realized: *Nobody knows I'm here.* The call from Mrs. Flint had come while she was on the road, nothing was on her calendar at work... She felt a sudden stab of fear, and wanted to grab her things and flee this place—right now.

She needed to call the office and let them know where she was, but she'd left her cell phone back in the car, on the passenger seat. How stupid! Taking a breath she said, "Mrs. Flint, may I use your phone?"

The old lady shook her head. "The phone quit workin'. Right after I called you, it just went dead."

Now the man at the sink moved forward, in Kathy's direction. Another sharp jolt of fear and her throat seized up. Then he walked on by and went to the doorway. He stood there a minute, facing the room, then turned and left and closed the door, killing the light.

"That's Bucky," said Mrs. Flint. "My boy."

Kathy just nodded, her heartbeat loud in her ears.

Mrs. Flint thrust her chin out. "Some think he's an ugly boy. Do *you* think he's ugly?"

*He's one of the ugliest people I've ever seen,* Kathy wanted to say. "Oh...no," she said.

"That's good," said Mrs. Flint, "but some people do. Been sayin' it all his life, what an ugly boy. They said it in Kansas, they said it in Texas. They said he was dumb, too, just 'cause he couldn't learn to read. But Bucky ain't dumb, he's far from dumb. As a matter of fact, he's a kinda mechanical genius. I don't care what it is, you give that boy somethin' to fix, he'll fix it. A stove, a clock, a car, you name it. Our truck, we got it for almost nothin' because it was so stove up, but Bucky fixed it. Runs like it just come outta the plant."

"That's wonderful," Kathy said.

"They said he was dumb, but he showed *them.* And strong? That boy can lift the front of a car off the ground."

"That's really something."

"You bet it is. He carries two eighty pound bags of cement at one time like nothin', like feather pillows."

"Amazing," said Kathy.

She looked at the pad on her knees and could barely make out what she'd written, the room was so dim. No lamps, the only source of electric light a ceiling fixture with a naked bulb. How dark did it have to get in here before Mrs. Flint would pull that chain? How cold did it have to get before she would light her stove?

Chilled to the bone, Kathy took a deep breath. She thought of the cell phone back in her car, she thought of her bright warm apartment. Swallowing hard she said, "So how can I help you, Mrs. Flint?"

The old woman puckered her toothless mouth. "You can't get me more money, right?"

"That's right, we discussed that before. You already get all the benefits you're entitled to."

"Well then you can't help me, you can't help at all."

Kathy shrugged. "So then why did you ask me to come here again?"

"I knew you would come anyway."

"What?"

"I knew you'd be back. People like you, you always come back, that's your job."

"Well no," Kathy said. "I mean if you didn't want me—"

"Oh yes, you'd be back. Always pokin' and pryin', trying to get me to do things I don't want to do."

"No, we want to make sure you're safe, that's all. That you're eating well, you're getting the things you need…"

The old lady's eyes went sharp. "You're here because of what *you* need, not what *I* need," she said. "You think I belong in a home, and you'll just keep comin' back till you put me in one."

With a shake of her head Kathy said, "Mrs. Flint, that's not true," and she suddenly had a mean thought: *For all I care you can freeze and starve in the dark in this dreadful place.* Then she shivered again. From cold? From fear? She said, "I'm sorry I didn't get my message across to you better, but…well, I just didn't." Slipping her tablet into her briefcase she said, "I'll leave you alone now, sorry I bothered you. Honestly though, if you hadn't called, I'd never have come here again."

The old woman's eyes were bitter now. "Oh yes," she said, "I know your kind, and you always come back."

Kathy stood. "Mrs. Flint, you have my card. If you ever think I can be of help, be sure to call."

To this, the old woman said nothing and turned away.

Kathy went to the door. She pulled on the handle. The door resisted, creaked, then opened. She stepped outside.

That giant was out here somewhere. She hoped she would spot him at work on his project, whatever it was, but the fog was too dense to see more than a few yards ahead and the daylight was almost gone. She heard nothing: no engines, no chopping, nothing, not even a crow.

As she started along the stony wet path she admonished herself, *Be careful, don't go so fast, or you're going to fall. And what's the big hurry, what are you thinking, calm down*—but she wanted to run. She just couldn't wait to get out of this horrible place and away from these horrible people, go home to her cozy apartment and take a warm bath, eat a nice quiet meal, read the paper...

At last, the end of the path, and—what?

Her car was gone. She'd parked it right here by the field, and now it was *gone.*

She looked at the fog-shrouded brush, then back at the field. Utter silence.

The giant had moved her car? He had no keys, she'd locked the doors, but... *He's a kinda mechanical genius.* She squinted hard at the field in desperation, darkness closing in, her heartbeat quick in the sides of her neck, so frightened she wanted to cry. *It's bigger. What is, the car?*

Then a rustling and crunching behind her, across the lane. She whirled...

And he sprang from the brush with incredible speed, the axe raised high above his head. Its blade caught the last of the silvery light, and helplessly shielding her face with her hands Kathy screamed in pure terror *"No!—"*

"You planted her good and deep," said Mrs. Flint.

The hulk in the doorway nodded.

"In her car."

"Uh-huh."

"And you put all her stuff in there with her. Her papers and stuff."

"I done it, Mumma."

"You smashed up her phone like I told you to and put all the pieces inside? And took care of the mess?"

"Uh-huh."

"Good, you done a good job this time. The coyotes can't dig her up if she's locked away in her car like that. We don't want no trouble like out there in Kansas or down in Texas, we don't want to have to move again."

"No, Mumma."

"They can't learn to leave us alone, can they, Bucky? I tell them I don't want no help but they just won't listen. Pry and prod, they just won't quit, so we have to *make* them quit."

"Try put you away."

"That's right."

"I'm hungry, Mumma."

"Well go wash that blood off your hands and light the stove and I'll make you a nice hot supper."

# THE GUARDIAN

When I was ten years old, I put my foot down. "Mom," I said, "you are not going to follow me everywhere this Halloween." I expected a pretty good fight over this, and I got it: "Danny, you're still too young to be going alone, it isn't safe."

"But Mom," I objected, "I don't go *alone,* I go with Noah and Sammy and Tom, and *their* mothers don't come. They haven't come for two *years* now."

"That's because they knew *I* was coming."

"No it's not, it's because they don't *worry* the way you do. Just because a dog nipped your ankle one Halloween when you dressed like a mailman—"

"Danny, it's not just that, and you know it," Mom said with an edge to her voice. "Young children get all excited on Halloween and don't look both ways when they cross the street. They get picked on by bullies."

"We *do* look both ways," I insisted. "*Always.*"

I didn't respond to the part about bullies, since there, she had a point. There was always the chance that we'd meet up with bozos who'd try to make off with our loot. It happened to kids sometimes. It never happened to us, of course, with Mom always there in the background. "I think you should wait one more year," she said, "before you go out alone."

There, she'd said it again: *alone.* "Mom, please," I said. "I wait one more year, and next year you'll say the same thing. I'm just so *embarrassed* when you're around."

Mom sighed. She was quiet a moment, and then she surprised me: "Okay. If you promise you'll stick with your friends, be really careful crossing streets and be back here by eight o'clock, I won't go."

I could hardly believe it. I'd won! I was gleeful, but still protested, hoping for more concessions. "But eight's too *early,*" I said.

"Two hours is plenty of time to go trick or treating, Danny. You promise you're back by eight o'clock or I'm coming along."

It was my turn to sigh—theatrically.

"And one more thing—don't you dare go to Quarryville."

"Of *course* I won't," I said.

Our little Maine town of Palmer was pretty and safe—except for Quarryville, the shabby neighborhood out on its western edge. The quarries had closed years ago, before I was born, and now they were used as dumps. On hot summer days, that area stank so bad you could hardly breathe. Nobody wanted to live there, but people did, poor people, rough people. My friends and I avoided the place, would never even think of going there on Halloween—but Quarryville would always come to us. Tough kids with only a hint of a costume, maybe a smear of burnt cork on their cheeks or raggedy towels around their necks, they'd arrive in gangs *demanding* treats, and if you didn't want a trick, a really mean trick like a broken window or punctured tire, you'd better come across.

"We don't even go *close* to Quarryville," I said, and thought of Butchy Drake, the meanest kid in school, a sixth grader. He lived in Quarryville.

"So that's the deal," my mother said. "You stay with your friends, steer clear of Quarryville and be home by eight."

I was really excited, but said very calmly, "Thanks, Mom. And please, don't worry about me, I'll be fine."

"Oh Danny," she said with a sad little shake of her head.

I couldn't really blame my mom for worrying like she did. Her only child going around without her on Halloween night for the very first time? Of course she'd worry. And then there was that terrible thing with Dad a few years back.

Dad travels a lot in his job, and one time in Cleveland he suddenly got real sick and needed to go to the hospital. Nobody knew what it was— food poisoning maybe, the doctors thought—but he was really, really sick and Mom had to fly out to Cleveland and leave me with Aunt Eileen. Dad recovered okay, but the incident hit Mom hard. It made her very alert to the fact that horrors can happen without any warning, just when all seems great.

This particular Halloween that I'm telling about—the last one I'd ever go trick or treating on, as fate would have it—my dad was in Albuquerque. My mom was always extra jumpy when he was so far away. Waiting for the other shoe to drop, I guess: on Dad, on herself—or on me. After that awful thing with Dad, if something bad happened to me, I didn't know what she'd do, but I was sure that nothing bad would happen on Halloween. I'd keep my promises to her, and all would be fine.

Mom was expert at sewing, and made my costume. She bought some tan-colored fabric and measured and cut and pinned and sewed, and presto, there it was, a lion suit. A tail, and a mane that I pulled up over my head. I made the mask myself, from a paper bag.

When the big night arrived—clear, cool, with a slice of moon—my best friend Noah came over at six on the dot. He was dressed as a Martian and Mom said she couldn't guess who he was. Then he lifted his mask and Mom, acting very surprised and delighted, dropped candy into his bag. As I ran down the steps of our porch with him Mom hollered after me, "Eight o'clock!" "I know!" I said. I had to be the only lion ever to wear a watch.

We went to the house next door, the Robertsons' place, and Sammy and Tom came running up. Sammy was dressed as a clown and Tom was a wizard. Tom's hat was black and pointed and covered with colorful stars and moons. I liked it a lot. We ran up the steps of the Robertsons' porch, rang the bell and the door opened up. "Trick or treat!," we yelled. Mrs. Robertson laughed and pretended she didn't know who we were—even me, who lived right next door—and gave us all candy. Some other kids came up behind us, and we left.

My friends plunged their hands in their bags and brought out some goodies and started to feast. I wasn't allowed to do this. That was another promise I'd made, and I vowed to keep it.

Trick or treaters were already filling our sidewalks—pirates and princesses, witches and werewolves—and only the little ones were escorted. I was just so relieved that my mom had stayed home. I was perfectly safe among my friends, and the cars on the street were just crawling along, being super careful. Excited and happy, we plundered the block, except for the house of the Wilsons, who always went out on Halloween and turned off their lights. Kids soaped their windows while they were away sometimes.

At the end of the block we turned down Marple Street. The houses were bigger and farther apart on Marple. The first one belonged to some people named Porter, Tom said. He rang the bell and the door flew wide and a monster with green skin and bulging red eyes boomed, "Welcome!" making us jump. "Mr. Porter!" Tom said, and the monster laughed.

"Tommy Hiller," he said, and asked who the rest of us were, and gave all of us lots of treats.

On the sidewalk again we were laughing excitedly, checking our bags, when we suddenly noticed a ghost beside us. It was shorter than us and was all alone, and its costume was just fantastic. Not simply a sheet with eyeholes in it, this outfit was silky and had a weird silvery shimmer—I mean it was really *cool*. And the mask, it had dark creepy sunken eyes and a wide purple mouth. Pretty scary, yet somehow sad—and it looked so *real*. As the four of us stood there staring, the ghost said, "Can I go around with you guys?"

A boy's voice, but not one we knew, and Sammy asked brusquely, "Well who *are* you?"

"Eddie Carter," the ghost replied.

None of us recognized the name. "You just move to Palmer?" Tom asked.

"No, I've been here a while."

"Well where do you live?"

"On Linden Street."

Linden Street. I knew where it was, but I'd only been on it once, with my dad. He'd missed the exit for I-95 and that's when we landed on Linden Street. It was narrow and lined with shabby houses and had no trees, not one. As we made our way back to the highway Dad said, "Your mother lived right near here when she was a child," and I was shocked. "Of course," Dad said, "it was nicer then."

Now I looked at the ghost. What was a kid from Linden Street doing all the way over here—alone?

Noah, the Martian, asked, "How old are you, kid?"

"I'm ten."

Our age, and that was good, but he sure was small.

To the three of us Noah said, "So what do you think?"

"I don't know," Sammy said, but Tom was decisive. "I think he should go back to Linden Street, wherever that is."

The ghost just smiled at this, then said in a quiet voice, "No, I think you should let me come with you."

"Oh yeah?" Tom said. "Why's that?"

I felt kind of sorry for the ghost—he looked so forlorn—and I said, "I think we should let him come."

We argued among ourselves while clusters of kids in costumes hurried past, then Sammy said, "Well what are we standing here for, we're gonna miss all the treats!"

We all took off, and the ghost named Eddie trailed along. We didn't say anything to him.

The next house we came to, Eddie stayed out by the curb as we mounted the steps of the porch. After we got our treats and were back on the sidewalk, I suddenly realized our ghost had no bag—and his suit had no pockets. "Hey, how are you gonna get candy without any bag?" I asked. He smiled and said, "I don't eat candy."

So why was he trick or treating? It didn't make sense. "You mean you just like wearing costumes?" I asked. I knew grownups who did that—dressed up in outfits and went around fooling their neighbors—but kids *never* did that.

Again, he just smiled.

We'd finished Marple Street and Coogan Street and were crossing Myrtle Street. Noah was in the lead and I was next. I turned to say something to Sammy, behind me, when suddenly Tom yelled, "Look out!"

The car had come out of nowhere, its headlights rapidly bearing down. Noah sprinted ahead, but my shock was so great that I froze. I was going to be hit!

Then a hand grabbed the neck of my costume, my lion's mane, and someone was pulling me backward, out of the street. The car roared past, just missing me, as teenagers leaned from its windows, jeering. It squealed around the corner and was gone.

It was Eddie who'd grabbed me. I thought: If we'd told him he couldn't come with us, I might be *dead*. I was numb all over and breathing hard, and here was the strangest thing: I hadn't felt like I'd been dragged, I'd felt like I'd *floated* away from that car—like one of those big balloons that you see in parades. My fear must have warped my senses, that's all I could figure.

I sat on the curb so my heart would slow down, and Eddie stood right beside me. He might have been little, but had to be really strong to pull me out of the street so fast like that.

The feeling returned to my body. I said, "You saved my life"—and thought of Mom, at home in the living room, worried. "But Eddie, don't tell my mom, okay? None of you guys, don't tell my mom."

Eddie nodded and said, "Your mom's really nice."

This startled me. I said, "You know my mom?"

"Not anymore, but I knew her a long time ago."

What? How could that possibly be? Before I could ask, Tom said, "The guys in that car are idiots!," and Sammy said, "What jerks!," and we crossed to where Noah was standing.

We did another block, and all was fine, but then, on Quentin Street, we saw a dog up by the corner—a dog with a piece of rope tied to its collar. I instantly thought of what happened to Mom on Halloween when she was a kid. "Pit bull!" said Tom. "Broke loose! I hate those dogs, they're mean—" and just as he said this, the animal charged.

We started to run—all except Eddie. Over my shoulder I saw him just standing there calmly, and then I saw something amazing. The pit bull leaped right at his face, and then suddenly stopped—in midair! It went stiff as a shirt on a winter clothesline, then fell to the sidewalk and whimpered and ran away.

"What happened?" I said as we came up to Eddie. "How did you do that?"

"Do what?" he said.

"That dog…"

"I guess he just changed his mind," Eddie said. "He didn't want to bite us after all."

We had done six more streets and our bags were bulging, when Butchy Drake showed up. He was flanked by two of his Quarryville buddies, Troy West and Bobby Marks.

He wore no costume, just a bandana around his head, but he did have a bag, a regular plastic shopping bag, and it was stuffed. We tried to hurry past him, but he grabbed Tom's sleeve. "Hold up, Mr. Wizard," he said, and his friends blocked our way.

It was hopeless to try to run in our costumes, they'd easily catch us. The five of us stood there, trapped. The smiling clown face Sammy wore looked utterly ridiculous, a stark contrast to how we felt.

Butchy said, "Hand over your bags."

The air was cool but I was sweating, and now my anger flared. "You leave us alone," I said. "Your bags are full, you don't need ours."

All three of the big guys grinned, and Butchy said, "Hey pussy cat, you mad?"

Swallowing hard I said again, "Just leave us alone."

Butchy narrowed his eyes. He said, "You know what, pussy cat, you sound a lot like Danny Wallace," and then he poked Noah's shoulder. "And who are you, freako?"

Noah said nothing, which led to another, harder poke. "You deaf or something, kid?"

Still Noah didn't speak—but Eddie did. "I think you should all leave now," he said.

At this, Butchy laughed. "Oh, yeah?" he said. "And who are *you*, shorty?"

"Just leave," Eddie said.

Butchy said to him, "Take off your mask."

"No," Eddie said, "I won't do that."

I admired the little guy's courage and said, "Yeah, don't do it." Then Noah chimed in, and Sammy and Tom. "Don't do it," the four of us said.

Then Troy gave Sammy a wicked hard shove that knocked him right down flat. He didn't let go of his bag, but candy came spilling out onto the sidewalk. "Take off your mask!" Butchy shouted at Eddie, and reached for his face.

His hand made contact with Eddie's head, and I still can't believe what happened. Suddenly there was this flash, this blinding light, and Butchy screamed. He jumped back quickly, holding his hand, a terrified look on his face. "You... What?" he said.

Then Troy came straight at Eddie and so did Bobby, and then—it was totally weird and fantastic—Eddie like stretched out long and started to *glow*. And he wrapped himself through and around the legs of the charging bullies and brought them down.

As they lay on the sidewalk moaning, Sammy got up and the four of us started to run. We turned the corner and ran till our legs hurt, our chests heaved, we just couldn't run anymore. We pulled up our masks and, gasping, looked around. To our vast relief, we saw no bullies.

Fighting for breath, Sammy said, "Did you see that? What Eddie *did?*"

"He *changed*," Noah said, gulping air. "I mean...he turned into a *snake* or something."

"And *light* was coming out of him," Tom said.

"I don't understand—" I began, and suddenly Eddie was standing right there beside us. He was not at all out of breath.

"I hope those three learned a lesson," he said with a smile.

Tom nodded, but Sammy and Noah stood perfectly still. Their faces were suddenly fearful.

"Thanks, Eddie," I said. "But how did you *do* that?"

No answer. We looked at each other, then Sammy said, "You have an electric thing, right? Like a shocker, right?"

"Yes, something like that," Eddie said.

"Can you show us?" asked Tom.

"I'm afraid I can't. I'm afraid that I have to be going now," he said, and then—he simply vanished.

The four of us stood there, stunned. "But...where'd he *go?*" Tom said.

"Impossible," Noah said.

"We better get home," Sammy said. "Right now!"

«« — »»

"You're ten minutes, early," Mom said when I came through the door. "I don't believe it."

She turned off the living room lights and we went to the kitchen. "Let's see what you got," she said.

I emptied my bag on the kitchen table. "Wow, what a haul!" Mom said.

"Yeah, I did really good," I said.

We both sat down. Mom said, "Some mini peanut butter cups, my favorite. I'm sure you can spare a few."

I gave her five. She popped one into her mouth and said, "You're a peach. Now look, don't stuff yourself."

"I'm not really hungry right now," I said.

"You've been eating."

"No."

"Honestly?"

"Honestly."

"Hmm," Mom said.

"Mom," I said, "this amazing thing happened. We met this new kid, Eddie Carter, he lives across town on Linden Street—"

Mom stopped chewing her candy. Her face lost its color. "Who?" she said.

"Dad told me you grew up there, in that neighborhood."

"That's right."

"Well this Eddie, he lives there, he did this incredible thing. Butchy Drake tried to steal our bags, but Eddie—"

I stopped. The only other time I'd seen Mom look like this was the night that she got the call about Dad, how sick he was out in Cleveland. She frowned at the table, the scatter of candy, and said, "Eddie Carter."

I thought of that weird thing that Eddie had said: *I don't know your Mom anymore, but I knew her a long time ago.* Impossible! I said, "You...*know* the kid?"

Mom was silent a moment then said, "I once knew a boy with that name, way back, when I was a little girl."

"Well maybe this kid is his son," I said.

"No, that can't be," Mom said. "The Eddie I knew was killed at the age of ten."

A quick bright chill went through me. "What?"

"Yes, he was a friend of mine. He lived in my neighborhood, on

210

Linden Street. His family was large and very poor, and I used to give him things. He was thin and pale and constantly hungry. I'd give him some of my lunch every day and it made him so happy. He loved Halloween. For once, he could stuff himself, and sometimes people would give us nickles and dimes. It was all the money he ever had.

"This one Halloween we went out together and Eddie as always was just so excited—and ran right in front of a car. Lying there bleeding, the last thing he said was, 'You're always so nice to me...someday I'll help you.'"

She stared at my eyes. "This Eddie, what did he look like?"

"I don't really know," I said. "I mean, I never saw his face, he was dressed like a ghost..."

"A ghost," she said, and her voice was small and strange.

I said, "But you can't be thinking... I mean..."

She looked at me quickly. "No, no, I'm sure there are still lots of Carters in that part of town, and one of them named a boy Eddie, that's all—maybe after the boy I knew."

"Yeah, maybe that's it," I said.

"What a strange coincidence," Mom said, and now she was chewing her lip. "So this Eddie you met stopped Butchy from stealing your bags?"

"That's right."

"He must be a pretty big boy."

"Uh-huh." After what she'd revealed to me, could I tell her the truth?

"The Eddie I knew was so small," she said, "the smallest one in our class, including the girls." Her eyes had a sad and distant look. "The poor little kid." Then sighing she said, "Well, honey, I'm really tired, I think I'll go up to the bedroom and watch TV for a while then go to sleep."

"I'm tired too," I said. And I was, completely exhausted.

And yet, when I got into bed, I couldn't sleep, kept hearing Eddie's words: *Your mom's really nice...I knew her a long time ago.* I thought of the Eddie killed by a car. *Someday I'll help you...*

My dreams were alive with demons and I tossed and turned till morning came.

And I never went out on Halloween night again.

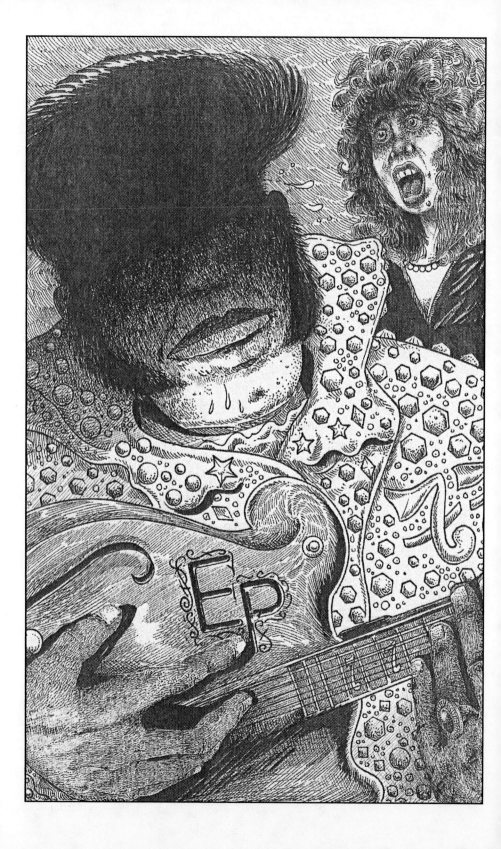

# WANT

They were on break. Linda Sue swigged her Pepsi. "I shoulda just kept my mouth shut about it," she said.

Arlene blew smoke. "All I asked's who you chose," she said in her high-pitched whine.

"Huh. *All* you asked?"

"Well I just wanna know. Jesus, who wouldn't wanna know, what's wrong with that?"

Linda Sue tossed her head. "First of all, I ain't really sure who they got. I can't do much choosin' till I see who they got."

"I thought they made you pick aheada time," Arlene said, pouting her purple lips and exhaling a thick white stream.

"Well they don't," said Linda Sue. "You're wrong."

A lie. Of course you had to pick ahead of time, and she'd known from the very first moment she'd thought about doing this who she'd choose.

Arlene took a long last drag on her cigarette, flicked the butt away. "You don't know who it's gonna be, I ain't goin' with you," she said,

"Well that's just fine," said Linda Sue. "I don't know why I asked you anyway, I'm sorry I did."

As she locked her car, she knew very well why she'd asked Arlene to come: she was scared to death. The parking garage was bleak and damp, with feeble orange-colored lights that looked like evil, dying suns, and her stomach plunged. Oh for God's sake, stop, she told herself, it's gonna be fine, it's gonna be great, that's why it costs so much.

Alone in the elevator, she took out her compact and checked herself. Her hair had been done just yesterday and looked real nice—high piles of brassy curls—and her makeup was also fine: green shadow on upper eyelids, black false lashes, glittery silver-pink lips. On the negative side, a chin pimple poked its sharp tip through her base, and her cheeks—

Were fat. Goddamn it, she still looked fat. She had damn near starved herself for almost a month, lost thirteen pounds, and...damn. "Who *cares* how you look?" Arlene had said. "It won't matter a bit to *him*." "Well it matters to *me*," Linda Sue had replied, "it matters a *lot* to *me*." Arlene had given that shrug of hers that Linda Sue hated so much. Pain in the butt, she thought as she snapped her compact shut and shoved it away—but I wish she was here.

The motion as the elevator stopped made her stomach feel worse. The doors slid open, revealing a small green room. The stern looking middle-aged woman behind the lone desk said, "Hello. May I help you?"

"I'm here for a two o'clock appointment," said Linda Sue, and her voice sounded thin in her ears. "Here's my card."

The woman took it and said, "Be seated, please."

A single picture hung on the wall; stark trees and a setting sun. A couple of vinyl chairs, and Linda Sue sat. Some old magazines on a brown plastic table. You'd think with all the money they made, the place would look nicer than this. She'd been paying installments for six months now, and she suddenly feared it had been a gigantic mistake. If she backed out, though, she'd lose half the money, that was the way it worked.

It's gonna be fine, she told herself, calm down. Too nervous to look at a magazine, she picked at a stray piece of cuticle on her thumb. She hoped he liked silver nails—

"Linda Sue?"

The man was short and thin and tanned, with black slick wiry hair. His black pinstriped suit was impeccable, his smile precise and empty.

She nodded. The man shook her hand. "Dick Harris. Follow me, please."

He turned and walked briskly down a long hallway, his sparkling shoes clicking against the fake marble floor. The walls were lined with photographs of dead celebrities, a thousand of them at least. No time for Linda Sue to examine them, Harris was moving too fast.

Stopping abruptly, he opened a door. With a brusque little bow, he held his hand out toward the room.

Now this is more like it! Linda Sue thought as she stepped inside. Her eyes widened. Why, this is...fantastic!

The room was huge and round, with a huge round bed in its center. Its windows were hung with gold velvet drapes, its snowwhite carpet was half an inch thick, its walls were a white and gold brocade with incredible velvet paintings in ornate gold frames: heads of tigers and horses, a shiny blue fish, and a fruit bowl so bright that it practically hurt her eyes. There were vases and vases of lush golden flowers, a bucket of champagne on ice on a white wooden cart, a credenza heaped high with all kinds of goodies: cold cuts and cupcakes and bowls full of candy, and frozen concoctions on ice. Also a jar of peanut butter. Gleaming gold and platinum records filled an entire wall.

"You approve?" Harris asked.

"Oh, yes," said Linda Sue, her eyes still wide.

"We're so glad. Please be seated."

She sat on a white plush couch, knees together, her hands on the purse in her lap. Across from her, in a golden chair, Harris said, "Now before you begin, I'd like to run through the procedures again."

"Okay."

"Would you care for a drink?"

"Oh, no, no thanks."

The crisp little man leaned forward. "The main thing you have to remember is, whatever you see, whatever you do, you're dealing with an illusion."

"I realize that."

"Of course you do. I just want you to be aware that it's all going to seem very real. *Unbelievably* real."

"Yeah, that's what they say."

"And it's true. We've used the information you gave us to fashion a drama that perfectly meets your needs. It's going to be as real—perhaps *more* real—than anything you've ever known before. But you have to remember—it *is* a performance."

"Okay," Linda Sue said, thinking: Come on, let's just do it!

"I'm so glad you understand," said Harris, reaching inside his jacket. "And here's the release for you to sign. It's our standard form."

He handed it to her. She tried to read it. "Will not be responsible...In case of...Under no circumstances...Liability limited..." Garbage, far as she could see.

"Okay?" asked Harris. He whipped out a pen.

"Sure," Linda Sue said.

"Good," Harris said, and watched her sign. He took the pen back, took the paper, put it away, and stood. "Your drama will start in a couple of minutes," he said. "We hope it is totally satisfying."

"Thanks," said Linda Sue, nodding.

Harris bowed once again, then left the room, closing the door.

She was suddenly very excited—and very afraid. Her heart made a squooshy loud sound in her ears. She reached in her purse for some gum, unwrapped it, popped it in her mouth, began to chew. Sat chewing on the edge of the couch, the excited feeling thick in her stomach and chest. Soon, any minute now. She wondered where—

Then a door to the left of the bed flew open and there—oh my God, there he *was!*

He tossed his head, his smile a sneer. His teeth were huge and shiny white. He jerked his guitar and nodded cooly and said, "Hello there, Linda Sue."

She was going to die. She could feel her heart swelling and straining, preparing to burst. She opened her mouth and no words would come out. Her gum was stuck to her teeth.

"What'sa matter?" he said in his mellow deep voice. "Cat gotcha tongue?"

"Oh," she squeaked. "Oh." She stared.

He looked marvelous, marvelous, better than ever. His brown hair was shiny and full, his complexion was bright, his eyes gleamed. His white silk shirt was open to the waist, and his waist was firm and slim. He wore gold lame skintight pants, black pointy suede shoes, and a golden chain that dipped down into the cleft of his hairless chest. "Oh my God," whispered Linda Sue.

"Love me, love me, love me, love me, love me," he bubbled, and strummed a soft mournful chord. He stared with his graybrown eyes. She could feel herself melting, her mind disappearing.

"Love me lovely, love me deep," he sang, and she thought she might swoon. She bit her lip and covered her mouth with her hands. He thrust his hips; the bulge in his gold lame grew prominent; she gasped. "And who's the gal I love?" he crooned staring down with his burning eyes.

"Why it's you,
Yes it's you,
Linda Sue."

Her mind was reeling. She didn't know whether to shout or clap or jump up and hug him or what, so she just stayed sitting.

"You like it?" he asked with another snide smile. Sweat shone on his wide tanned forehead.

She nodded.

"I'm so, so glad," he said, and strummed again, and this time sang "I Need You Like the Ocean Needs the Stream," one of his all time greatest. In his spell, she flowed over the ripples of song like a leaf in the stream he was singing about. Oh my God, oh my God, she kept telling herself, this is just so *real.*

He finished with a soft sweet chord, laid his instrument down, took a bright silver cloth from his pocket and wiped his flushed face. "Did it please you?" he asked, head cocked, his smile coy. "Now tell the truth."

"I...adored it," Linda Sue replied, her chewing gum lost in the gap between cheek and teeth.

"I'm so happy to hear that," he said. "'Cause I want to please you so very much—in any way I can. Mind if I take a load off my feet?"

"Oh—of course not," she said.

He nodded and sat in the chair where Harris had been. "We got all kindsa goodies," he said, "if you feel like eatin'.

"Oh, no. No thanks," she said.

"Well you got anymore of that gum?"

She felt paralyzed; then, "Oh, sure," she said, and reached in her purse and came out with a stick. He got up and took it, and as he did, his fingers grazed her hand. An electric thrill shot into her arms and chest. "I 'preciate it, thanks," he said, and sat again.

He tossed the gum wrappings aside—right onto the thick white rug— and shoved the stick into his mouth. "Now what wouldja like to hear next?" he asked. "Or you wanna just talk for a while?"

"Yes. Let's just talk," she said.

"Good, that's what I want, too," he said, "an' you wanna know why? 'Cause you're somethin' special, you really are. I knew it the minute I walked through that door. As soon as I looked at your sweet angel face, I said to myself, "This gal's somethin' special. This gal is the one you been waitin' for."

"That's...nice of you to say," said Linda Sue. Her heart was beating so fast, so fast...

Leaning back, his shirt spreading wider and showing more skin, he said, "You think it's just part of the show, I guess. You think it's just part of the act. You think I say that to all the girls, but it just ain't true. You're special. Real special. You're the one I been waitin' for—the one I want."

Linda Sue couldn't swallow. She shook her head. "I don't think you oughtta be sayin' this stuff," she said. "It's nice to hear, real nice, but it's not what I had in mind."

His eyebrows went up. "Oh yeah? I think it *is* what you had in mind.

And if I'm wrong? Can you blame a man for sayin' how he really feels?" Suddenly he was on his feet, and then he was sitting beside her.

He pulsed with heat; she bathed in his glow, and she suddenly felt so *alive.* "No," she said. "This ain't right. I mean, I was ready for—well, you know—an' I still am ready, but this…" She shook her head again. "It's just too much."

"Not at all," he said. "It's perfect. Touch my arm."

"What?"

"Go ahead, touch my arm."

She did, at the elbow; felt silken warmth—and she loved him with all her heart.

"Come away with me, li'l lady," he said, looking into her eyes, chewing gum.

She frowned and said, "I didn't think… I mean…I thought they didn't let…." She looked in those eyes, her heart swollen and hot, and said, "See, what I mean is, I'm only a factory girl. I put this tiny transistor thing, a component they call it, onto these what they call memory boards? I been doin' it four years now, and I'll probably do it the rest of my life. I don't have a boyfriend, the guys that I meet are so…plain, and all I wanted was just to…just…"

"I know, I know," he said, and he put his arm over her shoulder. Heat raged in her brain. "Years back, I used to drive a truck, an' I know how it is. I know what it's like to be you, 'cause I *was* you. And that's why I like you so very much. That's why—I *love* you."

His minty hot breath made her weak all through. "I wanta get outta there terrible bad," she said. "The work hurts my hands, it hurts my eyes, and sometimes I think…it's like already being *dead.* I'd love to go away with you, but the problem is, you ain't…you ain't—"

Sealing her lips with a blazing finger, he said, "Does this feel like I ain't? Just shush now, gal, I'm tellin' you, dreams can come true."

He took his hand down. Its imprint had branded her mouth; she was shaking all over. "But how does it work?" she asked. "I don't understand. Do I…buy you, or what?"

Tossing his head with a haughty sniff, he said, "Nobody buys *me,* ma'am. *No*body."

"But the thing is, outside of this room—"

Leaning forward he said in a soft voice, "Well doancha see? They never gimme a chance. And to tell you the truth, I never *wanted* a chance—till now, till you came along."

Her pulse fluttered into her throat. "But…" She thought she might cry.

"Come on, darlin', doan be a hound dog. You really gonna break my heart?"

She swallowed hard, dazed and confused. "I want you, I need you" she said. "Oh I need you so bad. But tell me somethin'—an' tell me true."

"What's that, sweet thing?" Spreading his arms he leaned back again, and one of his huge hands settled beside her hair. Its nearness gave her a neck full of goosebumps.

"Tell me true, now," she said. "Did you beat your wife?"

A snort. "Beat my wife, what a crock. Course not, li'l lover. I wouldn't lay a hand on a lady, you oughta know that."

"An' what about that stuff I read about those little girls? That you paid them to rassle in their underwear?"

"You know the papers, you know how they are. Anything to make money."

"Yeah."

She chewed on her tasteless stiff gum and believed him—with all of her loving heart. She squeezed her legs together, folded her hands and said with a little grin, "Did you really fly to Denver to pick up your favorite peanut butter?"

Laughing, he said, "Now that, I confess to, I *did* do that. An' a jar of it's sittin' right there, if you want a taste." He jerked his head backward.

"Oh no," she said. "I can't eat a thing. Not now. Not the way I feel."

He touched her arm; a thrill hummed in her veins. "I'll play you another song," he said, and reached for his shining guitar.

He strummed a chord, then sang:

"You're the gal
I got in mind.
The gal I looked
All my life to find…"

His oily baritone oozed its way into her open, defenseless soul. She squeezed her eyes shut; opened them carefully. Yes, it was real. *He* was real. This was actually *happening* to her.

He sang. She hung on his every word, intermittently chewing her gum.

"You're the one
You're the one…"

He blinked with heavy lids. "You *are* the one, li'l gal. I want you, I want you."

"And I want *you*," said Linda Sue, her whole body congested with love. "I want you so very much."

"I want you. I want you. I want you."

"I know you do. Oh I know it."

"I want...you."

"Yes, yes."

"I want...want...want..."

His fingers struck a chord that sounded wrong, and his smile this time was—jeez, it was really *weird*. And now as she watched his mouth as he sang, she saw that thing that happens in movies sometimes, when the lips and the voice are a little bit off, a little bit out of synch. Was she losing her mind? Was she starting to faint? Was this happening in a dream?

She took a deep breath and pinched herself, and it wasn't anything wrong with *her,* it was *him,* she was sure it was. His words were sluggish, gooey, slow; his fingers stumbled on the strings.

"You all right?" she asked, sitting straighter. "You feelin' okay?"

His shoulders heaved. His head weaved back and forth. His voice was droopy, an octave too deep, a forty-five record on thirty-three and a third.

"I...want...you..." he said, so slowly, so slowly, his wide jaw sloppy and slack. His fingers stopped strumming. His eyes had a blank, milky look.

"No!" Linda Sue cried. "You're doin' drugs! You're doin' drugs again! It ain't right, it ain't fair, I put that in the agreement—"

"I...I..." he said.

"Don't lie to me! You're doin' drugs!"

The guitar slid out of his sleepy hands; it dangled around his neck on its golden strap. "I..."

"It's the one thing I insisted on," she said. "No drugs. For God's sake, that's why you *died.*"

His jaw hung open. His tongue hung out.

She grabbed his shoulders. "Stop!" she cried. "Get aholda yourself! Don't do this to me! It ain't fair!"

"I want...I want..."

"Please. *Please.*"

His eyes struggled to focus. "It ain't...it ain't drugs..." He spoke with great effort, his breath coming hard. Her hands were glued to his shoulders. "It's...jus' that...we doan last...forever..."

His tongue made a whirring, clicking sound; his crooked eyes rolled back. "Love…me…cruel…" he said in a cracked, dull drawl. Then his breathing stopped.

"No, no!" screamed Linda Sue.

Then he started to tilt, his weight was too much for her quivering hands, and he fell with a terrible crash, the guitar sounding one harsh chord.

She sprang to the floor and shook him hard. "No! No!" she cried. "Get up! Wake up! Please! *No!*" And then she wept.

She was down on her knees, her face in her hands, and Harris was there beside her. "Linda Sue," he said. "Linda Sue, please, listen to me."

"No, no," she wailed. "He's dead. He's dead."

"He isn't dead," Harris said. "He's just—expired. It happens. Rarely, our maintenance program is truly superb, but it happens. We can start all over again, some other day. As a matter of fact, you'll get two dramas next time, with a brand new Elvis."

"I don't *want* a brand new Elvis," Linda Sue moaned. "I want *this* Elvis. But he's broke. He's goddamn broke."

"We can program another Elvis to be just the same."

"No you *can't*," Linda Sue said hotly. "This Elvis was special. This was *my* Elvis. There'll never be another one like him."

Harris sighed. "I believe I have heard this before somewhere."

"You just shut up!" snapped Linda Sue. "He was goin' to take me away. He was goin' to take me outta the factory, take me away to Graceland."

"We programmed that in. You requested that."

"I never did."

"Oh yes, it's right in the contract. You get double your money back or two dramas, it's up to you, it's our standard guarantee."

"And what about my *life?*" wailed Linda Sue, wiping her tear-filled eyes with her fingertips, "what about *that?* You killed my Elvis and left me alone and broke my heart forever, what about *that?*"

"*That* we cannot adjust," Harris said, reaching into his jacket pocket. 'Not responsible for broken hearts,' it says it right here. You signed the release."

"I know, I know, but—"

"Double your money back or two dramas, it's the best we can do."

Linda Sue closed her eyes: and she saw him again, saw him singing— to *her.* She choked on a sob and shook her head and rubbed the tears away; then opened her eyes again, sighing, and slowly leaned forward, touching her lips to the cheek of the fallen star. "Goodbye," she said, her voice broken and hoarse. "I'll love you forever and ever."

His marble eyes stared up at nothing. His skin was as cold as glass.

«« — »»

At the work station, Arlene said, "Was it worth it?"

"It was," replied Linda Sue. She stuck the component onto the board. Her wrists and fingers ached. Her temples throbbed.

"Would you do it again? Spend all that much money again?"

"Maybe someday. But not for a while."

"So who did you pick, anyway?"

"That's still nunna your goddamn business."

"I bet it was Elvis," Arlene said.

"It wasn't George Washington," Linda Sue said.

"I bet it was Elvis."

Linda Sue looked at the parts on the line. Through the mist that had suddenly filled her eyes they kept coming and coming, steadily, endlessly, thousands of them, like days.

# THE REAL THING

The Job Service guy looked up and said, "I just might have something for you."

Albert covered his mouth with his tattooed hand and coughed. "Oh yeah?" he said.

"I might." The Job Service guy was young, about twenty-four, with rosy round cheeks and a flop of dark hair hanging close to one eye. "Did anyone ever tell you you look like Santa Claus?"

"Well what do *you* think?" Albert said.

"Yeah, that's what I figured. Well Nelson's is looking for one, the sooner the better. You know where Nelson's is?"

"Of course."

"Here's the number to call," and he wrote on a pad, tore the sheet off and held it out.

Albert took it and read, "Mr. Hawkins."

"He called us this morning. One of his Santas got hit with appendicitis yesterday. He's in a fix.

"It's worth a try," Albert said. "Thanks a lot."

At the Palace Hotel he paid for a shower, and now he was down to a dollar, four quarters. He combed his hair and beard in the broken mirror, put his clothes back on. They were all that he had to wear and smelled pretty bad. He put on his overcoat, checked it for spots, rubbed the obvious ones with his towel till they faded away. The coat had held up fairly well and would hide his frayed, torn clothes.

225

He walked four blocks to Chestnut Street, stopped into a discount drug, spent a quarter on a trial-size aftershave. In a phone booth he sprinkled his coat with the sweet-smelling liquid, then made the call.

The office was dingy gray, with piles of papers all over the place. A wiremesh skylight with black blotches on it admitted a weak slice of sun.

"You ever been Santa before?" Mr. Hawkins asked. He was balding, paunchy, neat and trim, in pinstriped suit with vest.

"No," Albert said.

"There's a knack to it, it's not simply sit on my knee and what do you want, you have to relate. You like children?"

"I like them okay," Albert said, coughing into his fist.

Frowning, Hawkins said, "Sure, you can fake it, we've had a few Santas who faked it and did okay, but what we *really* want is a guy who's sincere. Understand?"

"Yes."

"You sure look the part," Hawkins said, "I'll say that much. Even your eyebrows—you'll hardly need makeup. The gloves will cover that tattoo."

"From my sailor days," Albert said, coughing again.

"Mmm. Your cheeks are a little thin, but other than that… Let me hear your ho's."

"What?"

"Ho-ho-ho. Let's hear it."

"Ho-ho-ho," Albert said.

Hawkins squinted and shook his head. "From the gut."

"Ho-Ho-HO!"

"Mmm. I'm going to have someone work with you on it."

"I'm hired?"

"No, not till I see you in action. And first, you need to pass a TB test. Take this paper to Dr. Higgins down the street, twelve forty-two. It'll take a few days to get the results."

"Yeah," Albert said.

"If we do take you on, we pay mimimum wage. You'd work four hours a day every day for the next two weeks—through Christmas Eve. We're open till ten, and you'll do the late shift."

"That's okay by me."

"Of course, if you're not any good—"

"I'll be good," Albert said. "I have a few days to practice."

"Come back when you pass the TB test, and Danny will show you how it's done. He starts at ten, so be here by nine."

"Okay."

"And one more thing. Cut down on that cologne you're wearing, kids don't go for that."


To Albert's great relief, the TB test was negative.

He'd had the cough for two months now; it was why he was looking for work. On the job application he'd put his address as "Box 0023 Water Street"—which was accurate, though the postal service might quibble. He *did* live on Water Street, in a box, and 0023 was the model number of the freezer that box had once held. Perhaps if it wasn't a *freezer* box it might not be so cold, Albert thought.

Whatever, he had to get out of that box, and soon. To stay in it all winter long would kill him—or put him in City Hospital. He swore he would never go back there again; it was worse than the street, that place.

Albert needed a room—away from the cold, away from the heavy wet air of the river. A room until spring and he'd be okay. With a couple of weeks at this job, he'd be able to pay for a room till the end of March and his cough would fade, he knew it would—once he had shelter with heat and a bed off the cold damp ground. Then a year from now his Social Security check would start and he'd be just fine. He wouldn't have to fight for deposit bottles with kids who had knives in their jackets and lacked all feeling in their hearts.

So all he had to do to survive this year was stay sober a couple of weeks. He had gone without drinking for more than three weeks five times in these past ten years, and now, with this job, he was sure he could hold out till Christmas.

He got enough money from bottles to wash his clothes, sat naked under his overcoat in the laundromat, a legitimate customer, paying for rich steamy heat with no fear of a cop coming up and demanding he leave. When he put on the warm clean clothes in the Palace, after another tepid shower, he felt like a king.

The fellow named Danny said, "You think: Santa Claus, the good guy, right? But to real little kids he's a monster, they're scared to death. And some of them kick and scream and cry while their mamas insist that they talk to the monster, bare their souls. So here you are, stuck with this screaming kid, and the lights shine down, and everyone's looking, and other kids wait in an endless line with their folks. It can get really bad. And you gotta be Santa, Mr. Nice, keep smiling and talking real sweet, Ho-Ho. Hey, you really do look the part."

Albert watched from the sidelines when Danny was Santa, and two of the kids backed out and two started crying, and one little girl threw herself on the floor and had something that looked like convulsions. But most of the kids were fine, and sat right up on Danny's lap, and Albert said to himself: I can do this. I really can.

But under the railroad bridge that night, in his freezer box, as a wet snow fell on the river, he couldn't sleep. He hadn't worked in seven years, and had never done anything even remotely like this. It was acting, that's what it was, he had taken an *acting* job. When he'd tried on the Santa Claus outfit he'd said to himself, I'm not *me* anymore—which felt good, surprisingly so. Thinking of this, he lay huddled against the cold, wide awake, as the dark wind howled.

In the morning he paced the gray city streets, every cell in his body craving a drink. Just a small one—to ease his coughing and steady his nerves. No! He battled the urge, walking quickly past wide windows brilliant with Christmas cheer—the trees, the garlands, twinkling lights—went into a store to warm his frozen face and hands, and there was a Santa, the line of children, the floodlamps. A photographer snapping the kids on Santa's knee. Tonight, that's me, he thought—and the doubts came on strong, and he wanted that drink worse than ever.

The day took forever to pass. He wandered in and out of five and dimes and drugstores, cafeterias. He couldn't eat, but God did he want a drink! At last it was five o'clock, and office workers clogged the sidewalks, hustling for buses and trains. Albert went into Nelson's, past glittering counters where perfumes were sold, and handbags, cosmetics. He went to the back, where the offices were.

"You're early, good," Mr. Hawkins said. "You might as well get your suit on now."

"Right," Albert said, and went to the room where it hung in a metal locker.

As he changed, his hands trembled. One small drink would set him up so fine… When he saw himself in the mirror, though, he felt a surge of confidence. This is the best I've looked in years, he thought. And I *do* look like Santa!

He dabbed red circles of rouge on his cheeks as Danny had done, then chewed on a mint. Bad breath is the death of Santas, Danny had said, and while Albert's front teeth were in decent shape (thanks, no doubt, to superior genes), his molars—what remained of them—required attention, and sometimes his mouth turned sour.

He had no watch and there wasn't a clock in the room, so he waited, standing, staring at blue linoleum and mint-green walls—a calendar with a winter scene of Vermont, a row of gray file cabinets. At last a knock on the door—Mr. Hawkins. "You ready?" "I'm ready," said Albert. The door came open, and Hawkins entered. He nodded. "You look quite good. Walter's coming off now and you're on in five minutes."

"Okay," Albert said, and coughed.

And then he was walking, with Hawkins beside him, through tables of towels and quilts to the toy department. Three dozen TV sets showed the same frantic scene. "Okay," Hawkins said, "showtime. I'll be watching."

Albert felt numb as he walked past the plastic reindeer, the blinking tree, and sat in the red plush throne. Floodlamps dazzled his eyes; his heart was pounding; he felt like he had a fever. He looked at the line of parents and kids and swallowed hard and coughed and cleared his throat. Near his foot sat a bulging red sack tied shut with a crisp white satin bow. In the background he saw Hawkins staring.

He focused on the first kid in line, a girl about four years old, and said, "Your turn to see Santa." His voice was a squeak.

He expected to hear some giggles, but no, this was serious business. The girl came up shyly, her hand in her mother's, and sat on his lap, her eyes watchful and wary.

"And what's your name?" asked Albert, hoping his mint had worked.

The girl simply stared. Albert realized that she was shaking.

"Her name's Melissa," the mother said.

"Hello, Melissa," Albert said—and thought of Laura. How many years had it been since she'd sat on his lap? Over fifty. And no other children had sat on his lap since then.

"What would you like for Christmas, Melissa?" His voice was not right, but better.

Melissa looked close to tears. Her mother said, "Tell Santa, honey."

"I..."

"What, darling?" Albert said.

"A..."

"What?"

"Go on, sweetheart," the mother said. "Santa's busy, he has lots of children to see."

"A..."

"What?" Albert said. He was clammy and burning.

"A doll."

"A doll," Albert said with immense relief. "A doll, and what else?"

The girl hung her head.

"A doll," Albert said, "good enough. And now Santa has something for you," he said, reaching into the basket that sat on a stand on his right. He took out a taffy and handed it to the girl.

Her pupils widened. She slid off his lap and his leg felt cool.

"Say thank you," the mother said, and Melissa did, staring down at her taffy, clutching her mother's hand and walking off.

*I did it,* Albert said to himself. *I did it, I'll be okay.*

The next kid came forward, a boy about five, and hopped right up on Albert's knee. He instantly started reciting his list, and Albert repeated the items, smiling, his voice at full volume now. *Repeat, but never, ever promise,* Danny had said. "That's plenty for Santa to remember!" Albert said winking and giving the boy his taffy. Next!

And on they came: the bold, the shy, the terrified, the greedy, the polite. The ones who said, "Are you the real Santa? Is that a real beard?" and "Real?" Albert would say, "go on, give it a tug!" And they would, and leave convinced, the myth preserved.

Hawkins watched from beside a Christmas tree. At last he gave a timeout sign, and Albert said, "Santa needs to see his elves for a minute, children, be right back."

"You're hired," Hawkins said outside the mensroom.

"Great," Albert said.

"Take a break every hour, stop at ten on the dot. You saw the clock?"

"No."

"It's off to your right, above the exit sign."

"Okay. Mr. Hawkins?"

"Yes?"

"I forgot to ask you—when do I get paid?"

"When you finish the job. In two weeks."

"Christmas Eve?"

"No, two days later, on Wednesday, that's when our checks are cut."

"*After* Christmas?"

"Yes. I meant to tell you that before."

"Is there any chance that I could…receive an advance?"

"No, that's out of the question."

"I'm in a bad fiscal position right now."

"Sorry, wish I could help, but I can't." Hawkins looked at his watch. "You're on again."

A few minutes into the session it dawned on Albert: he was a star! For one brief moment, he was the most important person in these children's lives. He resolved to let none of them down—not even the cranky, the surly, the stubborn. All got a pat on the back and a "Ho-ho-Ho!" and a taffy and went away pleased.

230

When his four hour stint was up, Albert was drained. The last time he'd talked to Laura—how many years ago? Seven? Eight?—she was teaching. Dealing with children day after day, their insecurities, their fears—he had a new appreciation of that now. Maybe he'd try to reach her again. This time he'd call cold sober and maybe she wouldn't hang up.

In the mint-green room he took off his costume, put on his only set of clothes and was just plain Albert again. He didn't much like that feeling—hated it, really. But later, hunched in his freezer box with the river flowing, flowing through the bitter night to the heartless open sea, he suddenly realized he no longer wanted a drink. And he had good dreams.

Each night he enjoyed the work more. He'd go in early, after his lunch at St. Bernard's, and warm himself amidst racks of clothing, stacks of luggage, tiers of sparkling gems. He couldn't wait to don his suit and take his place on the throne. He loved the feel of the kids on his knee, loved watching their awestruck faces. "Let's look at that camera over there and—peanut butter and pickles!" he'd say, and the kid would grin and the shutter would click, and he'd think of Laura so long ago. "And this is for you," he'd say and present the taffy and think: This is why I was put on earth. This is what I was meant to do, what I'm good at, and why did it take me my whole life to learn it? Why did it take an accident, pure chance? All those people who told me I look like Santa, and still, I never caught on. Good grief but I'm dense!

His desire to drink had vanished. His cough had improved, though he still bedded down in a freezer box. Though he still ate his lunch at St. Bernard's, he felt better than he had in years.

After each session as Santa he'd take his sweet time getting changed, chatting sometimes with Freddy, the night security guard, a sour, scrawny, chain-smoking guy of about sixty-five with a holster that looked in grave danger of sliding down over his hips. Albert didn't especially like Freddy, but hated to leave the warmth of the store and take the cold walk to Water Street. As he walked he would think of how his stock of days was diminishing. Soon, too soon, this job would end, and he would be plain old Albert again.

Three days before Christmas Eve, as a sad-looking boy expressed his fond wish for a pickup truck, Albert had a disquieting thought: Which of these kids would get what they asked for? Times were not good. How many of these who expressed their desires, cupping their hands to their hopeful mouths and whispering in his failing ear, would see those desires fulfilled? How many would wake up excited on Christmas morning, their hearts in their throats, and race down the stairs to a shattering disappointment? Maybe the kids who came to this store, to Nelson's, would get what they asked for, but what of the kids who had never set foot in a place like this, who lived in streets where Santa feared to go? Whose parents were out of work in this festive season, or drank up what money there was? What would those children think of Santa on Christmas day? They'd start to learn what all eventually learned: that little was as it seemed in this tattered world.

No, Albert thought as the sad little boy took his taffy and wandered off. They don't have to learn that now, at this age, at this time of the year—the way I did. There'd been no Christmas joy at Albert's house when he was young, with his father constantly drunk and his sick mother slaving to feed nine kids, cleaning toilets twelve hours a day. She would hurry out into the cold after midnight on Christmas Eve to scrounge an abandoned tree, drag it home and trim it alone and set out the handful of gifts. And once, when Albert had woken from restless sleep and crept downstairs to see the magic, see what Santa had left (for he'd been a good boy), he saw instead his drunken father trip and fall into the tree, bring it down in a shatter of ornaments, sizzle of lights. *I hate you,* he'd screamed in his head, and he vowed he would never become like his father. And then he grew up and joined the navy, and years went by and things went bad, and Laura, his precious Laura, had shouted the last time they'd spoken, "Your drinking put my mother in her *grave!* You're no father to me, I wish you were dead!"

"Mr. Hawkins?"
"What is it?" A frown, a sharp tilt of the chin.
"I really hate to ask again, but I wonder—"
"An advance on your pay."
"Well—"
"I told you before, it can't be done."
"Yes. Yes, you did."

On Christmas Eve Nelson's closed early, at eight o'clock. Albert's two hour shift went fast. He felt hollow and sad when the last child left. I can do it again next year, he told himself. I *will* do it again, I'm *good.*

With heavy feet, he walked to the back of the store, toward the changing room. The cleanup crew was already hard at work, trying to finish quickly: they had much to do at home on this special night.

The utility room was next to the changing room. Albert went in and sat down on a wooden box. With his head in his hands, he thought of the past two weeks. He'd loved the work, but had it been right, what he'd done? He hadn't promised anything, but kids that age would *think* he had, he knew they would, and he didn't feel good about that. Still holding his head, he thought of Laura, half a continent away—her husband, Mike, their kids. He hadn't called—had lost his nerve. Instead, he'd sent them a Christmas card. And once he got his check he would send them all presents.

He waited until the cleaning crew was gone, then left the utility room. Most of the lights were off and the store looked eerie, dead, the decorations drained of their festivity. And where was Freddy? Off tonight?

Still dressed in his outfit, Albert went to Santa's throne, bent down, and opened the large red sack with the satin bow. As he'd thought all along, it was stuffed with paper, a fake. "But *I* am not a fake," he said aloud to the empty store. "I'm real. And Christmas is real."

With change from deposit bottles he paid his fare, and saw that he had an excellent choice of seats. Most people had better things to do on Christmas Eve than cruise around town on a bus.

A guy in the back had a wiseguy smile but didn't make any remarks. When Albert got off, the bus driver said, "So this is where Santa lives."

"Used to live," Albert said as he hefted the sack down the steps.

The neighborhood looked worse than ever, and Christmas was when it usually looked its best. The walls of the redbrick houses were scarred by graffiti—none of that when Albert had lived here—and trash had collected against the marble steps. Plastic candles glowed red in the lace-curtained windows, and here and there a cutout Santa or wreath was tacked to a door.

The first place he went, a fat woman opened the door a crack and said, "We can't give nothin', we ain't got nothin' to give."

"Do you have any children?" Albert asked.

"Get lost," the woman said.

At the next house, a man's voice deep inside said, "Who's out there?"

"Some nut in a Santa suit," the woman said. Her hair was stiff and yellow, her mouth was hard.

"I've brought gifts for your children," Albert said.

"Call the cops!" cried the woman, slamming the door.

At the third house a hollow-eyed woman said, "Who sent you? Where are you from?"

"I'm doing this on my own," Albert said. Behind the woman stood two young children, a boy and a girl. Albert opened his sack and took out two presents, gaily—though far from expertly—wrapped. "Merry Christmas," he said, and handed the gifts to the kids, who looked stunned.

**233**

At the next house he stood on the steps for a while, trying to calm his heart, then pushed the bell.

He heard no ring, so he knocked. After a minute, the door came open. A man with sleepy eyes and a cigarette butt in his mouth said, "Huh?"

"Merry Christmas," said Albert. "I see you have a little girl. Are there any other children?"

"What? What's going on?" the man said, squinting.

Somewhere behind him a woman's voice said, "Who is it?"

"It's Santa Claus," said the man.

"It's not Joe. Is it Joe?"

"I once lived in this house," Albert said. "Can I come inside for a minute?"

The man hesitated, then, taking a drag on his cigarette, said, "Sure," and Albert stepped over the threshold.

So different, and yet—the same. And memories came rushing up: of Laura on that windowseat, reading her picture books; of Eleanor darning a sock in her chair.

"You used to live here?" the little girl said, coming up.

"I did indeed, sweetheart," said Albert, "long ago," and he reached in his sack. "Merry Christmas," he said, and gave her a gift. For a second she looked like Laura.

The man said, "Come on, what's the catch?"

"No catch," Albert said with a shake of his head. "No catch," and he turned to the door. As he went down the steps he heard the man say, "Gimme that package, don't open it yet."

He managed to give it all away, but it wasn't easy. And when it was gone and he stood on the corner holding his empty sack and shivering, snow coating his Santa suit, he knew he was not going to drink anymore.

Then, instead of the bus, a squad car came up, lights flashing, and both of the cops got out and the taller one said, "All done for the night, Santa Claus?"

"All done," Albert said.

"Time to come with us, then, I guess."

"I guess," Albert said.

The cop put his hand on Albert's head as he guided him into the car. "Arresting Santa Claus," he said. "Good thing my kids can't see me." He sat beside Albert and slammed the door. "You got any other clothes?"

"No," Albert said.

"They'll give you some."

The car took off. "Well, anyway, I finished," Albert said. "I thought you wouldn't come for a couple of days."

## 234

"The security guard saw you leaving the store with your bag," said the cop.

"Good old Freddy."

"An hour later we started to get these calls. You shook a few people up."

Albert looked at the snow falling out of a streetlamp. "I'd have paid for the items," he said, "but the manager just wouldn't give an advance."

"I'm sure the judge will sympathize."

"What will he give me?"

"Two months, maybe three."

"Spring," Albert said.

"Huh?"

"They won't let me out until spring."

"Yeah."

Albert leaned back in his seat, still holding his sack. No drinking till spring. And a warm place to sleep, and food for the winter, and once he got out—no drinking ever. He'd write to Laura and tell her that. And then when his Social Security check started coming, he'd get a room—an apartment, even—and she would come visit with Mike and the kids, and they'd have a fine time.

He looked at the empty streets, the cold snow, the fake candles in windows. "Well, I'm not a fake," he said.

"Say what?" the cop sitting next to him said.

"I'm real, the real thing," Albert said.

# CARNIVAL

The time line on the infowall said 4:45 and Haller tensed. He shuffled his papers, pretended to read. He glanced at Kroll, at his heavy face; watched him take his cigar from his mouth and rub his nose. Rub his nose with the back of his hand. Right hand. It was always the right hand, never the left.

Suddenly Kroll looked up. Ice spread through Haller's chest. He cleared his throat, examined his papers, tapped his console. The numbers flew by. He frowned at them and looked at Kroll and said, "Hey, Bill?"

Kroll tapped his cigar in his ashtray and shifted his bulk in his chair. "Yeah, Fred?"

"Calcom. I seem to remember a claim against them last winter, but I'm getting a 10122."

The sun behind Kroll's head: dull copper on darkening steel. Kroll smoked his cigar. "Calcom," he said, then he did it again—rubbed his nose with the back of his hand. Haller had never noticed it until he'd made definite plans. Seven years of sitting across from the son of a bitch, and he'd never noticed it. It was hard to believe—and frightening.

Kroll smoked his cigar. "Anita mentioned Calcom just the other day," he said. He stared at Haller, rocked back and forth in his chair. "Go ask Anita."

*Go ask Anita.* Superior bastard! "Thanks," Haller said, "I will." When he picked up the Calcom card, he noticed his hands were shaking.

Anita Molson was at her desk, leaning back in her chair, legs crossed.

She checked off a form with decisive strokes, then glanced at the infowall, saw Haller, smiled mechanically. "Hi, Fred." She checked off a few more lines, laid the form aside. "Can I help you with something?"

Anita had been promoted twice in the last five years, while Haller was stuck in the same old slot—and always *would* be stuck as long as Kroll was boss. He looked at Anita's soft full mouth, her pale gray eyes. Not even a hint of tension in those eyes. "Calcom," he said, bending over to show her the card. A minty flavor on her breath, and her body threw heat on his cheek. "I don't get any claims, but I seem to remember one."

Anita took the card from him and examined it quickly. His eyes traced the curve of her cleavage. "I seem to remember that too," she said. "In their Oregon district, wasn't it?" Her eyes.

"I think so," Haller said, and wondered again what her costume would be. As usual she'd given no clues. She was clever, all right: he had never guessed her costume yet in five years. Two of those years he had watched her intently, searching for the smallest hint of what she would become, but she'd given him nothing at all. This year it didn't matter, but he was curious all the same.

Anita tapped her console. Crimson numbers flickered past. "A claim in the Oregon district December 10th. Two hundred forty thousand dollars."

"I *knew* there was a claim," Haller said. He leaned closer, pretending to study the card; smelled the mint on her breath again, caught a whiff of her scent. The fragrance made his desire rise and his mouth was suddenly dry. She would change the scent, of course, and he wondered what kind she would use. "What the devil did I do wrong?" he asked with a frown.

Anita tossed her head and brushed her long dark hair away from her face. Her smile held just a touch of mockery. "You fed it a DL instead of a BL," she said.

Haller reddened. "Jesus, I've only been at this seven years. Thanks, Anita." He smiled, then saw Kroll watching, watching with steady eyes as he sucked his cigar. The jowly face turned slowly away, and Haller felt a chill. He looked at the infowall and the time line read 4:58, 4:59, 5:00, and then went blank, no numbers, just a dull pale steady blue. Then foot-high letters slid across the screen: THE MANAGEMENT OF MAYTEL CORPORATION WISHES YOU GOOD CARNIVAL.

*I'll bet they do,* Haller said to himself. His chest was tight and he took a deep breath, thanked Anita again and said, "Well, time to wrap things up. I'll see you Monday—and have a good Carnival."

Anita flashed another hollow smile. "You too, Fred." Haller's eyes stayed fixed on her a second, then he turned and went back to his desk.

Everyone straightening papers and closing drawers. Franks already had his jacket on and was saying a cheery goodbye to his side of the room. The infowall said 5:07 now and Haller, excitement pressing against his heart, sat down at his desk and pretended to study a form. From the edge of his eye he looked at Kroll, who was casually leafing through papers and smoking, as if this day were like any other, as if he had all the time in the world. Then suddenly and shockingly Kroll stared.

Haller felt his throat constrict as Kroll smiled insolently, sat up straight and tapped his papers on his desk and said in his husky voice, "Enough's enough." He set his cigar down, put the papers away and locked his drawer. "The rest can wait till Monday," he said, and stood up slowly, switched off his console, reached for the jacket on the back of his chair and slipped it on.

Sweat blossomed on Haller's brow. Kroll was fifty-two, but still had a fullback's build: forty pounds overweight and his stomach bulging, but still compact and strong in the shoulders and neck. He snapped his brief-case shut and nodded at Haller. "Have a good weekend, Fred," he said, cigar between his teeth again. "Good Carnival."

"Good Carnival to you, too, Bill," said Haller, forcing a smile. His voice didn't sound right. "See you Monday," he added, and his voice was better, and he straightened some things he had already straightened before as Kroll walked through the office and out the door.

Haller was the last to leave. He locked his desk, then stood there staring at the infowall, at the bright blue letters frozen there, THE MAN-AGEMENT OF MAYTEL CORPORATION WISHES YOU... A knot formed in his stomach, tightened, hurt. Abruptly he grabbed his briefcase and left the room.

The sun was behind the buildings now, dark orange and dim, and a chilly air swept up the street from the river. As Haller joined the crowd at the shuttle stop, he checked his watch. It said 5:35, and far in the distance he already heard the drums.

People scurried past in the quickening dusk, preoccupied, their expressions driven and tense. Spring equinox, and soon it would be dark. A cab appeared and was hailed by half a dozen of those at the stop. A woman was shoved aside and two men scuffled briefly before the smaller of them fought his way into the cab and locked the door. The woman in front of Haller shook her head and sniffed disdainfully. Haller thought of Anita, thought of Kroll. He tried to ignore the pain in his gut, but it was insistent now.

The shuttle pulled up, the doors opened slowly, and slowly the people filed inside, their faces edgy and bored. The driver watched the rearview mirror till everyone took a seat, then moving his arms in sweeping circles, he pulled the bus into the street.

The shuttle went three blocks and coasted toward its next stop. Haller watched a shopkeeper hurriedly pull an iron gate across the front of his store. Suddenly a sharp loud noise, and people flinched. The driver looked at the rearview mirror, his face tense and suddenly pale. Then beyond the front window four flashes of color, waving arms, deep raucous shouts. The figures turned the corner and disappeared. The driver braked to a stop and muttered, "Goddamn punks, can't even wait!"

The doors hissed open. Everyone had settled down again and looked at their hands or the floor in vague embarrassment. The new crowd made its way through the doors and the shuttle was packed. People stood over Haller, clutching the stainless steel bar above his head. Shoulder to shoulder, jammed into each other, they gazed past each other in silence. A briefcase banged into Haller's knee, a woman's waist was at his chin. Haller stared at the woman's belt through stifling space, then struggled up and through the crowd as the shuttle slowed again. When it stopped he edged his way through the door and stepped into the street.

The sharp cool air felt good on his skin as he started to walk. The last of the light was dying out and the drums were louder now. The streets in this part of the city were almost deserted: just a man in a suit on the opposite pavement, walking briskly; another younger man, his shoulders hunched, his hands in his jacket pockets, hurrying along.

Then suddenly a woman crossed in front of Haller, dragging a child, a little girl, by the hand. A child in the city during Carnival! In the poverty districts, yes—but here? Haller couldn't believe it. He watched as the woman fled down the pavement, pulling the child so hard her feet left the ground. Shaking his head, he went through the door of his apartment house.

In his living room, he stripped off his jacket and tie and unbuttoned the neck of his shirt. He sat on the couch, he thought of Kroll, he got up again and went to his kitchen and poured himself some strel. Drank it down in one gulp.

He had bought his half-liter allotment of strel two weeks ago, the first day the state outlets opened. He poured another shot in his glass and sat on the couch again. He sipped the powerful stimulant slowly this time, thinking: *Easy now, don't overdo it,* and took a deep breath and leaned back.

He thought of the woman and child again. They would never get out of the city now, they would have to find shelter for two long nights and a day, and during Carnival no place was safe. The last of the children and older people had left the night before—except for the poor, of course. He couldn't imagine how that little girl had been missed. He shuddered to think of what might befall her. At least he didn't have that worry, a wife and kids.

He finished the strel. The room was suddenly stuffy and warm and he opened the window. A gust of air rushed in and felt good on his arms and neck. The strel was already starting to work: he felt confident, strong and alert. He thought of Anita again and desire surged through him. He went to the bedroom.

He took out his costume and spread it across the bed as the strel rushed into his muscles and blood, making him taut and cold. He knelt and felt the costume's smoothness, touched its fur to his lips. It was beautiful, perfect: a jet-black jaguar with claws and teeth of steel. He had worked on the costume for all of six months, and now as he held it, felt its luxury, he filled with pride. His head was funny with strel as he thought: *A cat to catch a bird.*

Shivering from strel and excitement he took off his clothes, slipped into the costume and zipped it up. He fit the mask carefully over his head and stepped to the full length mirror that hung on the door.

Before him stood a lithe and deadly predator, all black except for its claws and fangs and the white and pink of its crotch. In other years, when his goals were different, Haller had filled the sexual border with rich designs that wound around his thighs and spread their colorful tendrils across his chest. This year, the border was a simple gash through which his genitals hung unadorned. This year he was not on the prowl for sex, he was after much bigger game: this year he was out to kill—to kill a bird.

He was positive that Kroll would dress as a bird. For months he'd analyzed Kroll's conversations, watched his every mannerism. Kroll had put crumbs on the windowsill for the sparrows to eat all month. And the number of times he'd referred to flight: his visit to the air museum, the gliding exhibition he'd seen down South. (With Wagner once, he'd even spread his arms to simulate the glider's wings.) Those pensive moments when he smoked and gazed across the city: he was dreaming of flying then, and Haller knew it. Kroll would be a bird for sure, and as Haller looked in the mirror and flexed his claws, he thought: *And I am the perfect cat to end that vile bird's life.*

His stomach contracted with hunger but he had no desire for food. He went back to the living room, sat on the couch, and listened to the drumming as it came through the open window. The beat was faster now and excited voices—laughter, shouting—rose from the street below. He clipped his strelflask onto his waistband, then went to the bedroom and took his billyclub out of his bureau drawer.

CARNIVAL

The billy was new and it was a beauty, longer than the standard model and with slightly more lead in its end. Haller took a few practice swings, tapping the billy's weight against his palm. It was two grams over the limit, but what the hell, they'd never pick him up for a minor infraction like that.

Billyclubs were the only sanctioned weapons during Carnival—but not the only weapons used. While knives had been outlawed years before, the revelers got around the rule by designing costumes with claws and beaks and fangs. As long as a blade was not detachable, it wasn't questioned. Of course, only troopers had guns.

Haller snapped the billyclub onto his waistband, strapped his genital shield to his left wrist, looked in the mirror again. The strel was almost at its peak and his juices surged. He looked at his jaguar head, his gleaming fangs, his vicious claws. He cupped his shield across his genitals and lunged at the mirror with his club. He was ready, ready to kill, and he closed the living room window, turned off the lights, and went through the door.

The moon was high and nearly full, the drums were loud. No shuttles now, no vehicles of any kind, just costumed figures capering in moon-bright dark. A blazing torch threw shattered streaks on painted faces, fur-covered loins, dark glistening pubic hair. Coarse shouts and throaty laughter—and from somewhere nearby, a scream.

Haller turned. Three figures on the corner—a spider, a ghost, and a shark with ragged teeth. They had an old man up against a building and were jabbing at him with their billyclubs, poking his stomach and chest and laughing harshly. The old man whimpered and pleaded and swore that he had no money, which only made the revelers prod him more. Young punks and their kid games, Haller thought. They hadn't learned to focus yet, to *use* the Carnival. Well, most never did, fools that they were. He watched the old man whine and cringe as the clubs came down. He felt a twinge of pity, but after all, the man had only himself to blame for his plight. If he'd missed evacuation, the least he could have done was stay inside. It was no guarantee of safety, God only knew, but to be old and on the streets in Carnival time, you had better be ready to die.

The shark brought his billy down again, and again the old man screamed. The ghost and spider laughed. Haller would have routed the punks in other years, but this year he had a mission, and to risk an injury to save an old man's life would be insane.

The street held dozens of revelers now. He joined them and started toward Center Square. From every direction they came, each doing the up-and-down Carnival dance to the pulse of the drums. Soon the street

242

was a river of beasts: tigers, leopards, bears and lions, panthers, zebras, wolves. There were monsters and gargoyles, gnomes and fairies, goblins and witches and trolls. There were birds—many birds: bright-feathered cockatoos, peacocks and parrots; dun-colored hawks and coal-black crows. There were fantasy birds, birds hatched in imaginations feral and dark—but none was the bird Haller sought.

The crowd thickened and swelled, and Haller was locked in its pulsating center, shield across his genitals, his right paw high in the air. The drumming grew louder, the dancing turned wild, the strel was icy fire in Haller's veins. He banged up hard against a buffalo that snarled and faked a swing with its billy, but Haller snarled back and cocked his paw and the buffalo bowed and laughed.

The crowd closed in and Haller was jammed against hot flesh. A bird of paradise strutted against him, rubbing her naked buttocks against his crotch. He didn't want it, didn't want to get caught up in it, he tried to back away but was once again squeezed against slippery flesh. He fought his primal urge—then desperately, impulsively, he freed his hand from his steel-tipped paw and slipped two fingers between the wild bird's legs.

For a second her dancing stopped: then it started again and she shrieked with excitement and Haller could feel her quivering wet on his hand. He thrust deeper, making her moan. Then the crowd surged forward, wrenching her out of his reach, and he stumbled, caught himself, was struck on the jaw by a flying elbow, and soon his erection was gone.

Far away in the back of his head, behind the drums, the choo-choo scream of chuffa-whistles, Haller cursed himself. He'd promised himself to avoid distractions and already had succumbed. He had to stay centered, keep his focus clear: only by doing that could he succeed.

The river of flesh moved steadily forward; at last it reached Center Square. Haller was wedged against pulsating bodies that stretched for blocks, stretched as far as the eye could see. On Tuesday he'd eaten his lunch in this very square, had placidly watched dull pigeons peck crusts of bread, watched women with bulging shopping bags sink wearily onto the benches to catch their breath. Now most of those women were far from here, the pigeons were roosting high up on the ledges of buildings, and Center Square was a dazzling explosion of feathers and fur and sweat and paint and steel. The drumbeats battered Haller's thoughts, buzzed in his breastbone, rattled his jaw and skull. On the lampposts the torches flickered and pulsed, throwing lightning across the grotesques. Paws thrust toward the silver moon, claws flashed. The crowd surged one way, then another, gaps opened and closed.

A tug at his waistband: quickly he whirled, shielding his crotch, lashing out with his claws. The thief jumped sideways, clutching its chest. A monkey, short and slim, and it screamed, "A taste, you bastard! That's all I wanted, a taste!" It staggered, its fur stained red. Raising his billy-club, Haller shouted, "I'll break your goddamn skull!" The monkey stumbled backward and disappeared.

The combat, brief though it was, had taken its toll. Haller was shivery, cold, his arms felt weak. The first rush of strel had died, and thin sharp pangs of humger cramped his gut.

It took him almost half an hour to fight his way to the edge of the square, another half hour to get to where the crowd was sparse enough to allow him to move unhampered. By then he was tired. Out only two hours and already tired. He couldn't afford to be tired so soon. He needed food; some food and he'd be all right.

The tavern reeked of smoke and alcohol. It was chaos, the end of the counter awash with beer and wet chunks of meat. Paws snatched and clutched, mouths sucked and chewed. During Carnival, food and drink were free—except for strel, of course—and anyone who ran short of strel would have to wait hours for more.

Haller grabbed a turkey leg from a steaming bowl. As he did, a hand closed over his crotch. A Siamese cat with pointed breasts and golden pubic hair. She stroked his organs. He pulled away. "Doesn't the big pussycat want to play?" she purred, and in spite of himself, he grew firm. "That's so much *better*," the Siamese said, and lowered her mouth to his groin. He jerked back sharply, his heart pounding hard in his head.

Near the wall, he devoured the turkey, swallowing meat in huge gulps. Revelers shouted, gorged themselves, and grabbed each others' genitals. Haller's mouth was dry: when he swallowed, the meat felt like stone. He finished it, went back to the counter and grabbed a mug of beer.

The cat was gone. He drank enough beer to quench his thirst and thought of Kroll. He took a sip from his strelflask, went back to the street.

A rhinocerous was relieving himself beside the tavern door; the urine splashed on the wall in a hard thick stream. On the pavement below lay the Siamese, her legs embracing the waist of a husky lion. The lion's naked flanks thrust into her; she gasped and groaned. Haller quickly turned into the street and thought of Kroll. That was all he would think of, Kroll.

Again he was carried along on the throbbing sea. Apparitions flashed before him, disappeared. A scuffle ahead and the monsters scattered. Two helmeted troopers, shiny and black, cracked their clubs on a vulture's skull. Haller watched as they dragged the bird off. It was some other vulture, not Kroll. He drank more strel.

**244**

For more than two hours he chanted and pranced and shrieked. The moon reached its zenith and started to fall, the air turned strangely warm. Hollow eyes swam in front of him; swollen mouths cackled and spit. Fangs, claws and beaks flashed past, flesh pressed his flesh. He shouted the chant at the top of his lungs, he pounded his feet on the pavement hard, he beat on the back of the creature in front as the creature behind beat him. It felt good, so good after such a long time—but not as good as in other years, because he was holding back, he was saving himself for the job he must do, the job he had to do this year or not at all.

He examined every hawk and eagle, every buzzard, every condor. Some had Kroll's swagger and bulk, but none had the gestures he knew so well he saw them in his dreams.

It was after four o'clock in the morning, after his third dose of strel had burned out, that Haller spotted the raven.

He had spun away fron the crowd and into a side street littered with papers and trampled food, was leaning against a wall, when he saw the bird in a doorway half a block down. It was stocky, muscular, shiny and sleek, with bright beady glittering eyes. For a long time it stood there motionless watching the crowd, then slowly it raised its right wing tip and brushed it against its beak.

Haller's heart sped up. He ducked further into the shadows. He opened his strelflask, drank, and thought: My God, it couldn't be better! He trembled, broke into a sweat. All he needed to do was wait till Kroll moved, then attack from behind. Kroll was older than Haller by more than eight years and slower, but heavier too, and as tough as a bull. It wouldn't do to confront him face to face. He drank more strel and moved cautiously forward past three male revelers pumping and sucking below a fire escape. The raven stepped out of the doorway and turned toward the street, his back to Haller—and Haller sprang.

A squad of troopers suddenly rounded the corner, shouting and swinging their clubs. The fox and gorilla fought furiously. By the time the combatants cleared out of the way, the raven was lost in the crowd.

Haller sat on a concrete step and cursed his luck. But he knew his target now, and from this point on it was simply a matter of time.

Through the dawn he searched for Kroll. He was carried up one street and down another, jostled, elbowed, pummeled on the back. The drums and chuffa-whistles pounded, chugged and groaned. Fireworks clapped overhead, streaking fangs and beaks with a ghostly red-white-blue. Just before the sun came up, a slender nun made a play for him and he let himself go, moved hungrily, black fur against black silk, till she cried and

245

clutched his back and his climax came. Then she whirled off into the dancers again and Haller, spent and dizzy, staggered into an alley and slumped on a doorstep.

He awoke with a start. Reflexively, his claws slashed out. Someone trying to steal his strel! The crocodile screamed, jumped back, its arms shooting into the air. A piece of its mask fell cleanly away, revealing a woman's cheek, ghost-white and then crimson with blood. Clutching her head, she ran.

Haller pulled himself to his feet and checked his strelflask: still half full. Thank God. He couldn't afford to be without strel now. Quickly he took a drink and plunged into the crowd.

The sun was already high and the air was warm. Haller couldn't believe he had fallen asleep. It had never happened before during Carnival, never in twenty-six years. He checked his watch. It was after nine, he had slept three hours. If he hadn't given in to that nun it would never have happened. He cursed himself.

There were bodies all over the place and the troopers dragged them away. The revelers ignored the fallen, pounding through their wanton dance, stomping their feet into vomit and urine and blood. As the sun grew hotter the stench grew strong, and Haller began to feel faint. He struggled to the fountain in Center Square and soaked himself with the horde, drank deeply from the mouth of a copper fish. As he wiped his lips with the back of his paw, black feathers flashed. He caught his breath. A redwing black-bird, not a raven. He took a drink of strel and resumed his search.

Shortly after noon, he stopped into a bar. He was feeling the weight of Carnival now, feeling it worse than he'd ever felt it before in twenty-six years. He went to the counter and snatched up a handful of fly-covered meat. He had no appetite, the meat was rank, but he made himself eat it; he needed its strength. As he moved away from the counter he looked outside—and the raven went by.

He dropped the rest of the meat and ran for the door. A pair of standing fornicators blocked his path; he knocked them down. They continued their act in the vomit and slime on the floor. He shoved a panda out of the way and burst outside.

The shiny black head of the raven was already half a block down. Haller pushed forward, banging against a tall green snake with a golden snout. Suddenly he doubled up in paralyzing pain: a blow to his testicles, hard and clean. He covered himself with his genital shield, gritting his teeth as agony wound through his groin. Stars burst in his eyes and he thought of the horrible sight he had witnessed at Carnival years ago: the castration, a bear losing everything with a murderous howl. He looked around but saw no assailant; the blow had been accidental. Slowly the pain subsided; he straightened up. When he looked down the street again, the raven was gone.

He searched all afternoon. The dancing grew slower, looser, the crowd thinned out. In the peak of the heat, at four o'clock, he was suddenly, shockingly tired. His heart started beating alarmingly fast, his left arm hurt, his mouth was dry. Wouldn't that be it, he thought: have a heart attack. Kill Kroll and *then* have a heart attack, wouldn't that be it. His pulse was in his neck, his head, too fast. He would have a beer. He had drunk too much of the strel and he had to slow down.

As he passed the alley beside the tavern, movement caught his eye. He stared at the spot, saw wooden crates, then flesh, a foot. And there, on the other side of the crates, lay a little girl.

She was naked. Blood ran from her mouth in a slow thick stream. He recognized the face: the girl he had seen with the woman the night before. Then behind him he heard a grunt and a cry, saw shapes in a doorway, a giant roach raising its billyclub high. Saw the woman, also naked, crouched against the door, arms shielding her face. Haller sprang, swung his billy, hit the insect's neck. The roach turned dully, swung, struck Haller's arm, and Haller cracked its temple, dropping it in its tracks.

The woman cowered in the doorway, whimpering. Haller felt anger, contempt, disgust—but mostly pity. Reaching inside his costume, he took out a key. "508 North 22nd, number 7D. Can you remember that?"

The woman nodded with terror bright in her eyes.

"Take the child and lock yourself in. Keep the lights off. If you're lucky, no one will find you."

The woman scurried forward and took the key, went to the child, lifted her gently. Turned and looked over her shoulder at Haller, fled into the crowd.

She'll never make it, Haller thought. A woman without a costume? Never.

He flexed his arm and winced. The spot where the roach had hit him was tender. Great, just what I need, he thought. He hurried out of the alley and into the tavern.

The smoke was so thick he could hardly breathe. In its purple haze a black Cleopatra was doing a sinuous dance on the counter, spreading her legs and squatting down. As Haller went to grab a beer she caught his hand and pressed it against her crotch. Making a fist, he jerked away, retreating through the crowd. Wiping her wet on his fur, he drank some beer. A blue baboon hopped up on the counter, entered the dancer from behind. She sank forward smiling, her head bent low.

By the time Haller finished his second beer, his heart had slowed—but now it seemed *too* slow, and somewhat erratic. His arm ached terribly, his head was thick, and all at once he was swept by a wave of despair.

Carnival would last just twelve more hours. At six in the morning the horn would sound, the streets would be cleared, and everything would be over for one more year. He told himself: *You have to find Kroll now!* But the voice in his head was distorted, distant, the lights in the bar seemed to flicker and fade, and suddenly all was black.

When he came to, his strel was gone.

Panic stricken, he jumped to his feet, clutching his chest. He still had his money, still had his watch, but his flask had been cut right off!

His head was splitting, his arm still ached, and he had no strel! His watch said 9:02. It would take him hours to buy more strel through an outlet, and he needed it *now!*

His mind was racing, yet blurry and dull. He approached a hefty boar, a boar with bloodred eyes and gleaming tusks. His arm was wrapped around the neck of an Indian squaw, and he pressed his muzzle close to her ear and laughed.

"Pardon me," Haller said.

The boar glared.

Haller's heart fluttered and skipped a beat. "I'd like to buy some of your strel," he said.

The boar laughed heartily. "Did you say *strel?* That's difficult to come by during Carnival, my friend."

"A shot," Haller said. "That's all I need."

The boar was silent.

"Twenty dollars."

The boar slapped Haller's shoulder and laughed again. "Twenty *dollars?* I thought you said you *wanted* strel."

"Thirty," Haller said.

The boar's eyes narrowed. "Make it fifty."

Haller cursed and produced a bill. The boar grabbed it, taking his flask from his waist. Haller sucked at it hungrily. "Enough!" the boar shouted, wrenching it back. Cursing again, Haller left.

The moon was high, the air was cool, the music was loud and fast. The chuffa-whistles started up and Haller danced, the strel racing into his veins. His frenzy grew, fresh confidence and power seized him as he slid through the flickering streets, shield over his crotch, his right paw high. Three times he circled Center Square, whipping himself to a cold hard sweat with the up-and-down dance, eyes wide and staring, muscles light and smooth.

248

The crowd was rough, much rougher than the night before. Beauties and beasts ran screaming with blood-streaked necks, torn costumes, torn flesh. Through the streets Haller danced, but found no Kroll, and at midnight, filled with bitterness, he joined some toughs who were smashing out windows. They were only a block from the Maytel Building when blackshirted troopers came swinging their billys, and Haller ducked into an alley. Winded, a pain in his side, his arm beginning to ache again, he leaned against the wall and closed his eyes.

A crash. He whirled. A garbage can came rolling at him from the alley's end, where two dark figures grunted and pumped on the ground. Haller watched in the feeble light—and with shock he saw that the figure on top was his bird.

Pressing himself against the wall, he watched the raven's flanks pump in and out. Slowly, breastbone tight and cold, hands quivering, he inched forward.

The figures thrust and rolled between the garbage cans. The woman, a shimmering mermaid, shuddered and groaned. Haller advanced, shield over his crotch, his billyclub tight in his hand. He could see the raven's feathers now, could see the mermaid's scales, and suddenly he stopped.

The mermaid was Anita. He didn't know how he knew it, but he did. That bastard Kroll! That filthy pig! Aflame with rage he lifted his billy, stepped out of the shadows and swung.

The raven lurched to the side and the club caught its back, not its skull. It yelped in pain and spun around, its stiff red organ spurting seed. It caught the next blow on its wing; then, roaring angrily, it ran. The mermaid shielded her crotch, slid up to the wall, her right arm over her head. Haller spit on her breasts. Then he turned and went after the bird.

Haller's strel had peaked. He cut through the crowd with amazing ease. Even so, by the time he reached the corner, the black feathered head had vanished.

To his left, shops shuttered with iron bars; to his right, St. Basil's church. He ran up the marble steps of the church and pushed on the heavy door. It opened slowly. Cautiously he slipped inside, his shield on his genitals, club raised high.

The vestibule was empty. He pushed on the inner doors, glanced around, quickly entered the church.

Dark, quiet, and warm. Votive candles flickered gently, casting red shadows on high brown walls. Far away in another world were the whistles and drums. Haller's breath was loud.

Then movement, up by the altar. Again! On Jaguar feet Haller raced down the aisle.

A short, slight figure in the garb of a priest was kneeling in front of the altar. Haller jumped from the shadows, his billyclub high. With a hoarse hard rasp he demanded, "Where is he?" His words echoed off cool marble and polished wood.

No reply. The small gray head stayed bowed.

Squeezing the figure's arm, Haller said, "I asked you where he went!"

A tired voice said, "Please, I am at prayer."

Haller squeezed harder. "Oh, so you want to play games!"

The figure turned. And Haller saw an ancient face, pale weary eyes. His startled mind recoiled, his grip relaxed. It was really a priest! Not a reveler in costume, but a priest! There were only a handful left in the city; he couldn't believe he was actually facing one. "Are you crazy?" he stammered. "An old man like you—here? *Now?*"

The withered mouth smiled. "God will protect his children," the quiet voice said.

Haller sniffed. "Yeah, God. You're lucky you haven't been killed!"

"I have prayed here during Carnival for fifteen years," the old man said, "and you are the first to interrupt. For who in love with wickedness would enter the house of the Lord?"

Haller laughed. "What you do is your business," he said with a sneer, "but I have business too. I know that raven's hiding here, now tell me where he went!"

"I have seen only you," the old man said. Red candlelight gleamed in his eyes. "I have been at prayer—"

All at once his expression changed. The watery pupils contracted, a shadow fell over the wrinkled skin and Haller crouched and whirled. The billyclub hummed past his ear, catching his collarbone.

Bellowing in pain, he swung. The raven dodged the billy, swung again, but missed. Haller gritted his teeth, swung hard, and cracked the black bird's skull. The raven wobbled, swinging wildly, missed, its genital shield slipped, slipped to the side, and Haller made his move—brought his billyclub up from below with all his might. The raven's howl resounded to the roof as Haller sliced its throat with a swipe of his paw.

The raven staggered, crashed into the altar. Its wings went limp. Its genital shield came loose, rang loudly as it hit the marble floor. Slowly the black-feathered mass crumpled into the aisle.

Dark blood flowed over polished stone. The raven made weak moaning sounds, then shivered and was still.

Haller's heartbeat was thick in his ears. It was over, over that fast! Kroll was dead!

A sudden urge to tear the feathered mask away swept over him. How he would love to see the look on that vile face now, that smirking face that would never mock him again.

The penalty for removing a mask was death, but who would know? The priest was lost in prayer again, he wouldn't notice if— Quickly Haller stepped forward, bent over the raven's body and lifted the mask.

It wasn't Kroll.

A numbness spread through Haller's chest. Trembling, he replaced the mask. He'd killed a total stranger—and Kroll still lived!

A clicking sound. He whirled. Too late: with its powerful wings the hornet rammed his club into Haller's throat, sending him reeling, knocking him into the votive stand. Glass smashed to the floor, flames sputtered and died as the hornet bent Haller backward.

"You fool!" said the hornet's husky voice. Its breath was black with the stench of cigars. You simple fool, did you think I didn't *know?*"

He banged his kneecap hard into Haller's crotch. Haller's scream remained trapped in his head; a feeble wet rattle was all that escaped from his lips as the hornet pressed down on his throat with the club. "You want to be account executive!" A laugh.

Candles fluttered around Haller's eyes, his hurt throat gurgled, he flailed his paws. "Account executive," the hornet said contemptuously. "*You?*"

The room grew darker, Haller heard the laughter die, his ears were filled with screaming engines, rushing waterfalls, he couldn't smell cigar smoke anymore, his throat and groin were huge with pain, the darkness rattled, his brain clicked red, then far away a tiny voice said, "Quit this house of God!"

And suddenly Haller could breathe again, the pressure at his neck was gone, he took wet gasping breaths as his vision cleared and he saw the priest with a huge brass pointed crucifix.

"Be sure your sin will find you out!" the old man cried, eyes gleaming in the candlelight, and jabbed at the hornet, who jumped back quickly, cursing. "Wickedness procedeth from the wicked!" croaked the priest.

The hornet cocked his club and the old man lunged; the crucifix ripped the stripes at the hornet's ribs. "Can a man take fire in his bosom and his clothes be not burned? Answer me!"

Haller dashed for the door. As he did, the hornet's wing lashed out and brushed his neck. He ran through the doorway, through the vestibule, into the street.

In the crowd, his neck began to sting. He touched it and his hand was wet. In a panic he pushed his way through the dancers, the beat of the drums banging into his terrified heart. Side hurting, heaving, throat congealed, blood streaming down his neck and into the jaguar fur, he elbowed his way through the capering beasts and ran so fast he was certain his heart would burst.

At last he was in his street, was in front of his building; ran through the bottles and papers and cans, ran over the bodies, looked over his shoulder and went through the door, half expecting to see the hornet. But no, and he took the elevator, leaned against the wall and felt the heavy pounding in his neck, behind his eyes. Clearing his throat, he coughed up blood. He left the elevator, hurried down the hall, unlocked his door, stepped into his apartment. Stood there listening.

No sound. The moon threw pewter bars across the floor. He bolted the door, left the lights off, went into the bedroom.

—And something was in his bed. He froze. Then he saw what it was: the child, the little girl. He remembered the woman then, saw her taking his key.

The moon was a sickly yellow on the child's face. The eyes were closed, the blood around the pallid mouth had dried. He felt the slender wrist, bent close. No breathing and no pulse: the girl was dead.

He backed away from the bed. In the darkness he opened the closet door and whispered hoarsely, "Come out!" and pain stabbed at his throat. "I'm not going to hurt you, come out!" He went to the bathroom, the living room closet. The woman wasn't there.

Cursing, he went to the bedroom again. "Couldn't even get rid of her for me, could you, bitch? You goddamn bitch, that's the thanks I get!" He opened the window wide, then lifted the child off the bed and threw her into the street. He managed to slam the window shut before she hit the ground.

He went to the bathroom, turned the light on, took off his mask. The cut wasn't nearly as bad as he'd thought. He washed it, pressed four sanistitches on it, went to the living room, sat in the dark. His throat was crushed, his breathing rough. He waited in the dying moonlight, heard the steady pulse of drums and chuffa-whistles far away, but heard no sound in the hallway beyond his door.

Thoughts raced through his mind. The raven: did he have a wife? Did he have any children? Where had he worked, what were his interests, what did his house look like? Hot bitter tears welled up as he thought: I *missed* him! Not a bird, a hornet! Christ!

He sat there listening, his body taut, his every nerve on fire, till at last in drizzling dawn the horn went off and Carnival was done. The drumming stopped, the air was still, a whistling tunnel of darkness sucked Haller toward dreamless sleep.

Kroll was already at his desk. He glanced up briefly as Haller walked into the office, then looked at his papers again.

Haller didn't feel too bad. He had slept all of Sunday and Sunday night, waking up only twice to urinate. The second time he woke, near dusk, he looked out the window and saw that the cleanup crew had dragged all the bodies away, and after that he slept twelve hours straight.

This morning he'd showered, shaved and changed the sani-stitches, hidden the huge black bruise on his neck with powder, managed to get some liquids past the angry lump in his throat. He would see the doctor about his throat tomorrow afternoon; he had already made an appointment.

He sat at his desk and opened his briefcase and Kroll said, "Morning, Fred. How was your Carnival?"

"Great." Haller said. "How was yours?"

"Real good," Kroll said. "I'm still feeling it, though. Getting old, I guess." He frowned. "It looks like your razor gave you a battle today."

Haller laughed as he fingered the sani-stitches. "Yeah, when I shave I'm in dreamland, Bill."

Kroll grinned. "I know just what you mean." He picked up some papers, leafed through them, and said, "Can you give me the dope on this Shales account?"

"Sure thing," Haller said. "Let me go get some coffee first. You want a cup?"

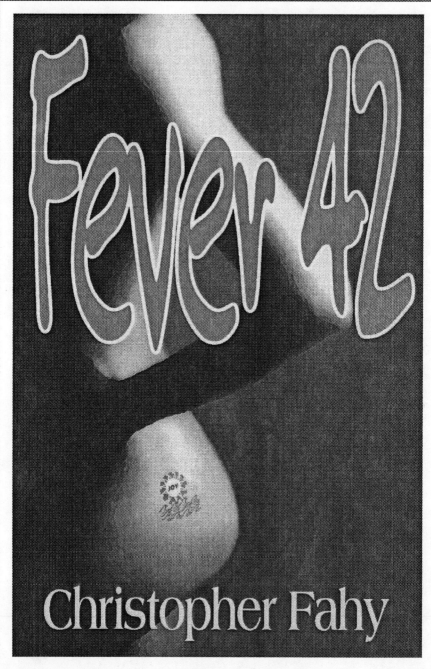

Release Date: June 2005

Trade Paperback        ISBN 1892950332        $14.95

# Fever 42

## By Christopher Fahy

"I thought that Chris Fahy's novel *Fever 42* was both wildly funny and surprisingly sad. The combination made me think of the early J.D. Salinger period. ... I think it will attract a lot of attention. Chris is a wonderful writer."
— **Stephen King**

"Ribald, erotic, hilarious, deeply serious and tragic, often all at the same time, *Fever 42* proves one of those rare books that restores our faith in the mainstream novel – and strangely, in humanity."
— **John Grant**, *Crescent Blues Book Views*

" ... Gut-wrenching... Takes off like a drag racer howling down a quarter mile track."
— **John Robinson**, *Portland Press Herald*

"All the thrills and spills of a runaway mid-life crisis — from the safety of your armchair.. delightfully scandalous."
— **Michael Kimball**, author of *Undone* and *Green Girls*

" ... A narrative that drives you like an out-of-control second-hand Dodge station wagon on a ride that makes you worry for your own strange trajectory."
— **Jack Ketchum**, author of *Off Season*

Ted Wharton, 42, a teacher at Whitman High in Somerside, New Jersey, lives a routine suburban life with his wife and kids. Disenchanted after fifteen years of teaching, going thru the motions at work – and home — he feels the clock is ticking. Then it happens: on the same day that one of Ted's colleagues drops dead of a heart attack, Joy, 17, a bright and stunningly beautiful senior in one of his classes, makes a play for him. And he puts up no resistance. Fully alive for the first time in years, he revels in his wild trysts with Joy – many at Whitman High. Living on the edge, obsessed with Joy, but realizing the ultimate disaster this will become, tries to end his relationship with her. Only to see his world spiral out of control.

A tragicomical tale of desire, deceit and betrayal, *Fever 42* is a thunderbolt of a novel, an unforgettable joyride.

| Trade Paperback | ISBN 1892950332 | $14.95 |
| Trade Hard cover | ISBN 1892950464 | $29.95 |

## OVERLOOK CONNECTION PRESS

www.overlookconnection.com

Printed in the United States
64700LVS00005B/241-291

9 781892 950734